Royal
Dispatch

Jennifer Margaret Fraser

Integrated

PUBLISHERS.COM

Library and Archives Canada Cataloguing in Publication

Fraser, Jennifer Margaret, 1966–, author
Royal Dispatch / Jennifer Margaret Fraser.

ISBN 978-0-9947299-2-7

I. Title.

Editor: Michael J. Marson, B.A, MCPM, Integrated Publishers
Proof-reader: Tom Brown
Cover Designer: Simon B. Troop, CS Creative
Front Cover Image: Simon B. Troop, CS Creative

Integrated Publishers: www.integratedpublishers.com

Available from Amazon, Kindle and other online stores

DEDICATION

for my mother, Janet Isobel Fraser

Fraser is a great story-teller and *Royal Dispatch* was a gripping read. I couldn't put it down, but I didn't want it to end. That's when I know I really enjoyed a book!

— David Thomas Critchley
RCMP Chief Superintendent

A well-told tale of suspense set in scenic 1957 Victoria, Canada, RCMP Inspector Kent Riley, has a secret past that ties him to one Flynn Dolan of the Northern Ireland Nationalists, considered the Irish National Army's most prolific bomber. Dolan is using the pretext of the Royal Visit to set a bomb and capture the Queen so that Ireland might be set free. Riley and Constable Michael Callaghan, a 23 year-old child prodigy, battle to find and stop Dolan. Five Stars: A compulsive and dramatic read with an ending that is deeply satisfying.

— J.R. Rogers
Best-selling author of *Mission to Morocco* and *The Cypriot Agent*

Royal Dispatch is an incredibly fantastic read. A world has been created that draws you in such that you don't want the story to end. Every sentence, every page, contains vital character and story detail too important to rush through despite the thriller's pace.

Royal Dispatch brings me to a place and time I have never imagined, but feel I have intimate knowledge of now. The characters are real and true. There are surprises. Characters you can hear, feel, touch, and smell. This book is an insight into the human condition at a time of great change, with really interesting parallels with today's world. This is Canadian *noir*, and shows darkness can exist anywhere, even on an island on the edge of the world. I read it like a film, though it felt more liberated than one, yet structured to keep you compelled. Once you open the book, the countdown starts, the clock is ticking.... will it blow?!

The politics are raw and despite the Irish struggle being reduced to a slightly hackneyed noble cause, I still went with it. Like many Irish people and many more British people, I have deep dislike and disrespect for monarchy. But again, you gave it humanity, which is quite a feat, given they are the source of great pain, inequality and social injustice. I connected with Queen Elizabeth II and her humanity.

— Stephen O'Connell
Filmmaker

Royal Dispatch is the exciting tale of RCMP investigator, Irishman Kent Riley, a lone wolf who finds himself in Victoria, British Columbia, in 1957 specially assigned to investigate a mysterious art theft and the possible negligence of the local RCMP Detachment that left one officer severely wounded and another in a mental ward. Reluctantly straddled with a young and over-eager Constable Michael Callaghan as his assistant, Riley uncovers a plot led by a ghost from his past to kidnap Queen Elizabeth and Prince Phillip in a few short days during their visit to the provincial capital.

The tale grips you from beginning to end, from when two Mounties unexpectedly face a hail of bullets in an ambush to the violent confrontation at the famous Empress Hotel that leaves cops and kidnappers dead. The characters are tightly drawn with no excessive description or needless jabber. One is pulled into Riley's thought processes while he puts aside his own Irish dislike of everything British and pieces together how the initial art theft might mean the life of the Queen. An excellent read for those who love crime novels.

— Mark Thorburn
Author, Historian, Teacher

JENNIFER M. FRASER

dispatch 1. a message dispatched or sent with speed; esp: an important official message often in cipher sent by an officer of the diplomatic, military, or police service of a government 2. the act of putting to death: killing

PROLOGUE

Victoria, Canada
Monday July 1, 1957

"My mother said that to be thirty, and not have a job, is a sin," Liam said turning away from the sea and the wind, cupping his hands over a match.

"But you have a job, you do, Liam," Flynn insisted.

Liam could barely hear him. When the cigarette was lit, he handed it to Flynn. Pulling his collar up against the wind driving off the ocean, Liam shivered. He drew his dark coat closer and checked once again that it was fully buttoned, even though it scratched against the scruffy beard covering his chin. Shuffling his feet, he tried to ignore the cold as he glanced up at Flynn, who was facing the sea like he might walk into it and never come back.

Liam forcibly made his voice deeper. "Flynn, are you *sure* they'll be calling in Kent Riley?"

"How many times will you be asking?" The wind whipped through Flynn's dark hair. Squinting, he raised his face to it. The cigarette glowed in his right hand. He held it low beneath his hip.

"And what if they don't?" Liam persisted.

"They'll be calling Kent. Don't you be worrying about that."

"How do you know?"

"I can feel it." Flynn raised his hands up to the wind.

"Jesus and Mary," Liam muttered, "he'll never agree to be working with us again, will he?"

"He might be, he just might," Flynn replied.

"I'm telling you, Flynn, you think too much of Kent Riley."

"I trained Kent myself, Liam." Flynn's tone brooked no argument.

"Well, I'll be telling you right now, it won't be me blowing myself up along with her Highness and I doubt it will be Kent Riley either." Liam wanted to walk off the beach and quit the whole damn plan.

Flynn pulled on his fingers listening to each click as the bones snapped in place. "Listen Liam, you weren't to be knowing this yet, but I'll tell you now." Taking one last drag of his cigarette, he threw the butt onto the wet beach and rubbed it into the sand with the toe of his shoe. "I've found a man who'll be rigging up a remote for us," Flynn said.

"Remote? How do you mean?" Liam pulled a dark green hood over his face.

"It's a radio controlled device so the bomb gets triggered when you're at a safe distance."

"Why'd you—"

"So you don't go blowing yourself to bits," Flynn replied, cutting him off.

Flynn's eyes were as dark as his hair. Moving towards the boat, he picked up a heavy leather bag and hoisted it to his shoulder.

"Come on, Liam, it'll be eleven fifty-two. Time to move."

Liam grabbed Flynn's arm at the base of the sea-wracked steps. "Can you be telling me one more time?"

Flynn turned to him and spoke as though he were introducing a play. "You stay in the shadows when we reach the patio." He took a deep breath. "Take the path to the left, wait while I open the gate and we go in the front door. Don't touch it, don't touch anything." Flynn turned to Liam. "I'll be the one to open it. It may take some time."

Liam's heart began to pound.

"The studio will be down the hall to the right."

The sketch of the floorplan was crammed into Liam's pocket. He resisted the temptation to pull it out and consult it one last time.

"You best be watching the steps into the living room, staying close to the wall." Flynn looked at him sharply. "Not a bloody sound, Liam. I'll be the one doing the talking. Let me tie him up. And yourself, you'll be keeping your gun sights on him. You'll not be letting your eyes leave his. Do you have it fixed in your mind then?"

Liam nodded.

Standing in the shadows of windswept evergreens, Flynn and Liam watched Charlie Crawford through a large window as he worked on a canvas. He was etching in white the outline of a massive horse. Then he began to apply what looked like black tar to the canvas with a sharp knife, muttering to the horse as if it could hear him. The wind rattled the windows of the studio, but he didn't seem to notice. Putting down the brush heavy with tar, the painter ran his thumbs up and down the legs of the horse, shading and blending as he went. Then pulling the knife from the waistband of his trousers, he used it to nick away bumps and bubbles with the blade.

The horse loomed. It arched its dark neck toward the painter. Crawford shut off the lights for a moment and all Flynn and Liam could see was the horse's white outline forming a contrast against the black tar background. Flynn released air through his teeth. The wind howled, waving trees in the darkness, the sea surging up the rocky beach below. The painter clicked the light back on. Carefully he wiped the knife and tucked it back into his waistband. Flynn and Liam watched as he selected a slender brush from a paint-spattered table, dipped it in white paint and murmured at the creature that almost seemed to strain against the canvas' confines as he approached. Dabbing along the horse's legs with the paint-soaked brush, he peered closely, then pulled the knife again and using the sharpened edge, he cut away at the white line, concentrating its light.

Flynn stirred and motioned to Liam. He flashed a grim smile that made Liam's heart go cold.

"For Ireland, then." Flynn whispered as he pulled down his hood.

● ● ●

Although she'd worked as an RCMP dispatcher for almost four years, Sylvia James had never done a night shift before. This was a shift normally reserved for E-Division's regular officers. Even so, Victoria was quiet – almost boring. Kicking off her heels, she swivelled in her chair and gazed up at the expansive radio system banked up against the wall. Her headphones lay over to the side. A silver microphone sat on its round base before her. She studied the reel-to-reel that cluttered the counter and went over the buttons she'd have to push if a call came through. Damn thing. A "prototype". Staff Sergeant Jones liked the term and used it often, but for Sylvia it was just one more thing to think about.

Gwen entered the office. She smiled weakly. Sylvia took a sip of her ginger ale and lit up a cigarette to offset how tired she felt.

"Why the sad face, Gwen, come on."

"Oh, I don't know." Gwen looked down and fiddled with her hands on her lap. "Who knew that a broken heart would make me feel so sick?" She laughed as if to lighten the moment.

"Have some ginger ale," Sylvia said. "You look as pale as a ghost. Come on, it'll perk you up."

Gwen shook her head, eyes filling with tears.

Sylvia rose from her chair and kissed Gwen on the cheek. "Come on, kid, it's not so bad. There are lots of other fish in the sea."

The line buzzed. Gwen grabbed the receiver while Sylvia clicked on the reel-to-reel machine and pulled on headphones to check it was recording clearly.

"Police Department – what is the nature of your emergency?"

Sylvia pulled on headphones so she too could listen to the call. "Backup" was another term Staff Sergeant Jones liked to say.

"Look, a deer has been hit by a car on the road out Ten Mile Point way," said a man's voice. "Can you get some of your boys to take care of it? It's hurt pretty bad."

"On Arbutus Road?" Gwen asked.

"Yes, that's it."

"We'll send a car right away. Could I have your name and—"

There was a hard click as the man hung up without even so much as a 'thank you'. Sylvia pulled off her headphones.

• • •

Not much longer until Constables Vittorio Cervide and Marcel Chausseur's shift would be done. It had been a quiet night so far, two 'drunk and disorderlies' and a 'domestic'. Still Vittorio felt tired. He pulled over, left the engine running as he rubbed his eyes. The radio suddenly crackled to life.

"Calling Car Twelve, Dispatch, do you read me?"

It was Gwen on the line. Why was she working Simon Boyer's late shift in Dispatch tonight?

"Car Twelve, go-ahead," responded Marcel from the passenger seat.

"There's a wounded deer on Arbutus Road. Take care of it." Gwen's voice sounded tense, almost unnatural.

"10-4. Car 12, 10-17 – en route" said Marcel into the mike.

"What's Gwen doing working tonight?" Marcel asked.

"I don't know," said Vittorio turning the car around. "Should be Simon Boyer. I thought you had lunch with him today?"

"He had to go out of town and said George Murphy would be on shift tonight."

"Marcel, when are you going to tell me why you called off your engagement?"

"Never. I don't want to talk about it. Let's just say, like all women, Gwen can't be trusted." Marcel put his hands on the dashboard. "Look there's an injured deer out there for you to shoot. Come on."

Vittorio angled the car down the dark wet streets, noting that the wind was picking up. Cruising slowly down Arbutus Road, he eventually saw the animal up ahead, moving weakly near the centre-line. It was sickening to watch the beast trying to rise and slumping back to the wet pavement. Marcel had turned his head so as not to see. Vittorio smiled. His partner could take down an assailant twice his size or remain completely calm walking into a bar brawl, but Marcel could not stand to see the wounded deer struggling in the car's headlights. Vittorio got the Remington from the trunk of the car and went toward the animal, talking softly. He could hear Dispatch coming in again. Gwen shouldn't be working at night. The deer twisted around at Vittorio's approach, increasing its efforts to get away. He rubbed his hand on its flank, noting the badly shattered leg. He took a few steps back and positioned the rifle. Whispering an apology, he pulled the trigger and the gunshot cracked through the night air. The deer lay still.

Marcel suddenly flashed the headlights at him. Vittorio picked up the dead animal and moved it over to the side of the road. It was surprisingly light and warm. Public Works would be by to pick it up in the morning. Marcel honked the horn lightly and Vittorio hurried back. "What is it?"

"10-83, but get this, they're stealing some guy's art collection."

"What's the 10-20?"

"4040 Telegraph Bay Road. Thieves may still be present."

"10-82?" Vittorio gunned the engine.

Marcel was scanning the road map and didn't hear him.

"10-82?" Vittorio asked once again.

"10-10," Marcel said and at the look on Vittorio's face firmly stated, "Negative," adding, "The homeowner is safe at the neighbour's house next door."

"Sirens?"

"No, let's surprise them."

Vittorio made a sharp U-turn and they plunged down the hill. "What if they're armed?"

"Dispatch didn't call in a 10-82," Marcel insisted. "I just do what I'm told. Turn here."

"How can you see?" It was absolutely pitch dark.

"This is the way."

Marcel had a feeling for the city that Vittorio admired. He manoeuvred through downtown traffic like a cabbie and his sense of direction was always spot on. The tires screeched as Vittorio hit the corner a little too sharply. The trees were close together and the houses were far apart. They flew down the road. Vittorio angled the car around a curve and they plunged down a hill.

"Slow down!" commanded Marcel.

Vittorio hit the brakes sharply and the car skidded left.

Pointing at a low house down a driveway, "There it is," Marcel said. Then he spoke into the mike. "Dispatch, Car 12, 10-23."

The house was dark, but Marcel must have somehow seen the numbers. Vittorio pulled over swiftly against a wet bank. He opened the car door and pulled out his revolver. Wrapping both hands around the cold grip, he slipped out of the car leaving the door ajar. His adrenalin shot up as he got low and skirted along the edge of the drive toward the house. It looked like a rancher. Marcel must be behind him, but he couldn't hear him.

Then he heard Marcel speaking urgently from a distance: "Dispatch, Car 12. 10-32. I repeat 10-32."

10-32? Marcel must see something he couldn't see if he was calling for additional units. Were the thieves armed? Christ, how did Marcel know that? Vittorio hesitated for a moment. Just as he turned to call over to Marcel, he saw two dark figures out of the corner of his eye by the front door. He couldn't make out their faces in the night. Their faces were blacked out. He pulled his gun forward and yelled "Police – don't move! Put your hands in the air. I repeat—"

A shot exploded in the silence and Vittorio felt searing heat on the side of his head. It was like someone had taken a knife and jabbed it into his brain. He fell to his knees and rolled sideways, holding his hand on the wet, burning side of his head. He couldn't feel his ear. He closed his eyes. He dimly heard Marcel's voice.

"Car 12 to Dispatch, we've got a 10-33—"

Marcel must still be in the car. Vittorio wanted to tell him to stay in the car where it was safe.

"It's a 10-33 – I repeat a 10-33. Vittorio's been hit!"

"Car 12 to Dispatch," Marcel was yelling. "Vittorio's down. We've got a 10-33! Send all units! I need 10-64, 10-64. I need an ambulance!"

His uniform soaking in the driveway's cool dampness, Vittorio whispered into the dark: "it's serious. We've got a 10-33. There's an officer down." He tried to stop the blood that was now leaking onto the ground and pooling at his cheek. His whole brain was screaming. Then it all went black.

● ● ●

Constable Chasseur strode rapidly down the lower corridor of the RCMP Detachment. He'd entered directly from the parking bay and so far hadn't seen anyone.

The heavy door to the Dispatch room resisted slightly as he pushed. Sylvia jumped up when he entered and Gwen gasped. Marcel's hand went unconsciously to his chest where Vittorio's blood felt slightly sticky to his touch. His stomach heaved.

"Your uniform!" exclaimed Sylvia. "What's happened to your uniform?" Marcel found himself trying to somehow brush the blood off. The reel-to-reel was within reach.

"Is Constable Cervide alright?" Gwen asked, her face pale and strained.

"What the hell were you thinking?" Marcel cried. "Were you trying to get us killed?"

"What are you talking about, Marcel?" Sylvia asked.

"I'm talking about Vittorio being shot!"

"Calm down," Sylvia pushed the door fully shut. "You're yelling."

"I'm talking about radioing us not to use our siren. I'm talking about getting no backup. Doesn't 10-32 mean anything to you?"

"You didn't call for back-up." Sylvia cried. "We didn't tell you not to use sirens! Why would we? We radioed you 10-82 and to use 10-30."

"What the hell happened out there Marcel?" Gwen asked. "I called the ambulance, you never requested backup."

"What are you talking about no sirens, Marcel?" Sylvia demanded.

Fingering the knife in his coat pocket, Marcel examined the reel-to-reel. He looked over at Gwen. Avoiding his glare, she lowered her head even farther, then hand on mouth she jumped from her seat and went rushing out the door. Perfect.

Sylvia turned on Marcel. "Now look what you've done!"

She gazed at the open door for a moment then added. "I'd better see if she's okay. I don't know what you're talking about. Tell me about—"

"Vittorio's in surgery." Marcel replied. "You'll both be fired or worse."

"We didn't do anything wrong."

"Fine. Go see if she's alright."

"Why do you care so much all of a sudden?" Sylvia's eyes flashed angrily.

They could hear Gwen retching in the little bathroom down the hall. Sylvia stormed out the door, leaving Marcel standing in the Dispatch room alone.

Sylvia was speaking outside the bathroom door in a soft voice. His hand went to the small cross hanging from the chain around his neck and he closed his eyes. "Forgive me. *Forgive* me."

Marcel looked at his watch, right on schedule. He checked the corridor one more time. Sylvia had gone into the bathroom. Quietly, he pulled the door shut. Unbuttoning his stiff shirtfront, he removed the substitute reel and laid it on the counter. Flicking open the small knife blade, he sliced the magnetic tape. Carefully removing the reel of tape from the machine, he stuffed it inside his shirtfront, wincing at the cold metal against his chest.

He took the substitute reel and inserted it. His hands were shaking slightly. He willed them to stop. Threading the tape through the spools and sprockets, he took a tiny piece of adhesive from the inside of his wrist and attached the ribbons of magnetic tape. Turning the machine on, friction caught the tape and pulled it taut. Marcel took a last glace around Dispatch as if he had forgotten something. He opened the door and listened. The sound of running water and girls' voices came from the bathroom. Without a sideways glance, he walked rapidly past and exited the building by the back door into the rear parking bay.

Driving through the empty streets, Marcel noted the lights were on at Constable Dan Smythe's house as they had agreed. Dan stood on the porch smoking. His light hair looked grey as he hunched against the wind. The neighbours might wonder about a second RCMP vehicle parked outside Dan's place, but then they'd probably just think it was routine police business. No one was awake at this time of night anyhow. Getting out of the car, Marcel was hit with a blast of damp wind on his face. Once when he'd had a fever, his mother placed a cold compress on his forehead. He could hear her humming *À la claire fontaine*. A wave of homesickness for Montréal and his family washed over him.

Dan didn't say a word, his eyes darting down the street both ways. He held the door open and Marcel went down the dark hall into the lit kitchen. A reel-to-reel tape machine was sitting on the table, a near duplicate of the one in Dispatch. Where Dan had secured it, Marcel did not want to know. There was a short blonde woman with faded lipstick standing by the fridge.

"I'm Bonnie," she said as the three sat down at the table. Marcel gave Dan the stolen reel and watched as he mounted it onto the spindle and threaded the tape onto the hub. Dan flipped the power switch and waited for the empty reel to spool up and load the thin magnetic strip.

"Won't the Staff Sergeant be able to see the cut in the tape when you splice it back onto the one in Dispatch?" Marcel asked.

"Trust me he'll never even notice it. And no one will be able to hear the difference either," Dan said.

"I still think we shouldn't risk it and just do a new recording," Marcel insisted.

"Are you kidding?" Dan's anger was palpable. "It would take forever and the longer we use Bonnie's voice, the more obvious it will be that it's not Gwen or Sylvia speaking."

"I know, but what if they figure out the call was erased and re-recorded."

"I'm telling you, Marcel, they won't notice. Flynn's had me practicing on this machine for months."

"How much time do we have?" Bonnie asked.

"No time." Dan replied, turning on the radio that was sitting on the counter. He fiddled with the nobs until he got the frequency right and opened the window above the sink. Wind rustled into the room blowing the thin curtains on either side.

"What do you want me to say?" Bonnie asked.

"Just be quiet. We first have to erase the 10-82 and 10-30." Dan put a piece of paper before her. "Read this out. You're going to call in a 10-83 and then here—"

"What's a 10-83?"

"It means a break and enter – then you're going to say 'no sirens,' I want you to say it quietly, pull back from the microphone when you say that part, okay?"

"Alright," said the woman, "but what's 10-82 and 10-30?"

Dan looked like he might lose it, but he patiently answered the question. "10-82 means 'weapons' and so 10-30 is 'use caution.' Marcel, you've got your script?"

"Yeah – I got it Dan," Marcel showed him the paper.

"You've got the part about backup, 10-32?"

"Come on, Dan! We've got to hurry. I have to get this tape back to Dispatch or we're done for."

WEDNESDAY

JENNIFER M. FRASER

CHAPTER ONE

Investigator Kent Riley sat at a heavy wooden table waiting for Deputy Commissioner, Richard Tepoorten. He'd been scheduled to arrive in Victoria for VIP duty on Thursday, but there had been a violent art theft leaving a member badly wounded. Most likely unrelated to the pending Royal Visit, the Deputy's assistant had said, but the next thing Kent knew, the Deputy Commissioner had sent a car and Kent was on a red-eye flight out to the west coast.

The room must have belonged to some provincial bureaucrat. A large bookshelf overflowed with annual reports and stacks of paper. A grey painted desk took up one corner and was cluttered with two phones, envelopes and a box of pencils. One wall was now covered in RCMP blueprints and maps. Tall windows looked down upon a quiet harbour. A woman hurried in and put down two cups of black coffee. "The Deputy is on his way," she said closing the door behind her.

The farthest west Kent had ever been was Saskatchewan to attend Depot. Even though he'd been briefed on the flight out from Toronto, he couldn't help expecting the young city, named for Queen Victoria, to be some sort of antiquated outpost at the far edge of the country, a final fort or frontier town. Instead Victoria appeared to be well established and had an air of vitality about it. The scale and grandeur of the grey stone Legislature, and the ivy-covered Empress Hotel facing it across the harbour front were impressive to say the least.

He'd worked in Québec, Ottawa and Toronto, but being on an island with the expansive sea beyond reminded him more of Ireland than Canada. As another ocean breeze gusted through the open window, he felt a sudden rush of jumbled memories. His breath faltered for a moment – Sarah's scarred neck; his father holding the box of his mother's ashes; flying over the sea to get back to Belfast – Flynn Dolan's twisted face and, his father fighting back tears on the long journey home.

'She would want us to be burying her at home, Kenny,' his father had said.

Kent knew islands and he knew the choppy, white-capped Atlantic, but this was the Pacific, he reminded himself. A different ocean – a different time. He pulled his pen and notebook out as the Richard Tepoorten entered the room. Kent stood to shake his hand.

"Thank you for coming on such short notice, Investigator Riley."

"Of course, Deputy."

The Deputy Commissioner put down the files he was carrying and took a drink of his coffee. He extracted a photograph from the file. "This is Vittorio Cervide."

Kent studied the face. He couldn't be much older than thirty, but his black hair was receding off a high forehead. His eyes were neutral as they stared back at Kent.

"On Monday night, at approximately zero one hundred," continued the Deputy, "Constable Cervide was shot in the head."

Kent stopped writing, and he looked up, waiting for the Deputy to resume.

"Constable Cervide has undergone surgery, his right ear was irreparably damaged, but they no longer believe he suffered any permanent brain damage. He is out of surgery and is recovering at the Royal Jubilee Hospital."

Kent let out a deep sigh. Well at least he wasn't killed. Not many survive a bullet to the head.

"He'll likely have vertigo, and a possible concussion. He was unable to talk yesterday. There's a constable posted outside his door at all times. When he is well enough to give a statement, I'll let you know."

"What was the time again?"

"Approximately zero one hundred. Cervide's partner – a constable named Marcel Chasseur," he paused and extracted another photograph from the file and handed it to Kent. Chasseur's eyes were hooded. His mouth, although pulled into a military expression for the photograph, seemed loose. Kent didn't like the look of him.

"Two years on the Force, served in the Royal Canadian Navy for two years before that. Trusted, tough, but a little too quiet, you know. Single, from Montréal, family's French. Father's a retired shopkeeper. Constable Chasseur's been all nerves since the shooting."

"Nerves?"

"Can't sleep or even settle, won't talk to anybody. He has trauma-like symptoms. He's currently under observation in the Psychiatric Ward at the Jubilee."

The Deputy's short choppy sentences broke the narrative down so it was easier for Kent to take notes. He flipped the page and took a quick sip of his coffee. He had trouble imagining this former Navy man with the hooded eyes being so shaken by a non-fatal shooting. Nervous? Sleepless? That made *no* sense. He recorded the words with a sense of disbelief. Whatever had happened must have been a hell of a shock. The Deputy Commissioner waited for him to catch up.

"It seems there was a problem in Dispatch. They use civilians in E-Division during the day."

"Civilians?"

"I know. The Staff Sergeant says it's an 'initiative', a way to employ young women. They all want jobs, just like during the War. Staff Sergeant Jones says they don't have to pay them as much so it saves funds that are desperately needed elsewhere."

"Might save money, but their job is to—"

"I'm not saying I agree with it," the Deputy raised a hand. Kent leaned back in his seat and Tepoorten resumed.

"So on Monday night, two *civilians* took the call. They're running a project where they record the calls on a reel-to-reel. The Staff tells me the frequencies were good and the signal was clear. No major weather issues, but it was windy. System had just been through a routine check – no on-going electrical or transmission problems." The Deputy raised his hands and then dropped them. "How could Dispatch make such an error?"

"Sorry, Deputy?"

"In one night, we end up with a near-priceless sculpture stolen, one member wounded in hospital and the other locked-up in the psych ward – three days before the Royal Visit?"

What error in Dispatch, Kent wanted to ask, but knew better than to interrupt. Tepoorten got up from his seat and walked over to the desk in the corner as if looking for something to throw across the room. "Civilians," he said, shaking his head, but then added quietly. "The two girls had immaculate records up until now."

Kent stretched out his legs and opened his hand to the morning breeze from the window. He would have liked to ask about the art robbery so that he knew what thieves they were talking about and what sculpture was stolen, but he knew from experience that the Deputy Commissioner needed to tell the story in his own way. He always started with the individuals involved and offered details that others would skim over. The Deputy believed that 'God was in the details.' Tepoorten was thumbing through the file again. Kent waited.

"It seems the break-in occurred just before twenty-four hundred hours at the home of one, Charlie Crawford, an artist from Texas. I've never heard of him or seen his work, but apparently he's a big deal in New York –

paints modern stuff – looks like a child painted it to me. His house is on the ocean in Cadboro Bay. His wife is Susan Macmillan, as in the logging family 'Macmillans.' Thankfully Mrs. Crawford wasn't home at the time. The thieves were pros. Alarms dismantled and telephone wires cut – tied Mr. Crawford up – but in the end only took the one piece. A sculpture, if you can call it that."

Tepoorten pulled another photograph out of the file. Kent scanned the image of a burnished golden head, lying on its side, its eyes closed. It looked like a woman sleeping with lips like moons. It was very stylized, life-sized and somehow erotic. He read the caption at the bottom, *Sleeping Muse* – Constantin Brancusi.

"Is it gold?" Kent asked.

"No, it's bronze, but this sculpture is still worth hundreds of thousands to the right buyer. Our preliminary report says it's the only thing they took even though there were several other high-value pieces and paintings, not to mention Mrs. Crawford's significant jewellery collection."

A targeted heist was always more worrisome than a run of the mill robbery.

A discreet knock, and Tepoorten's assistant Miss Lennox opened the door a crack. "It's Neville Heath, from London for you Sir."

"Damn, tell him I'll call him back in fifteen–no twenty, minutes."

"Of course, Sir." She bowed out and secured the door softly behind her.

The Deputy looked down at his watch and then lit a cigarette. He offered one to Kent.

"No thanks."

"Seems the thieves underestimated Mr. Crawford," said the Deputy. "Apparently he carries a knife at all times. Supposedly, he paints with it. He managed to cut the ropes they tied him to a chair with, slip out and run to the neighbour's house while the thieves were otherwise occupied. Dispatch took the emergency call at twenty-three-fifty hours and routed Cervide and Chasseur, to attend the scene. They called in a 10-83, but no record of weapons."

"Dispatch called a 10-82, but it was heard as 10-83?"

"I don't think so. Not according to the report."

"But surely Crawford told Dispatch the intruders were armed and dangerous."

"He did." The Deputy shook his head. "However, Car 12 went to the scene without sirens. Constable Cervide got out of the vehicle and practically stumbled into the thieves just as they were exiting with the Brancusi sculpture. One of the men fired a shot striking Cervide in the head, and in the resulting chaos, they both escaped. It seems Dispatch gave Constables Cervide and Chasseur the wrong code. They were totally unprepared."

"Unacceptable. They should both be let go immediately."

"It's all captured on tape."

"That ought to make firing them that much easier."

"There was a delay with backup as well," the Deputy sighed. "Wounded cop, stolen art and armed thieves unaccounted for – and the Royal Visit is seventy-two hours away. Riley, the papers are already all over this."

"How so? Who talked?"

"Don't know. It was supposed to be kept quiet, so we've got a leak."

What next? This was a mess. Kent was starting to regret taking the assignment. Not that he could have actually refused.

"It makes the force look inept, not exactly what we need days before the Royals arrive. Although it could all be unrelated, these events have set Premier Bennett and all of E-Division on edge."

Kent imagined the local papers filled with their share of cartoons depicting the RCMP as a bunch of fools, sporting big Stetsons, astride knock-kneed horses.

"Mostly in Victoria the force deals with drunks, domestics and petty crime." Tepoorten tapped ash from his cigarette into a shallow, cut crystal dish. "You might have the occasional fist fight or quarrelling neighbours. I want to know *why* an art heist now and *why* was an officer was shot. It's too close to the Royal Visit for my liking."

Kent started to see that the Dispatch error could be connected to the impending visit. He didn't like the look of it either. He put down his notebook and pen. Time was not on his side. "Do you want me to use a polygraph on the civilian dispatchers?" He asked.

"No, no lie-detectors." The Deputy lowered his voice, "Don't forget that the Press will be all over us if there's any hint of an internal screw-up. There cannot be so much as a whiff that we suspect one of our own. If we use the polygraph, what with the leak, we'll be all over the damn papers again."

The Deputy Commissioner picked up a letter opener and passed it from hand to hand. "I need you to get to the bottom of this and keep it under wraps. Internally, do whatever you need to do. I've already got the approval for any phone taps you need. Publically, I want everyone, including the Press, to become bored with this story and move on to covering the Royal Visit." The last three words hung in the air between them.

"Today is Wednesday. On Saturday, Queen Elizabeth II and Prince Philip arrive in the harbour to begin their tour of Victoria. We have less than seventy-two hours to figure out if there are any risks to their safety."

"What will my role be on Saturday if everything goes as planned?"

The Deputy extracted several papers from his file and handed them to Kent. "You will brief Her Majesty and Prince Philip at eleven hundred hours in the Premier's Office."

17

The events of the day were listed and followed by extensive details regarding protocol, location, directions.

"They have a series of appearances throughout the day that you will attend with Her Majesty and the Prince. At seventeen hundred hours, you will escort them from the Premier's Office through the underground tunnel to the basement of the Empress Hotel."

Who knows about the tunnel? Kent wondered.

"From there, you will then escort them up to their room on the seventh floor via a service elevator. The lift has been disabled for the past two weeks, supposedly for repairs, but we've shut it down as part of the security protocols."

Kent located the time on his schedule and perused the directives regarding room assignments on the seventh floor.

"Once the Royals are safely in their suite you will secure the immediate area."

The Deputy got up and gestured to one of the maps. "This is where the decoy will travel." Kent joined him and followed his finger as he pointed out the route. "While you're securing the Empress Hotel, the media will follow the decoy cavalcade taking the Queen's stand-in to Government House. Members have been brought in from as far north as Whitehorse and as far east as Newfoundland to make a show of securing the place. Lieutenant Governor Ross has been exceedingly co-operative in this matter and has given our staff full access to Government House."

The Deputy Commissioner resumed his seat and Kent joined him at the table. He reached for his coffee, but it had grown cold.

"Nothing in the evening?" Kent asked.

"The Queen has made it quite clear that she is fatigued from a very busy schedule in Washington State and insists she and the Prince have an evening off."

The Deputy tidied the papers back into his file. "She and Prince Phillip will dine alone in their room Saturday evening."

"Who will have access to the tunnel and service elevator?"

"No one but you and the Queen's man, Fenwick Chisholm. He came to Victoria in advance to get a lay of the land as it were."

Kent wrote Fenwick Chisolm down in his notepad.

"Who knows about the decoy going to Government House?" He asked.

"Staff Sergeant Jones has been told that the Queen will be at Government House and that two Ladies-in-Waiting will be staying in the Vice-Regal suite on the sixth floor of the Empress Hotel."

The Deputy took Kent's schedule and flipped through to the fourth page and pointed out the locations with names adjacent.

"The Vice-Regal suite is where Jones' men will be posted in twelve-hour shifts starting Friday morning until the Ladies-in-Waiting, along with the Queen and Prince, leave at zero nine hundred on Sunday."

Considering the theft and the leak, the complicated precautions made Kent feel more at ease.

"Only you and Fenwick Chisholm will know that the Royals will in fact be located on the seventh floor in suite 704. Your suite, 702 will be right next door and Chisolm's room is on the other side."

"No protective policing around her room?! Is that even—"

"Just you and Chisholm. He's been positioned in a turret room down the corridor for weeks now, except for a brief stint in Ottawa to check on the last leg of the Royals' North American tour. The Queen will be better protected if *no one* knows she's in that room."

"Because no one is protecting her," Kent spoke slowly wrapping his mind around the unusual idea, "so she won't be a target."

Tepoorten nodded. "Exactly." His face clouded. "The part that galls me is Prince Philip has said to the American Press that he likes how 'rational' security is in Canada in contrast to the Americans. And then he has the damn foolery to add: 'If they plug us, they plug us.'"

Kent thought it best to distract him. "Who exactly is Fenwick Chisholm?" He asked.

"He's her Head of Security."

Kent raised his eyebrows.

"I know. I asked our liaison, Neville Heath, if we could fully trust him. According to Heath, Chisholm was captured in '44 by the Nazis during a night raid behind enemy lines in Austria. He was held in Stalag 17-B as a POW for eighteen months."

"It's a bloody miracle he's still alive."

"King George took a personal interest in his return."

"In exchange for—"

The Deputy ignored his question and went on. "Since Chisholm's release, he's been assigned to the Queen's Guard and personally responsible for the Queen's safety."

Kent's throat tightened. "He knows about me?"

"We'll put Members all over Government House where the decoy is staying, in case anyone tries to cause trouble. The Empress Hotel staff has been informed that two of the Queen's Ladies-in-Waiting will spend the evening in the Humboldt Wing, on the sixth floor, in the Vice-Regal Suite. There will also be reporters at the hotel interviewing these Ladies-in-Waiting as they make their way to their room. While everyone is focused on Government House and the Vice-Regal Suite, you will ensure the Queen and Prince are safely established in 704 with you on one side and Chisholm on the other." Tepoorten straightened his shoulders. "She's an extremely important young lady who needs our protection."

No, Kent thought, she's not. She's the head of an Empire built on oppression.

"How will I recognize Chisholm?" Kent asked.

"Look at his hands."

Stalag 17-B must have been a living hell. Kent could not imagine the relief Chisholm must have felt as the door to his cell opened and he exited at the behest of his King.

On a short-leave between deployments, Kent had been having tea with his father when Parliament issued the decree that the two princesses, Elizabeth and Margaret, should be evacuated to Canada and most Brits seemed to agree. Sending her children to the safest place in the Commonwealth seemed like the prudent choice to make, but the Queen Mother held fast. And when London was being bombed into the ground, the Queen had issued a statement: 'the children won't go without me and I won't leave without the King and the King will never leave London.' Kent could practically hear her voice even now.

Kent willed himself to think of Queen Elizabeth II as Second Subaltern Elizabeth Windsor. It wasn't fair to hold her responsible for Britain's loathsome treatment of Ireland. He made a conscious effort to remind himself that Princess Elizabeth Windsor had spent the war years as a military driver and mechanic. Besides, Kent had sworn an oath to this woman, the RCMP's Honorary High Commissioner when he joined the Royal Canadian Mounted Police. He'd made a promise to her, a promise to this duty-bound, imperial leader, this 'lady'. He must never forget that oath.

Kent and Sarah had been in Norfolk when King George VI died. 'Oh Kent, the King's just died and Elizabeth is so far away.' Sarah had cried hard and wouldn't leave her spot by the radio for the whole day. She never changed out of her nightgown. The Royal Family might as well have been her own family the way she carried on. Kent made the mistake of saying to her that when the King was sick, Elizabeth really shouldn't have been off on tour overseeing her vassals. Sarah's furious voice had filled the room.

'What!? Vassals? Do you know what Princess Elizabeth has been doing in Kenya, Kent? I mean do you really know? She opened the Kenya Farmers Association.' Sarah strode around the room swinging her arms. 'She went to a Masai tribal gathering and held an event for women of all communities in Mombasa.'

Kent had tried to calm her down by coming over and stroking her hair and then kissing her. She pushed him away. The last thing she'd said as he slouched out the door was, 'She went and toured the Royal East African Navy, Kent. You should be ashamed of yourself. Her father just died.' Kent decided a long walk was the best course of action and when she'd settled down, to beg her forgiveness.

"I'm going to give you several numbers where I can be reached," the Deputy said, snapping Kent in an instant back to matters at hand. "I've told Staff Sergeant Jones that you'll be handling the case. I don't fully trust him."

"Why?"

"I'm not sure. He's a bit of a drinker. He's an idealist."

Kent put a question mark beside Jones' name. "Can I access Special-I?"

"You won't need to. You've already been assigned an expert," Tepoorten glanced down at his file. "Constable Michael Callaghan," he read, "a specialist in technical operations. He has a mechanical engineering degree from the University of Toronto. From what I gather, he's a bit of a genius – graduated top of his class. I'm told Callaghan's the best there is."

"But Deputy, you know I work best alone." Kent learned the hard way that the more people who knew something, the more people got hurt along the way.

Tepoorten ran a hand over his face. He jotted down a series of telephone numbers on a piece of paper. "Look Riley, keep me informed as you investigate. You can't call me too often on this one. We can't afford missing any details with the pending Visit."

Kent figured he could keep some sort of Special-I expert alongside if it made life easier for the Deputy. Kent gathered the files and put them with his notepad into his briefcase. "I'll find out what's going on, Deputy."

The Deputy Commissioner shook his hand, looking hard into his eyes the way fathers do when their sons go off to war. "I know, Riley. I know you will."

CHAPTER TWO

Flynn Dolan knocked on the warehouse door. The alley looked drab in the summer morning with its rubbish bins and dusty gravel. The door opened slightly, and Scotty opened it a bit further, taking in Liam O'Rourke standing slightly behind Flynn and off to the right. He glanced up and down the alley and then let them in. Flynn resisted looking up as he heard the man with the rifle shift his feet slightly on the catwalk above.

Scotty searched him and Liam for weapons. A wiry man in his fifties, maybe older, he smelt like stale cigarettes. Taking Liam's case, Scotty opened it on a small table by the door, rifled through the stacks of bills, fastened it shut and returned it to Liam. "Come on then boys," he said, "Henry's waiting."

They walked down the narrow path through the stacks of boxes. Flynn's nose crinkled with the dusty air and Liam let go a resounding sneeze that echoed in the tomblike space. Boxes were stacked in every direction as far as they could see in the dim light. They made their way to Henry's office in silence. Scotty used a patterned knock and the door opened. The guard let them pass, a knife gripped in one hand. Henry motioned at him. The guard kept his gaze on Flynn, but let his hand drop.

Henry was sitting at his desk, his grey head illuminated by a green desk lamp. "Come to see the Royal quarters have you?"

"That I have, Henry – that I have."

"Well, go on then. Rooke, show Mr. Dolan where we'll be putting her Majesty upon her arrival. I'll wait for you here."

Unbeknownst to Flynn the guard they passed at the door had silently followed them across the room and was now standing directly behind them. As they made their way deeper into the warehouse, Rooke didn't speak and Flynn wondered if he was a mute, maybe lost his vocal chords in the War. Maybe he couldn't speak English.

Flynn pulled absently on his fingers easing blood into the joints. "So, how long is it that you have been working for Henry, Rooke?"

"Forever."

So he wasn't a mute after all. His accent sounded Eastern European. "Where are you from?" Flynn asked.

"Istanbul."

Rooke opened a door that had several locks on it. Flynn and Liam entered. There was an army cot on one side and a metal pot on the other.

"What's the pot for?" asked Liam.

"For her to be pissing in." Flynn replied in a flat voice.

"She will be needing a bathroom, Flynn."

"She'll be needing a prison, Liam."

Rooke didn't make a sound and nothing about their exchange registered on his closed face.

Liam was shaking his head. "She should maybe have a desk, Flynn. Somewhere she can sit to write. Maybe she'll want to be writing some thoughts down."

"It's not a writing place, Liam. It's a prison. Her Majesty needs to know what it's like to be without freedom. Just be glad I haven't arranged for her to be beaten by the guards." He spoke through clenched teeth, "I could have her beaten to death – would you prefer that then, Liam?"

Flynn walked out of the room and Rooke locked it up behind them. Liam kept his head down.

"Weep all you want," Flynn said, "but weep for the Irish, Liam. Don`t you be weeping for the Queen that has British soldiers and Ulster Loyalists to do her dirty work. She'll know what it's like to be dirty, Liam, dirty and without hope and without dignity."

Liam grabbed Flynn's arm tightly as they walked back through the dust. Flynn shook it off in disgust.

Henry sat toad-like in the green dusk. He was the banker that never gave you a loan. "Well now, Mr. Dolan. Is the room to your satisfaction?"

"Yes, it'll do, Henry, it'll do."

"Have you got the money?"

Liam pulled out the leather case and unclasped it, laying it in front of Henry.

"Here's twenty-five thousand dollars." The down payment as agreed.

"And the rest?"

"When we bring her, there'll be twenty-five more and twenty-five again when we take her away."

"Alright," Henry nodded slowly, opening the case and surveying the bills stacked inside.

As they approached the heavy door back into the alley, the shoes above scraped on the metal of the catwalk. Flynn took deep breaths of the dusty air to push a sudden rush of emotion away. He owed his father this. It was love, a son's love for his father, rising in his chest.

Liam followed him out, but remained quiet. Flynn could tell he was harbouring disagreement, but the Queen was within Flynn's grasp and they both knew it.

Liam patted his arm and rasped out. "You can trust me, Flynn. I'd do anything for you, anything to see your plan work. We owe it to so many people, Flynn, so many people."

Flynn indulged, just for a few seconds, the vision of telling his father that he had taken the Queen. That she now was the prisoner and Ireland could take its rightful place in the world. Ireland would finally make Britain pay for years of poverty, starvation and shame. He would use a quiet voice. Man to man. Showing his father that what he had suffered was not in vain. Flynn wanted him to know that he had a daring son, a son willing to risk his own life for his country and was about, against all odds, to bring the Empire to its knees.

Ruining his reverie was a sudden flashback to his father's broken body, the bruises on his face, his mother's tearless eyes as she washed the once powerful body for burial after it was brought home from Crumlin Road Gaol.

He shook off the image. "Come on, Liam. Let's be reading the paper in the hotel lobby. Perhaps we'll be catching a glimpse of Kent." Flynn pulled a soft cap from his pocket and tucked his dark hair away.

"You think the robbery would have brought Kent out this quick?"

"I can't be knowing, Liam, but I have a feeling, especially after I took care of Constable Cervide." God he hated them.

"Dan said Kent was scheduled to be arriving on Friday," Liam said, "but since the shooting there'd been a whole series of calls placed out of the Staff Sergeant's office. Dan's thinking it might be about Kent."

They made their way down Douglas Street, turned toward the Inner Harbour and took the steps leading into the Empress Hotel. Flynn settled into a wing-backed chair in the great lobby while Liam skirted around for some newspapers left behind by hotel guests. He sat across from Flynn on a velvet brown couch and he rustled the pages in front of his face in a weak attempt to blend in. Flynn began to study the people around them, seeking a glimpse of his old friend, 'RCMP Investigator' Kent Riley. Ah, it'd be so good to see Kenny again.

Flynn couldn't sit still. He folded up his paper and strolled over to a shop window while studying the reflection of well-heeled people enjoying their little sandwiches and cakes. Forcing down the bitter taste of resentment that filled his mouth, Flynn gazed into the shop window. He took in a sharp breath as he spotted Kent crossing towards the reception desk briefcase in one hand and a suitcase in the other. Kent slowed for a moment looking lost in the grand lobby.

His hair was still the colour of embers when you blew on them to keep the fire going. Flynn had known, even as a boy, that Kent Riley would grow up to become this man. He'd singled him out. Kenny was a skinny kid, but Flynn had taught him how to box, how to harness his body's agility and speed. Taught him how to control it and to control others. Kent was the younger brother that Flynn should have had.

So just like clockwork, like Dan said, Kent had been called in to investigate the Brancusi theft, the 'mistakes' in Dispatch and the shooting. Not many men could shoot a man's ear off in the dark. Flynn smiled at the terrible irony that Kent, this trusted protector, was in fact the most dangerous individual to have anywhere near the Queen. When Flynn needed Kent, he knew exactly how to get him. And Constable Smythe had assured him that he would deliver the genius – this Michael Callaghan who knew how to make the remote they needed for the bomb. It was almost too easy.

"Did you see him? Kent's here, just like you said." Liam's voice made Flynn jump. He hadn't heard him approach.

"Yes, I saw him." Flynn could still see Kent as he now strode through the lobby and waited in front of an ornate lift. "I told you they'd be calling on him." A stooped porter approached and took Kent's suitcase. They entered the lift and the doors shut. Flynn still watched as if Kent might somehow reappear.

"Shall we be going then?" Liam asked.

"What?"

"I said, shall we be going then?"

"Right," Flynn tried to concentrate on Liam.

Flynn took one last look at the lift where he'd last seen Kent and turned on his heel.

Ever since Kent abandoned him, Flynn found he was always looking for him. And now, finally, he'd brought him back.

CHAPTER THREE

Kent hesitated for a moment in the lobby of the Empress Hotel as his eyes adjusted from the summer light. Driving in from the airport, with wild forest on either side, he had not expected to discover Legislative Buildings that could have been designed by Wren himself or to step across the threshold of a grand hotel better suited to Paris.

The Empress was enormous and stately. It must have hundreds of rooms. It faced the Harbour with the Legislature off to the left side as if it were an after-thought, a lady-in-waiting to the Grand Dame herself. This hotel was a place worthy of a Queen. Under huge chandeliers well-dressed guests were greeting one another and setting off for a day of sightseeing. Others were taking tea at little tables. Shops selling neatly laid out jewellery, handbags, scarves and haberdashery were built into the hotel interior.

At the end of the immense polished front desk, a clerk with salt and pepper hair caught Kent's attention with a slight tilt of his head. Kent approached and the man placed his hand flat at the edge of the wide desk. He had a slender gold ring on his left hand, and stamped into the metal was the RCMP crest.

"Hello Mr. Laurier," said the man.

"Good-morning," Kent replied.

"How was your flight?"

"Fine, thank you."

"We have you in room 602. A porter will assist you with your bags up to the sixth floor. I'll summon him now." The man handed him three keys. One must be for his seventh floor suite and the other one?

"Were you able to meet your friend at the Legislature, Mr. Laurier?" the older man asked brightly, as if they were exchanging information about local sites a tourist should take in while visiting the city.

"Why yes, thank you," Kent replied in the same light-hearted tone, "that meeting did take place."

"It's almost eleven hundred hours and your office called from Toronto asking me to relay a message to you. Your meeting with Mr. Jones is set for thirteen hundred."

Kent nodded.

"If there's anything you need, please don't hesitate to contact me here at the front desk."

Kent suddenly felt exposed and wanted to get to his room. Gathering up his briefcase and luggage, he made his way to the lift. He could sense someone's eyes on him, but he didn't have the energy to figure out who it was. Maybe the Staff Sergeant was keeping tabs on him. He rolled his tense shoulders while waiting for the lift to arrive. Hopefully there was a gym with a punching bag somewhere in this very large and opulent hotel. He should have asked his RCMP contact at the front desk. A man approached rapidly on his right and Kent instinctively tensed until he noted the porter's uniform.

He glanced down at the man's hands. Several nails were missing and there was a large square graft on his right hand where he must have suffered a serious burn. His left hand was without a thumb – Fenwick Chisholm.

"Please allow me take your valise for you, Mr. Laurier," the porter said. "Did you have an agreeable flight?"

Noting the slight Oxford accent, Kent handed him his suitcase, but held onto his briefcase. "Thank you. I did as a matter of fact."

They entered the lift along with a tall well-dressed woman and an equally dapper, but rather stout man.

"What floor, ma'am?"

"We're on the third floor, thank you."

"And what floor is your room, Mr. Laurier?"

"I'm staying on the sixth floor," Kent replied.

The porter stared ahead. He had thinning hair and a weathered face. His eyes were a bluish grey and he was several inches shorter than Kent. He had a bit of a stoop. After the couple exited on the third floor, Chisholm's back immediately straightened and, when the door slid open again, he moved swiftly into the corridor – the Queen's man.

"What time is your meeting with Staff Sergeant Jones?" Chisholm asked.

"Thirteen hundred hours according to our contact at the front desk" Kent glanced around to ensure they were alone. "I had the feeling in the lobby that someone's already watching my movements, Chisholm."

"Are you sure? Who, hotel staff?"

"I don't know. Do you think Staff Sergeant Jones wants to keep tabs on me?"

"Possibly, but I doubt it." Chisholm gave him a sceptical look. "Always go to the Humboldt Wing, sixth floor, when taking the lift. I have 'Mr. Laurier' registered in room 602, which is down the hall from the Vice-Regal Suite, and you will use that room except during Saturday when you will be staying beside the Royals in suite 702."

"The constable at the front desk gave me both room keys and a smaller third key."

"Yes we've had Constable Macdonald undercover at the front desk the past two weeks. The little key he gave you is for the turret room up on the seventh floor where I've been stationed. It's on the other side of the suite where Her Majesty and Prince Philip will stay."

"By the way, how did you know it was me standing outside the lift?"

"The Deputy Commissioner told me to watch for a tall Irishman." Kent heard a tinge of disdain in the man's reply and felt the most common feeling of his life growing up – resentment. It had only been about seven minutes and he already disliked Fenwick Chisholm.

"What's the status in the hotel?" Kent asked.

"So far, there's nothing to report. I do not expect any trouble during the Visit. I know the Deputy Commissioner has been concerned by the possible breach in Dispatch that could be connected to the Crawford robbery and shooting. However, I feel confident that events will proceed as planned."

"This is exactly why we shouldn't use civilians in key roles like Dispatch," Kent asserted.

"Agreed. I have done countless tours with her Majesty and frankly, her brief stay in Canada worries me far less than the time she just spent in America. My Washington counterpart assured me it was absolutely routine."

Kent used one of the three keys to open the door to 602 and Chisholm hefted his suitcase up onto a luggage stand while he explained. "More than one-half the staff here are Brits so I blend in nicely. I have the key to 704 where Queen Elizabeth and Prince Philip will be staying. If you need access, you can obtain the key from me."

Kent's Edwardian room was painted in pale blue. There was a buttery coloured couch and two patterned wingback chairs with a wooden dining table beyond. The walls had meticulous drawings of sailboats and larger seagoing vessels that likely depicted the local landscape.

"The locks were recently changed. Throughout the Visit, you will conduct all business here on the sixth floor – no one else is booked into or permitted on the sixth or seventh floors."

"Are the floors blocked off?" It seemed to Kent that anyone could have taken the lift to this floor.

"No, it's a technique we've been using with great success for the last two years. It was designed by a psychologist in Geneva."

Kent fought the impulse to scoff.

"London refers to it as RIPS, for 'right in plain sight'. The theory is, the VIP does not have any visible protection – officers are assigned to a decoy instead. The VIP thereby does not attract attention and is less open to possible attack. So far it's worked flawlessly."

Kent wasn't sure what to think. It went against his training and instincts.

"Report to Tepoorten if you see anyone on this floor. It's most likely they stopped here by mistake – there's no reason for anyone to be on this floor."

"I've never done VIP protection this way."

"The Vice-Regal Suite next to this room will be manned as of Friday by Staff Sergeant Jones' men and all entrances and exits to that floor will be guarded as well. Again, this creates an illusion and attracts attention to this floor instead – thereby deflecting the focus from the Royals."

There appeared to be a bedroom off to one side and a bathroom. Kent pushed the door slightly ajar to confirm.

"How will I contact you?" Kent asked.

"We will do a check-in at twenty-one hundred each night in the turret room," Chisholm replied, "and at other designated times if necessary. Not even Constable MacDonald at the front desk knows I am stationed there. Do you have time for me to show you the layout up on the seventh floor before you meet with Jones?"

Kent looked at his watch. "Yes, if we're quick about it. I'd like to get a bite before the meeting."

"Good. Won't take long. That will still leave time for some lunch."

"We're six floors up and the Queen will be seven," mused Kent, "would it be possible to reach these windows from the ground?"

"Only if you're Sir Edmund Hillary," Chisholm assured him.

They went down the hall and up the cement stairs, making sure that no one else was below. Chisholm led Kent to 704 and opened the door. Kent felt awed by the pale golden wallpaper, veined marble topped tables, and plush sofas in a blue and yellow stripe. Sarah would have felt utterly at ease here, but Kent instantly felt too big like he might knock a dainty knick-knack over or smudge the rich carpet with his shoes. Crisp navy curtains framed the large window that gazed out at the Inner Harbour. There was a narrowing of the harbour at the far end and then it opened up to the Pacific. Kent pushed open the bedroom door and entered. The bed was enormous and covered in a rich brocade with a whole host of matching pillows. He looked in the large empty closet, then into the bar area with its shining glasses and empty flower vases.

Chisholm stood at ease by the door, legs slightly apart and damaged hands behind his back. "I've heard from Tepoorten that you served in British Intelligence in the final year of the War," he said, almost sounding respectful.

"I think the Deputy may have made it sound more than it was. I spent many wet, bleak hours on a boat in the North Sea picking up torpedoed sailors and sending in weather and shipping reports," Kent explained.

"How old were you?" Chisholm asked.

"I joined up on my eighteenth birthday so by then I was in my twenties."

"Why did you leave Ireland?"

"When de Valera declared neutrality, when he refused a united Ireland," Kent's hands clenched, "and *then*, when he wrote to Germany with condolences on Hitler's death, my father decided we had to move to America."

"Is your father—"

"He was a clockmaker, but everyone in Ireland is a de facto politician."

Chisholm smiled. "*Did* you move to America?"

"No, we came straight to Canada instead. My father's got an uncle in Toronto who sponsored us."

"Do you like it in Toronto?"

Kent thought for a moment. "It's deathly cold in the winter, but not so gray as Dublin or London. I serve at the pleasure of the RCMP so I am rarely in Toronto."

"Your wife's from London, so I've heard, how does she fare during the Toronto winters?" Chisholm asked.

"My wife died two years ago," Kent replied.

Chisholm's eyes showed a brief glint of surprise. "Oh, I'm sorry. I had no idea."

"The Deputy spoke to you about her then?"

Chisholm's brow creased. "No, I don't believe that he did."

"Well, then who?"

Chisholm remained silent for a moment. "An officer I met at RCMP Headquarters in Ottawa," he said slowly "when the Deputy Commissioner and I were going over the plans for the Royal Visit. Back about a week ago."

"Who was he?"

"I don't remember, a constable I think, light-coloured hair – fairly tall fellow. He said you'd married a British girl and at the time I thought he was trying to put you in my favour." Chisholm looked askance.

"How would he know you and I were going to be meeting or working together?" demanded Kent. "Maybe this is our leak – the informant who went to the papers."

"The constable should not have known about any of it," Chisholm mused. "I think because I was meeting with the Deputy Commissioner and at Headquarters, I didn't register at the time that it was irregular."

This made Kent trust Chisholm in a grudging way. Men who identified their own mistakes rarely made the same ones twice. Kent searched his own mind for a tall, blond haired cop and came up with nothing.

"Bloody hell, I have no idea, but I'll be calling the Deputy and alerting him." Kent went to the phone sitting one of the marble tables. He pulled out the paper with all the contact numbers on it the Deputy had given to him earlier and dialled. Chisholm remained at the door straight-back, eyes ahead. He looked like a soldier awaiting inspection.

"Deputy Commissioner? It's Investigator Riley."

"Yes, Riley, what is it? Have you connected with Fenwick Chisholm?"

"Look there's been some kind of – it seems a constable told Chisholm back in Ottawa last week about, about my wife, Sarah. He didn't mention that she had passed away so—"

"Riley, I'm sorry."

Kent tried to keep the mounting fear from his voice. "Chisholm can't remember who it was." An image of Sarah's face, twisted in fear and pain as the knife trailed across her throat, flashed across his mind. "I understood that no one other than you and Miss Lennox were even to know that I would be working with Chisholm. The meeting Chisholm is referring to occurred more than a week ago."

"Chisholm and I were ironing out some details to do with Ottawa," the Deputy explained, sounding more like he was talking to himself than Kent. "That said, no one should have had that information. What did he look like?"

"Chisholm doesn't remember exactly, blond hair, tall. Why would he mention Sarah? That seems to be very specific."

"I'll look into this, Riley, and get back to you," the Deputy Commissioner said. "Miss Lennox may have talked, although I doubt it. But if she did, you won't see her when you and I meet next."

Kent put the phone down and put his palm on the cool marble of the ornate table. Then he turned it over and rested the back of his hand on the stone. He thought about Chisholm's tortured hands.

"You better go, Riley, if you're going to make your meeting with Staff Sergeant Jones. There's a place called Sam's Deli up Government Street where you can have a soup and a sandwich. Turn right as you leave the hotel and it's about two blocks up on the right."

Chisholm opened the door a crack, peered into the corridor, and then opened it widely. As Kent passed him into the hallway, Chisholm put his hand on his arm. "I am sorry about your wife Riley, I truly am."

CHAPTER FOUR

At lunchtime, the Matador was full of smoke and voices. Men sat at tables and leaned against the bar. Young women floated around, teasing and flirting. Their skirts were short and their shoulders bare, just the way Paul O'Rourke liked them. Two guards flanked the heavy steel door. They used a series of whistles as a warning system, but so far this month there'd only been one close call with the cops.

Flynn and Liam were playing gin rummy. A cigarette girl came by and Paul grabbed her and she fell easily onto his lap with much giggling.

He crooned into her ear. "I've booked a room for us, gorgeous, just say the word."

"Oh, Mr. O'Rourke, you know I love a man in uniform, but I have to get my beauty sleep," she said, pulling herself away from his grasp.

"Why don't you call me 'Paul', and I'll be showing you other ways to exercise your beauty."

Blushing, she strolled off, glancing over her shoulder at him.

Flynn put his cards down on the table and reached for his coffee. He pulled on his fingers and the joints clicked into place.

Liam put his cards down as well. "You've got to stop doing that, Flynn," he said crossly.

"When did you ship the sculpture, Paul?" Flynn asked.

"Yesterday afternoon, should take three days by train," Paul told him.

"When will he send the rest of the payment?"

"Half later today and half on the day he receives the sculpture," Paul explained.

Dan Smythe entered the club dressed to blend with the crowd. Liam raised his hand slightly and he came over. Unbuttoning his jacket, Dan pulled out a chair and sat by Flynn. Paul leaned back so he could look at him. "How might *Constable* Marcel Chasseur be doing this morning?"

32

Dan smiled. "Crazy. The boy's crazy as a loon."

"They bought it?" Flynn asked.

"Hook, line and sinker." Dan said with a smile.

"The doctor bought it?" Flynn wasn't convinced.

"He's sold," Dan assured him.

"The Staff Sergeant believes the boy's gone mad?" Liam was almost laughing.

"Not so much." Liam's face fell.

"But enough." Dan said reaching out to pat Liam's arm, "enough."

An older woman came by and set down a pint of beer in front of Dan. She marked their chit and faded back into the crush of men. Flynn lit a cigarette and inhaled deeply. Paul stared boldly at the cigarette girl and she smiled back at him from across the room.

Flynn rounded on Dan, who began drinking as if to soothe an unquenchable thirst. "Did you get anything out of the cop I shot?"

"No, I couldn't get near him," Dan failed to cover up his surprise at this attack.

"What do you mean?" Flynn accused.

"The Staff has a constable in the room at all times," Dan's voice rose.

"Are you telling me you couldn't get past one of your own men?" Disgust was creeping into Flynn's very tone.

"I couldn't very well question Cervide with another cop sitting there, now could I?" Dan's mouth tensed.

Flynn stood up, pushing his chair back. Liam stood slowly as well, putting a hand on his shoulder. "Now, now, let's be keeping everything quiet-like – we're not wanting any attention."

Flynn sat again stiffly. He swept his cards into a pile. "That wounded cop is at best a witness or at worst a threat and we need to know what he knows now!"

"*You* missed him," Dan said sadly.

Flynn's black eyes went a shade blacker. "*I* took his ear off on purpose. *I* didn't *want* to be killing him, you bloody fool."

Liam rubbed his scruffy beard. "That's right, Dan, that's exactly right."

"Do you know, Dan," Flynn said quietly, "how easy it is to kill a man?"

"I didn't mean—" Dan blustered.

"Do you know how hard it is, in the dark, to shoot a man's ear off?"

"Look Flynn I'm sorry. I'm just tired."

Flynn's voice dropped. "I've been planning that robbery and the securing of Kent Riley and the goddamn kidnapping of Her Highness for over a year now. I have been living in this Godforsaken town among its Colonial citizens full of their English teas and pretension until my soul is sick with hatred. And you want to say that I missed the bloody mark?!"

"Flynn, I'm sorry. I wasn't—"

"Shut your gob, I'm done." Flynn's chair dragged on the floor as he shoved it back. Looking down at the chit, he threw a few coins on the table. He slowly pushed the cards off the edge and the three men watched them fall onto the floor. He walked out of the Matador and not even Liam had the courage to follow him.

Liam looked over at Dan, his chin quivering. "Jesus and Mary, are you a Goddamn idiot?"

Paul didn't care for this in-fighting, as other priorities were rising. "Liam," he said, with a wink to his cousin, "I need a break as much as Flynn does. I'll be back shortly."

Grabbing a bottle from under the table, he came up behind the cigarette girl and took her hand. "Come on Nora, I want you to be putting down your wares. Aren't you such the dedicated little shop keeper?"

She didn't pull her hand away and instead followed his lead. He gave Mrs. Leary a nod and she opened up one of the back rooms. "I've got a rich drink for you, my beauty." He whispered in the girl's ear and she squeezed his hand.

The room was dimly lit with a bed off to the left, a wooden dresser and burgundy chairs on either side. As she took the big box of cigarettes from her shoulders Paul slapped her hard on the behind, his hand making contact with her stockings. She took in a sharp breath and spun around trying to pull down her short flared skirt.

"Don't do that, Paul, it *hurt*," she pouted.

"That's how I like it. I want to see you being feisty and wicked."

She smiled unsurely. "You said you'd get me a drink."

"And here it is my beauty." He handed her a cut-crystal glass half full of vodka. He sat heavily on a velvet chair by the bed. She took a tiny sip as he pulled her over onto his lap.

"What is it?" she asked crinkling her nose.

"Pure Russian vodka, a shipment just came through the docks and we nicked a bottle or two for ourselves. It's guaranteed to make you the most wicked of girls."

"What if I don't want to be wicked?"

Paul put the glass down on the table and began kissing the girl's neck and undoing her sequined dress.

"Not so fast, not so fast," she protested. "Give me more of that drink."

Breathing heavily, Paul handed her the glass and she drained it. He slid her dress off and heard a tiny *click*. He stopped moving, stopped breathing. There was a barrage of talking and music outside the door. There it was again, a faint *click*. What the hell?

"What's the matter?" she breathed. "Did I do something wrong?"

Some blighter was playing a pipe of some kind in the smoky room beyond. Paul swivelled his neck. Chairs were scraping and glasses were clinking on the table tops, but what was that sound? It was a mechanical sound and it was close. He remained deathly still. Was it the cocking of a gun, the opening of a blade? Paul turned slowly back to the girl and pulled her dress back up.

"Hey what's wrong with you?" Nora asked.

He stood her up and got up slowly off the worn velvet of the chair.

"Don't you like me anymore?" she teased.

Paul put his finger to his lips, made a slow pivot in the room, now listening for the shutter of a camera. He shoved a handful of bills at Nora and pushed her out through the doorway. She looked like she was going to cry. Mrs. Leary's watchful eyes widened, but she locked up the room and shot Paul a disapproving frown. Paul skirted around the card game, past the guards and pushed through the steel door and burst into the street. He went down a couple of blocks and then doubled back along the laneways.

The Matador looked tired and run-down in the daylight, especially from the back entrance. He knocked at the warehouse door and he could sense he was being observed from above, but he didn't dare look up. After a few moments, the door slid partway open and a lean, grungy man of about fifty or so looked him over. "Can I help you?"

"I want to talk to Henry."

'Oh, do you?"

"Yeah, tell him Paul O'Rourke is here to see him. Liam O'Rourke's my cousin."

Who says he's here?"

"Flynn Dolan says."

"Stay here and I'll see if Henry's available." He closed the door in Paul's face. Paul waited. After a few minutes the door slid open – this time just enough for him to walk through.

"Stand still, I got to check you out." He could smell the smoke on his breath as the man frisked him and then gave some sort of sign to the dark above them. Paul glanced up and saw a man with a rifle in the shadows up on a catwalk. He was led down a narrow path through dusty boxes to a closed door. The man gave a patterned knock and a voice called out. "Okay, Scotty, bring him in."

Paul's eyes had to adjust to the light. There was an ample man seated at a big wooden desk. The only light source in the room was a curved desk lamp with green glass.

"So what's this about Flynn Dolan?"

"I'm part of his crew."

"What can I do for you?"

Paul noted in the shadows two men looking ready to spring. Both had hands in jacket pockets as if they never released their weapons. Henry, in the pool of green light, hunched forward in his chair eyeing Paul closely.

"I said, what can I do for you? I don't have a lot of time. Scotty says you're sent by Flynn Dolan, what does he want?"

"Being at the Matador just now, I heard clicking noises in one of your backrooms," Paul said. "I was wondering what it might have been then?"

Henry started laughing drily. "It was nothing, Mr. O'Rourke, nothing at all – unless I need a favour."

"A favour?" Paul's stomach lurched.

"You know, money or assistance or maybe just silence."

"You're taking photos then? You're saying it's a camera."

"Yes, pictures. The men who find out about the pictures are rarely in a position to share the information – not if they want to live. Do *you* want to live, Mr. O'Rourke?"

"I want to buy some pictures from you."

"Pictures of yourself or someone else?"

"Myself." Paul felt his skin burning. The night came back to him. The girl's bloody screams and the thrashing of her body – having to hit her to shut her up – then the broken sobbing. She had to have been a virgin. It was a mess, a bloody, Goddamn mess. Flynn owed him for that. He owed him a lot. His eyes darted around the room. The men at the back still hadn't moved, but one wrong move and he knew they would kill him. It was a sobering thought, enough to make him swallow his shame and do what it took to get the damn pictures back. "How much do you want for them?"

Henry stared at him. "What're they worth to you?"

"I'll be wanting them for my own pleasure – so not very much – but I've got a fancy on for this girl and maybe she'll come back to me if I show her the pictures of us together."

"Is she married?"

"Yes, I believe so. How about I give you fifty?"

"I have business with Flynn Dolan, Mr. O'Rourke, and out of respect I'll make you a deal. A hundred and fifty and they're all yours, but not a word. If I hear so much as a whisper about this matter – you'll regret ever coming to see me. Understood?"

"Understood."

"Now what day was it?" Henry got up slowly. He pulled out a drawer in a metal filing cabinet to the right of his desk. Paul took a step forward and one of the thugs subtly shook his head. He immediately stepped back in place.

"It would have been a Thursday, part way through May – May 17th."

"What time?"

"It was late at night, about eleven."

Henry's fingers clicked through the file folders. He pulled one up on the desk and positioned the light so that it poured out fully on the images when he opened it. Paul swallowed. The two men stared at him without moving. Henry closed the folder. He studied him.

"There aren't any photographs of you, Mr. O'Rourke, none."

Paul felt a wave of relief followed by a wave of fear. "Does that mean no one took pictures of my room that night then?"

"Yes," Henry replied slowly, "which is a surprise, but perhaps that is the case."

"How can I be sure?"

"I think we're done here, Mr. O'Rourke."

Paul started to sweat. Flynn had best not know about this slip up. Maybe because Henry had failed to supply the images, he wouldn't say anything. Glancing at the two men flanking the door, Paul figured that speaking again was not wise. He'd just wasted Henry's time and now one more person on the street knew about the blackmailing racket. Paul took a backwards step toward the door.

Henry said to him softly. "Quiet is the name of the game, Mr. O'Rourke. This meeting never happened, no one ever finds out about this, not even Flynn Dolan."

Paul felt a rush of relief. He almost smiled. Henry was not planning to talk to Flynn, well not unless it brought him something he needed, and God willing he didn't need anything from Flynn.

"Not a word," Paul said and exited without a backward glance. Standing outside the door was the scruffy older man. They walked in silence down the dark corridor of the warehouse and out the sliding door. Paul gave him a brief nod and set off down the street in the dusty sunlight of the alley.

CHAPTER FIVE

Kent arrived at the Detachment ten minutes early. The officer at the front desk looked at his I. D. and buzzed him in through the gate that separated the waiting room from the entrance.

"Good Morning, Investigator Riley. Please take a seat and Staff Sergeant Jones will be with you momentarily. Would you like a coffee?"

"Yes please, just black, thank you." The desk clerk went down the hallway to fetch it. Kent gazed at the RCMP crest hanging above his desk. He'd never liked the bison as a symbolic creature. It lacked the dignity of a stag or lion. He mouthed the motto, *Maintiens Le Droit*. Would the Royal Visit require him to maintain the law or bend it? He joined several other men in the waiting room and picked up a newspaper.

The clerk returned with his coffee and handed it to him. "The Staff Sergeant will be with you shortly."

A couple of uniformed officers entered through double doors to the right of the entrance. "Ah, you must be Investigator Riley." One of them said with ill-disguised respect.

"Yes, I am. Good morning."

One was almost as tall as Kent with light coloured hair. The other one was shorter, built like a bull and sporting a regulation buzz cut. They came over and the smaller man introduced them.

"I'm Constable Timothy Rogers and this is Constable Dan Smythe."

"We fought over the chance to work with you," Smythe said, "but the Staff Sergeant thought Mick Callaghan was the only man for the job." The two men started laughing.

Kent felt like telling them that whomever the Staff Sergeant had assigned, he was unlikely to last a day.

"You'd better watch yourself with Callaghan," the tall cop added, "he's the only guy that had to go through Depot twice." More laughter ensued. The clerk at the front desk frowned.

"Oh come on, Larry, you've got to admit it's pretty funny."

A young man approached briskly. At the sight of him, the shorter constable turned away from Kent. The tall one, Constable Dan Smythe, Kent made a note of his name, gave him a look of pity and the two walked back the way they came. Kent watched Smyth for a moment more then turned as Callaghan approached – black shoes squeaking – glasses glinting in the overhead lights. His uniform didn't seem to fit properly. Constable Callaghan looked so young, Kent felt like checking his I.D.

"Good afternoon, Investigator, I'm Constable Michael Callaghan."

"Afternoon" Kent said, shaking his hand. Callaghan had a surprisingly firm grip.

"We're to go to the Staff Sergeant's office now. Please follow me, Sir."

They walked in silence down several corridors. Kent liked a man that knew how to be quiet. He studied the young cop. Constable Callaghan was portly and the sort of man you couldn't recall the features of when someone pressed you to describe him. The two entered Staff Sergeant Jones' office for their briefing.

"Sit down gentlemen, sit down. Larry got you coffee, Investigator Riley, ah good, now let me see."

The office was strewn with papers and files. A crystal decanter sat on the back shelf with several glasses. Framed photographs of the Staff Sergeant, in red serge, atop a gleaming black horse adorned the wall. There were also several pictures where he was posing with people Kent assumed were important. On his desk was a silver framed portrait of a handsome woman and two children, probably in their teens by the look of it. The Staff's face was Old World decrepit – like a British landowner from a bygone age who drank sherry and ate too much pheasant.

"Let me see, let me see. Where is that file," the Staff Sergeant muttered. "Constable Callaghan will take you to see Constable Marcel Chasseur who was present the night of the shooting. Then he'll take you to the site of the robbery, Mr. Crawford's house, and hopefully you'll have time to meet with the two female dispatchers as well."

Kent noticed that Callaghan was taking notes.

"The dispatchers, Sylvia James and Gwen Heller, have been suspended until further notice – which has been challenging to say the least with this flu going around. Some of my most reliable – ah there it is." The Staff shook the file free of the other papers on his desk and sat heavily back down in his chair. "Gentlemen, I don't want anyone else to know about this case or how you are proceeding," he paused for a moment, then lowered his voice. "I would like to avoid any further involvement – even among my own staff. The fewer people that know about Dispatch's error, the better. That said, come and talk to me anytime for whatever you need and I'll see that you get it. Here's my home number, call me at any time, day or night." He pulled out an elaborately carved silver cigarette case, and leaned towards Kent, "Smoke, Investigator Riley?"

"No, thank you."

The Staff did not offer a cigarette to Callaghan, who had the look of a man more likely to enjoy a lollipop.

Surveying his notes, the Staff said, "I know the Deputy Commissioner has briefed you about the robbery so there's no point in going over the events again. Do you have any questions I can answer?"

Kent watched him closely. "When did you first hear that we had a member down?"

The Staff Sergeant put down his cigarette carefully. "I got the call shortly after zero one hundred, Tuesday," his features registered the stress of that night.

"And what did you do?" Kent asked.

"I dressed and went straight to the hospital."

"Did you see both men, Constables Vittorio Cervide and Marcel Chasseur?"

"Constable Cervide was already in surgery. Constable Chasseur was so shaken from the night's events that he didn't come to the hospital until several hours later and by that time—"

Kent cut him off. "When did you secure the reel – the tape recording from Dispatch?"

The Sergeant's eyes widened ever so slightly.

Kent pressed him. "The Deputy Commissioner told me that the exchange between the officers and the dispatchers was recorded as part of a special pilot project you were running here."

"Yes, yes, the prototype, well let's see—" The Staff's face was sweating slightly and he mopped it with a handkerchief he had pulled from his breast pocket. "I believe I secured the recording at about zero eight hundred, Tuesday."

This was a significant gaff and all three men knew it. Jones had not secured the tape recording of the incident for hours. Kent would have gone immediately to Dispatch, not the hospital.

"Could I please have the reel now? I'd like to take it back to my hotel room and listen to it." Kent got up. He thought much more clearly when he was moving. There was little space in the office, especially for a man of his size. The other two men seemed to retreat slightly into their seats so he could pace. The Staff Sergeant called for the tape recording to be brought up.

"Constable Callaghan needs to be in a suit, not a uniform," Kent said. "I don't want any attention drawn to us as we look into this." He addressed the young cop. "How long until you can be ready?"

"Ten minutes," the boy replied glancing over at Jones. "Permission to change, Staff Sergeant?"

Jones scowled at him. "Go, go and change, Callaghan. For God's sake go and change." The boy hustled out of the room. Kent waited until the door closed.

"Why does he wear glasses? How is it possible?"

"He's an exception and—"

"Constable Callaghan is too inexperienced to be working on such a case," Kent insisted.

"Investigator Riley, I conferred with the Deputy Commissioner about Constable Callaghan and we both think he's the best match with you for the job. In terms of technical operations, Constable Callaghan is exceptional. Trust me. It will make up for his lack of experience or the fact he wears glasses."

"A couple of officers said he had to do Depot twice. Is that true?"

"Yes, I'm afraid that's true. He failed the fitness portion of the program. And some other minor exercises."

"What minor exercises?" Kent really didn't want to know.

"But he attained a perfect score on the written exams and he's a fine shot. That has only ever happened once before."

"Usually, I work alone."

The Staff's lips tightened. "I'm following the Deputy Commissioner's instructions," he said. "Do you want me to contact him?"

There was a quiet knock at the door. "Come in," the Staff Sergeant called out. A heavy-set, black haired cop entered with a box. Removing the lid, he showed the reel and a thin tightly wound rope to Jones.

"Yes, that's it, thank you." The cop handed the box to the Staff and slipped back out without speaking.

"No, no, don't bother the Deputy Commissioner with this," said Kent. "He's got enough on his mind with the Royal Visit. I can handle Constable Callaghan, but so much as one mistake and the kid's off the case."

The Staff gave an exaggerated sigh, then stood and rocked back and forth on his heels. This was clearly a man who had risen up through the ranks over many years. He had a commanding air, but wasn't quick. He hadn't followed protocol and properly secured the Dispatch tape. Instead, he went to the hospital to be the man of the hour – the caring leader protecting his men and ready to talk to the Press. The Deputy Commissioner had warned Kent that the Staff Sergeant was a drinker and an idealist.

He had opened up the box again and handed Kent the reel. He held up the thin, tight coil of rope. "This is what they used to tie up Mr. Crawford. I've had it run through our lab and it's standard. You can buy it in any hardware store, but take it if you think it might help."

Kent put the reel and the coil of rope into his briefcase then signed the evidence forms Jones pushed across the desk.

"We dusted for fingerprints at the Crawford residence," the Staff said. "The thieves wore gloves. There's nothing. They wore masks so Mr. Crawford didn't see their faces. And it was too dark for either constable to get a good look before the shooting started."

Kent took a sip of his now tepid coffee and watched the Staff Sergeant carefully. "How well do you know the two civilians in Dispatch?" He asked.

There was the briefest moment where anxiety touched the Staff's face.

"They are on paid leave until this is all sorted."

"You didn't answer my question – how well do you know them?"

"Well let's see now," Jones replied slowly. "I believe Sylvia James has worked here for three years or maybe four. Her parents live in Vancouver. She began as a receptionist. Then she worked for a time as my secretary. She has been part of the civilian pilot project in Dispatch for close to a year. I can contact Records if you think it's necessary."

"And the other?" Kent asked.

"Gwen Heller has worked at the station for almost two years and has been part of the pilot in Dispatch for going on ten months. She's—" Jones trailed off with an awkward smile.

"She's what?" Kent asked.

"She's very nice." Jones said weakly.

"When can I interview them?"

"They're very upset and Ms. Heller appears to be—" The Staff Sergeant seemed to be struggling to find the right words.

"Please arrange for Miss James meet me at the Empress Hotel, room 602 at nineteen-thirty and Miss Heller thirty minutes later."

"Are you sure?" the Staff asked. "There are many rooms here that you can use."

"I'm quite sure," Kent replied. "That will be all for now, Staff Sergeant Jones. Thank you."

Jones paused for a moment, clearly not used to being told when a meeting was over. Then he lifted a set of keys from a hook on the wall. "The car you've been issued has all the bells and whistles, but most civilians won't notice that it's police issue."

After giving an awkward little knock, Callaghan appeared in the doorway, dressed in an ill-fitting dark suit. It looked as if he'd borrowed it from his father for a funeral.

Rising, Kent gestured for him to move ahead, "After you, Constable."

In silence, the two men walked into the parking bay and located the car. Callaghan added an irritating little skip to his gait in order to keep up with Kent's longer strides. The car Jones had assigned them was a pale blue Plymouth Fury. The subtle air intake on the hood was the only indication of the high performance package lying beneath its unassuming exterior. Kent took the driver's seat, but did not start the car. After a great deal of fidgeting, Callaghan finally settled in the passenger seat.

"How old are you, Callaghan?"

"Twenty-three, Sir."

"Don't be calling me 'Sir'. I was told you had an engineering degree from the University of Toronto."

"I went to university at fifteen!" The boy smiled and pushed up his glasses. "Guess you could say I'm a fast learner."

"When did you complete your training at Depot?"

"I finished almost three years ago. I had to do the program twice."

"You know, normally they don't take recruits who require glasses."

"I know, but my university professor contacted them directly without me even knowing and put in a good word. He said that—"

"And you've worked in Victoria since then?"

"No, I was stationed in Québec City first, then Whitehorse for six months, and the rest of the time in Victoria. They needed someone for technical operations." Callaghan paused and then said quickly. "I heard about what you did in Québec."

"What was it that you heard exactly?"

"I heard you stopped a kidnapping, saved the man, but didn't even—"

"Do you like being a cop, Callaghan?"

"Yes, Sir."

"Call me Riley. Why do you like being on the Force?" Kent had yet to turn the key and start the car. He looked straight ahead.

"I like it because I can outsmart lesser minds," said the boy with great seriousness.

At this, Kent stopped his interrogation and looked over. Callaghan looked right back at him, eyes unblinking behind the round steel rimmed glasses.

He started the car.

"Out east, we prefer Dodge, not Plymouth," said Kent.

The boy adjusted the rear-view mirror for Kent, positioning it perfectly. "I'll have you know," the boy announced primly, "that the Plymouth Fury has a 318 cubic inch V8 that produces 290 horses at the rear wheels," Callaghan paused then made up his mind. "It's faster than the D-500 Dodges you use back east."

Kent didn't bother responding to convey a clear message. He put the car in gear. But apparently, the child prodigy was not done. "It's also got twin 4-barrel carbs. That keeps it humming!"

Again Kent didn't reply, but even that didn't seem to register.

"The Plymouth has twelve inch brakes," Callaghan ventured, finally seeming to pick up on the mounting tension in the car. Nonetheless, he was unable to stop himself and suddenly blurted, "Dodge only has eleven inch drums, Sir."

Kent pulled out to the edge of the lot and stopped. "Callaghan, can you do something useful now, like telling me how to get us to the Royal Jubilee Hospital?"

"Yes, Sir!"

Sunday could not come soon enough.

CHAPTER SIX

Flynn Dolan leaned back from the table covered in wires, putty, and TNT. Looking like he wanted to wash his hands, Paul hovered by the sink, what with his cigarette girls and filthy lust. God how Flynn hated the look of him.

Liam and Paul hadn't said a word since the Matador. They were all waiting for Constable Dan Smythe's call. No one dared to speak until that happened. Liam shooed Paul away from the sink and poured a glass of water that he placed before Flynn.

Drinking the cold water cleared his mind. Returning his thoughts to the bomb on the table, Flynn picked up the detonator just as the phone jangled loudly on the kitchen wall. Paul and Liam froze. Flynn pushed his chair back from the table.

Wiping his hands on his trousers, Liam picked up the receiver. "Hello?"

"It's Dan." Liam announced. Then listened intently.

"Well?" Flynn's voice came out tense.

"Dan says he's in," Liam said with barely suppressed excitement.

Flynn smiled and Paul let out a ragged breath while Liam listened on the line. "Hang on Dan," Liam said into the phone.

He looked at Flynn. "Kent Riley met today with the Staff Sergeant for a briefing," Liam explained. "Just as we hoped, Riley's working with Constable Michael Callaghan, the wiring expert."

"How's he looking?" Flynn asked lighting a cigarette.

"Michael Callaghan?"

"No, how does Kent look?"

"We just saw him at the—"

Flynn's mood darkened and Liam asked Dan the question, then hung up the receiver. "Kent looks good," Liam reported. "Dan said that he looks fast and strong."

Flynn nodded slowly. "We'll be having Kent with us soon enough, which means we're right on task."

"It's more important that we got the electronics specialist, Flynn, if what you said about the remote is really true," Liam said.

He always knew how to spoil a moment.

"Everything's going according to plan," Paul said quietly. Still hovering at the sink, he looked nervous. What was wrong with him?

It didn't matter. They had Kent now *and* the electronics genius.

Flynn suddenly felt warmed by the afternoon sun beaming into the brightly painted kitchen. Even the bomb components had a glow of light and energy about them that seemed missing before.

"Pack this up, Paul. I'll be going for a walk," Flynn announced.

"Do you want me to come with you?" Liam asked reaching for his coat.

"No," Flynn replied, "I'll be going alone to think a bit."

CHAPTER SEVEN

Royal Jubilee Hospital was too warm and smelt like disinfectant. A nurse directed them to Vittorio Cervide's guarded room.

"Let's hope Constable Cervide's well enough to talk," Callaghan said brightly.

"You'll be waiting outside," Kent said. "The man cannot be talking to everyone."

Kent left Callaghan chatting amiably with the other constable stationed in the corridor. He entered Constable Cervide's room slowly and quietly. Cervide's head was bandaged and blood was seeping through where his right ear should have been. His eyes fluttered slightly and he tried to sit up in alarm.

"Constable Cervide, I'm Investigator Riley – please lie back down. No need to move on my account" Kent assured him.

Cervide moaned with the effort of shifting back into a supine position.

"Can I ask you a few questions?"

"I gave a statement to Constable Smythe this morning," said Cervide in a strained voice. It was clearly an effort to speak.

"Really? Did Staff Sergeant Jones send him?"

"Yes, I believe so."

That was the tall constable with the light hair. The one that fit Fenwick Chisholm's description of the cop in Ottawa who mentioned Sarah. The Staff Sergeant didn't say anything about getting a statement taken by Constable Smythe. Kent pulled his notebook out of his pocket.

"Could you tell me about the Dispatch radio call that directed you to the robbery."

"I didn't hear it. My partner took the call."

"Constable Marcel Chasseur?"

"Yes, that's right."

"And why was it that you didn't hear the exchange between your partner and Dispatch?"

"I was several feel away from the squad car dealing with a wounded deer. It had been hit and was lying on the road. I had to shoot it. Then Marcel shouted at me that we had a 2-11 in progress; we got to the house and I—" Cervide swallowed.

"Did you proceed to the scene with the siren on?"

"No, Marcel said Dispatch called a 10-83. I was surprised."

"Strange."

"Yeah, I asked Marcel why and really we didn't have time to even think about it. Got to the house and I was approaching—" Cervide's eyes clouded.

"Where was Constable Chasseur as you approached the house?" Kent asked keeping his tone neutral.

"I thought he was right behind me," Cervide said uncertainly.

"He wasn't at the car?" Kent pressed.

"No, he was going to come, that's right, but there was another call from Dispatch. Then I saw the intruders."

"So to be clear, Chasseur stayed at the car and you went toward the house alone and then you saw the intruders. What did they look like?"

"I couldn't see. They had dark hoods pulled over their faces and then they started shooting. It all happened so fast."

"How many shots?"

"I don't know. I don't remember." Cervide closed his eyes. "One second I was shouting for them to drop their weapons – and then the next minute I was face down on the ground."

"Where was Constable Chasseur when they began shooting?"

"He was – he was there too." Constable Cervide's brow furrowed.

"With you? I mean beside you or behind you?"

"I'm not sure. I think he was coming to cover me," Cervide said, "I know he'd be right there, but everything happened so quickly. We were completely unprepared." The constable's hands lay limply on the white knit blanket.

"I'm going to speak with Constable Chasseur shortly," Kent said. Cervide nodded his head imperceptibly and winced with pain.

"Is it okay if I ask you some more questions tomorrow after hearing his version of the events?" Kent asked.

"Of course. Marcel's okay isn't he?"

"Yes, yes, he's fine, not injured. He's had a nervous reaction."

"Nervous?" Cervide repeated the term as if Kent was twisting the truth. "He's *not* a nervous cop, Investigator."

Kent patted the young cop's inert hand. "I'm going to find out who did this to you, Constable Cervide. I promise you."

"I know you will." Cervide closed his eyes again.

As Kent and Callaghan returned to the Jubilee hospital's main floor, both scanned the signs for the Psychiatric Ward. "Callaghan, did the Staff Sergeant say anything to you about having Constable Smythe take a statement from Constable Cervide this morning?"

"No Sir, he didn't." Callaghan pushed his glasses up higher onto the bridge of his nose.

"I'll need you to set up a reel-to-reel for me in 602," Kent said. "I'll be needing it tonight by nineteen-thirty. I worry the Staff Sergeant left the Dispatch reel unattended too long. I need to talk to those dispatchers and I want a record of it."

"Affirmative, Sir."

"Please call me Riley." Kent glanced over in irritation at issuing the reminder, but Callaghan, oblivious as per usual, was peering at the hospital directory.

"Ah, now I remember!" the boy said. "The psychiatry wing is down this way. We'll need to sign in with the station nurse and perhaps the doctor too."

Kent did not want to know about Callaghan's previous experiences with the psychiatric unit. He followed him in silence to the nurses' station that stood before the closed doors of the ward. An older stern-looking nurse was speaking into the phone, and she put down the receiver and looked up at them. "Dr. Barbery?"

"No." Kent showed his badge. "I would like to speak with Constable Marcel Chasseur."

"Just a moment please."

She went over and pulled out a file. She read through and said, "Investigator Kent Riley?"

She looked down at the badge more closely. "You may see Constable Chasseur for a brief period, ten minutes at the most. He's in Room 8." She grabbed a pen from the desk and jotted a note down on the sheet. She gave the two men an appraising look. "I am sure you realize that Constable Chasseur is in a state of shock that we are monitoring closely. You must be careful not to aggravate his condition." She put the file away and faced them. "Please sign here."

Kent took the pen, scanned the sheet and scrawled down his signature. Callaghan did the same in a flowing, dramatic fashion.

The nurse checked the clock on the wall. "The psychiatrist, Dr. Mason, will be here in a few minutes. You may want to speak with him as well."

"Thank you. I do, please send him along when he arrives."

Kent and Callaghan entered through the sealed double doors. The air felt humid in the corridor and the two remained silent. The ceiling seemed low and there was a lack of natural light. Someone screamed and both men jumped. Still they didn't speak.

Watching the numbers on the door, Kent stopped. "Here we are."

Beside the door was a posted sheet that read: *Marcel Chasseur, room 8. Access Limited.* Kent looked up and down the hallway for an intern or nurse on the off chance Chasseur became agitated or violent, but the corridor was as empty as it was quiet. He motioned Callaghan to remain outside. The boy's eyes widened with ill-concealed disappointment behind the glint of his glasses. Kent wouldn't have been surprised if he'd stamped his foot in protest.

Chasseur sat in a chair staring out the barred window at the passing cars. Even though he was a large powerful man, he looked deflated.

"Good afternoon, Constable Chasseur. I'm Investigator Kent Riley. I'd like to ask you a few questions."

Chasseur turned in the chair and stared at him, fingering a gold cross that hung around his neck. He faced Kent and then stood slowly, as if a great weight was bearing down on him. The Constable looked searchingly at Kent for so long it was uncomfortable, almost embarrassing.

Kent tried again. "Well, can we talk, Constable Chasseur?"

"Yes, yes we can talk." The Constable's eyes flitted nervously around the room. "I'm sorry there isn't a seat. Can you sit on the bed?". Chasseur went to sit back down in his chair, but abruptly got up again and began to pace nervously. Then he sat down again and clasped he knees to his chest.

"Who's at the door?" He asked, his voice rising. "There's a man out there in a dark suit. He's looking at me. Who is that? Why is he here?"

Trying to keep the tension out of his voice and out of the room, Kent replied. "Oh, that's my partner. Do you know Constable Callaghan?"

"Partner?" Marcel paused for a long time and his face crumpled. "My partner! It's all a lie. Car 12 to Dispatch, it's a 10-41. I repeat a 10-41. Vittorio's been hit! Send all units! I need a 10-64, 10-64." He started rocking and raised his voice even higher. "Where the hell is backup!? Jesus Christ, help me. Vittorio's down!" He started rocking violently.

Kent went over to calm him down and Chasseur started screaming.

"Get away from me! Don't touch me."

Callaghan came into the room. "Stand down, Sir."

For a second, Kent considered pinning Callaghan up against the wall and reading him his rights. He reluctantly stepped out of the boy's way as Callaghan pushed by. He approached Chasseur and spoke to him firmly while taking the man's face in his hands to stop the rocking.

"Calm down, Marcel."

Constable Chasseur seemed startled into following the boy's orders. He took a deep, shuddery breath. Callaghan spoke more quietly, but still held the constable's face and looked directly into his eyes.

"Your partner's okay. Vittorio's going to make it." Chasseur tried to turn away, but Callaghan held him secure.

"Look at me. You know me, Marcel. It's Mick Callaghan."

Something crossed Chasseur's face that showed he was returning to the here and now. A tear slid down his cheek. His knees were shaking. Callaghan's voice became soothing.

"That's it. Vittorio is on the mend. He's resting right now. Marcel, you got him help and he's going to be fine."

Chasseur gripped his arm, "but they said no sirens when they should have called a 10-72, they were armed, my partner, I lost my—"

A grey haired nurse came into the room carrying a plastic box of medication. She halted abruptly at the sight of the two men. Callaghan released Chasseur's face and took a step back. "He's become quite agitated," Callaghan said sounding guilty.

"I can see that." The nurse pushed open the door widely suggesting all too clearly that they should exit immediately.

"Well, I am *not* surprised," she said with annoyance to Kent, while looking at her patient.

"Did Dr. Mason authorize this visit?"

"We signed in at the nurses' station and were given express approval," Kent said. "This is a police matter."

Chasseur had bowed his head and was muttering unintelligibly to himself.

"Mr. Chasseur should not be questioned at this time," the nurse said brooking no argument. She put down the medicine on the counter and straightened the coverlet on the bed. When she straightened back up, she seemed surprised to see they were still there. "Please return to the nurses' station," she began to close the door, "and Dr. Mason will meet you there."

Callaghan scooted out of the room and Kent went to follow, but then stopped. The nurse busied herself lining up the medication on the other side of the bed. "There, there Constable Chasseur. You need to rest and I have some medicine here that's going to help you stay calm and feel better."

Kent moved the door back open and Chasseur turned at the sound. The man's eyes were red-rimmed and dark circles clouded his otherwise handsome features. Chasseur smiled like a man whose heart was breaking.

"She's a whore," he hissed.

Kent opened the door further. "Who is a—"

"Excuse me," the nurse said wheeling around, "I thought I told you it's time to leave. Please!"

There was nothing Kent could say or do with the nurse right there. He bowed out of the room shutting the door behind him. Callaghan was not in the hallway. Kent hurried down the stifling hallway and through the double doors so as not to miss the doctor. The boy was chatting animatedly with the psychiatrist at the nurses' station. It almost made Kent forgive him for interfering with his questioning of Chasseur.

Dr. Mason ushered Riley and Callaghan towards his nearby office. He looked to be in his late fifties. He was slender with a trim grey beard and dark brown eyes. He wore a tailored suit and over that a white lab coat which was the only indication that he was in fact medical staff. When they entered his office, Mason removed the lab coat and hung it on a coat rack to the left of his desk. Callaghan and Kent sat on a maroon leather couch while the psychiatrist took an upholstered chair across from them. The phone rang and he answered with a quick apology. The desk was completely clear except for the telephone and a pad of paper. Books lined two walls and a large window dominated another. Dr. Mason finished his call.

"I have just heard from Nurse Reynolds that my patient became quite upset when questioned, Investigator," the doctor noted in a somewhat disapproving tone.

"I actually had not yet started asking any questions, much as I needed to," Kent looked severely at Callaghan. "In fact, I had barely said hello. Then Constable Chasseur panicked at the sight of what he took to be a stranger peeking through the window."

"I'm not a stranger," Callaghan interjected, "I know Marcel. We've worked together for six months now. In fact, it may have kept him relaxed if I had—" The boy trailed off as Kent's face flushed with anger.

"What did he say when he became upset?" asked Dr. Mason.

Kent got up and walked over to one of the bookcases. As he spoke his gaze wandered across the spines of books, trying to recall Chasseur's exact words. "He seemed to return to the night of the shooting. He was feeling let down – betrayed. I think he felt betrayed by Dispatch or maybe by the thieves who shot at them. He was speaking of—"

Callaghan jumped in. "He was absolutely reliving the shooting because he was reliving Vittorio being shot at with the 10-41 and called for a 10-64!"

Riley felt a rush of disbelief that this young excitable cop had the gall to interrupt him. He was already proving to be more trouble than he was worth. Kent had to get rid of him and fast.

"10-41," the doctor pulled a small notebook out of his pocket. "What does that stand for?"

"It means he was hit!" Callaghan blurted.

"10-41 means 'Information Confirmed'" Kent asserted, "and Constable Callaghan is assuming he called in a 10-40 meaning 'possible hit.'" Kent absolutely had to wrest back command of the discussion.

"And when Constable Chasseur was in discussion with you, he employed this term again?" queried Dr. Mason.

"Yes," Kent said with conviction, before Callaghan could open his mouth. The doctor flipped to earlier pages in his notebook. "Was there anything else he said that may shed some light on how he's feeling?"

"He said that the nurse was a 'whore'," Kent informed the doctor.

"I didn't hear him say that!" Callaghan gasped.

"Nurse Reynolds, a whore?" The doctor let out a short bark of a laugh. "I highly doubt that." Then he added, "Men who are traumatized often express angry sentiments against women because they feel vulnerable." Seeing the puzzled look on the two men's faces, he added. "It's an attempt at regaining masculine control."

Kent returned to his seat, thinking that restless pacing and staring at books did not make him look at all as if he was in 'masculine control.' Callaghan never moved a muscle, except to polish his glasses like he was some sort of bloody jeweller.

The psychiatrist stood. Putting his white coat on again, he opened up the door. Both Callaghan and Riley got to their feet. Kent's mind raced as he considered various ways to get Dr. Mason to give him permission to talk again with Chasseur. He needed the constable's story and he needed it now. Regardless of what kind of fits Chasseur put on.

"Whore eh?" mused Dr. Mason. "That's interesting, that's helpful. Would you gentlemen be able to return again tomorrow morning? Say at ten o'clock?"

Kent's shoulders eased. What good fortune.

"I'd like to repeat this exercise," the doctor went on. "An exercise where you enter the room, the same way you just did now."

Callaghan interrupted eagerly, "Both of us?"

Kent's bright mood darkened. The doctor looked him in the eye and replied. "Yes, both of you. Indeed, the combination is vital I believe. The patient seemed to respond negatively to Investigator Riley and have more of a rapport with you, Constable."

Callaghan looked up sweetly at Riley with his round face and shiny glasses. Kent imagined whipping his glasses right-off his face and jumping up and down on them and then kicking them violently around the room. Keeping his face impassive, he met Callaghan's eyes and held his gaze until the constable stopped glowing at him.

"Thank you, Dr. Mason." Kent shook his hand. "We'll be returning tomorrow then at ten o'clock."

"Excellent, thank you."

Kent took a step forward so that he was encroaching on the doctor's space. The man faltered slightly. Kent said with a tone that left no room for doubt. "You need to describe to me in detail anything you learn about Marcel Chasseur's condition, statements he makes, references to the night of the shooting, anything and everything – the nurses as well. Please inform them of that immediately."

"You have my full cooperation as well as that of my nurses."

"I know that I do," Riley told him taking a step back. Much to Kent's amazement, Callaghan inserted himself into the near impossible space and shook the doctor's hand warmly and rather vigorously.

They exited the building without speaking. When they reached the Plymouth, Kent realized he was starving.

"How about something to eat, Sir?" Callaghan asked mercifully. "I know a great little diner around ten minutes from here."

"Fine, Callaghan. Please, for the last time, call me Riley."

"Yes Sir, Riley, I mean."

He directed Kent to a stately hotel positioned right on the ocean. While the Oak Bay Beach hotel was elegant with sweeping views of the sea, the diner within was full of chattering women decked out in their Sunday best. Kent couldn't think of a worse place to eat a meal after a day like this. There were white doilies and too much furniture. There wasn't any room for the elbows of a man his size. The ladies slowed their chatter at the sight of the two men and Kent found himself smiling and nodding like a fool. He really needed to shoot Callaghan. They sat across from each other at a little square table and a stout woman bustled over to take their order. Kent glanced through the menu.

"Afternoon, gentlemen! Oh, Constable Callaghan it's nice to see you again! You must have the day to yourself. I barely recognized you without your uniform."

Callaghan grinned sheepishly as if he was on holiday.

"And a fine day it's been today. I hope you gentlemen have been enjoying the sunshine! Now, what'll it be? The special is roast beef with Yorkshire pudding and I believe it's just ready now."

"I'll have that!" the boy said joyfully.

"I'll have a plate of fish and chips, thank you, and a pint of beer."

"Fine, fine." The lady said. "And you young man, a spot of beer for you as well?"

"Yes, ma'am, that would be dandy."

Kent despised Callaghan even more for having a term like 'dandy' at the ready.

Replaying the meeting with Chasseur and the constable's hysterical fit, Kent wondered what approach he would use to figure out just how traumatized Marcel Chasseur really was. He had certainly dealt before with madness as a defence. He could hardly wait until he met with the two dispatchers. There was so little time. It was Wednesday and the Queen would arrive on Saturday morning. Less than three days away.

"Sir, are you there?" Riley looked up to find Callaghan waving his hand dangerously close to Kent's face. The waitress arrived with the beer in glasses sweating in the warmth of the restaurant.

"Your food won't be but a minute, gentlemen."

"What's our next step?" The child prodigy drank from his beer and smacked his lips with pleasure. His whole round face creased with enjoyment and Kent almost liked him for a brief moment, which Callaghan spoiled by repeating the question a little louder as if Kent was slow to understand it the first time.

"Next steps, Sir. What's the plan?"

"I'm thinking Callaghan. Give me a moment for heaven's sake!"

Callaghan pulled back, "Sorry, Sir. Think away!"

"I need the reel-to-reel for the interviews. You and I need to hear that tape before we meet with the dispatchers. We'll need two machines. I also want to see the painter, Charlie Crawford, and go over the crime scene."

Kent drank from his beer and it was cold and tart, just as he liked it. Despite the many, many ladies, this place had one or two redeeming qualities.

"I have heard it said, Sir, that you prefer to work alone."

"Yes, Callaghan. That is in fact true, I do."

"And why is that?"

"My feeling is that the fewer people who are involved, the less likely they'll get hurt."

Callaghan looked slightly afraid, and Kent felt guilty, oddly paternal and angry all at once. "Don't worry, Callaghan, you and I are partners on this case. I'm stuck with you, whether I like it or not."

Callaghan was listening intently, but his brow was furrowed. Kent tried again.

"We're working together and I will make sure that neither one of us gets hurt along the way."

The boy cheered up.

"Now, I want to prepare for the interview with the girls from Dispatch tonight." Kent drank more beer, and talking more to himself, he added. "I'll see each of them separately first and then maybe I'll put them together and ask a whole different set of questions so that I can figure out how they interact."

"You know that they live together, Gwen and Sylvia."

Kent put his beer down with a clunk. "What! No, no one informed me about that minor detail."

"Well they do." Callaghan announced officiously.

"Why didn't the Staff Sergeant mention that?" Kent wondered out loud.

"I'm not sure." Callaghan replied as if Kent had directed the question at him.

"I need you to bug their place as soon as possible."

"Yes Sir, I'm good at that."

"I've used the metal wire system, but it can be difficult to work with," Kent said.

Callaghan shook his head. "Wire is way too complicated, plus it has poor fidelity."

Kent was about to reply, but Callaghan was not yet done.

"What really frustrates me with wire is it tangles and kinks, but it also requires a very strong current to imprint the signal."

Kent jumped in to keep Callaghan on task. "Both dispatchers will be at the Detachment tomorrow at zero nine hundred. So that gives us a sixty to ninety minute window to bug their phone before meeting Dr. Mason at the Jubilee Psych Ward."

"I prefer the cellulose acetate plastic tape," the boy intoned slipping into one of his trance-like lectures.

"That should give us time to get the gear prepped and ready to go." Kent tried again to wrest his attention back to the task at hand.

"It's because the tape's coated with iron oxide which—"

Hopeless.

Kent struggled to remove his suit jacket in the warm restaurant and hung it on the back of the chair. Remarkably, this was enough to stop the relentless lecture as Callaghan reached over to straighten the jacket and fuss like a mother hen making sure that Kent's suit jacket didn't get wrinkled. Kent eased his shoulder strap and glanced around. Caught up in their conversations, the chattering diners appeared to take no notice of the gun holstered under his left arm.

Once Callaghan finished fussing, Kent asked: "Can you check that 602 is clear, Callaghan, and then put a device on the phone that allows us to record calls? Can you get that done by this evening?"

"Yes, Sir, I can sweep the room and I can install a pressure-actuated microphone that we can use to record any telephone calls."

Kent's immeasurable suffering may well be worth it if the child prodigy could have that all done by the time the two dispatchers arrived.

The waitress arrived with their food. She put down a steaming plate of roast beef for Callaghan and fish and chips for Kent. Slipping the bill under the peppershaker, she asked "Another round, gentlemen?"

"Yes, thank you." Kent broke into the batter of his fish and took a bite. He could not believe the taste. Instead of the salty, waxy white fish of Toronto, here he was biting into rich buttery layers of flavour. The dish transported him back home to the newspaper wrapped fish and chips of his childhood. Callaghan was watching him, and grinning, which was very irritating.

"Isn't the food grand?" Callaghan took a sip of beer and leaned in like he was about to impart serious information. "My mother brought me here the first time and I've come back at least once a week since! I don't usually eat lunch out. I pack a sandwich, but once a week I like to treat myself. And I bring mom along once a month for luncheon on Sunday." Callaghan took a considerable bite of his roast and chewed it with apparent bliss.

The waitress returned with the fresh beers. She added them to the bill.

"Everything alright here gentlemen?"

"Do you have a bit of horseradish?" Callaghan asked through a mouthful of roast beef.

"Yes, I'll just be a second." She gathered up the empty glasses and hurried off.

Callaghan cut his food first into bites and then ate them methodically. Kent gazed at him in wonder. "So Callaghan what is it your father's doing?"

Callaghan smiled gratefully at the waitress who had returned with a little dish of horseradish. "He has an appliance shop in town, *Electrolife*," he said, spooning sauce onto a corner of his plate. "He fixes appliances, toasters and lamps and vacuums even. He can fix pretty much anything that plugs into a wall socket."

Kent sipped his beer and watched Callaghan take a piece of Yorkshire pudding and swirl it around in gravy before lifting it to his mouth.

"How about *your* father?" The boy asked Kent, taking a draught of beer and smacking his lips.

"In Belfast, he was a watchmaker and in Toronto, he works with the electricians who maintain the subway line."

"When did you move to Canada?" Callaghan dipped one of his carefully cut pieces of roast beef into gravy and then put a tiny dollop of horseradish on it.

"After the War. What about you?"

"I spent my childhood in Vancouver, but when I left to attend the University of Toronto, my parents moved across to Victoria and set up shop. My mother and father are from Edinburgh originally, but I've never been. My older brother, James, was born there though."

Leaving the chips on his plate, Kent finished off his fish. "Are you almost done, Callaghan?"

The stricken look on the boy's normally pleased face nearly made Kent laugh. Callaghan had only eaten half of the food on his plate, but if he kept up with the careful cutting and dishing out of precise amounts of gravy and horseradish, they'd be here forever.

"I'm almost done, Sir, just hang on one more minute."

Riley pulled the bill from under the peppershaker and looked it over. He gathered some money from his pocket and put it on the table.

"Let's go see that Texan painter, Crawford and then you can set us up with the reel-to-reel back at the Empress." Kent stood. "Where's your equipment being kept then?"

"It's at the Detachment. Won't take me a minute to grab it." The boy was standing, but still shovelling in bites and chewing rapidly his last few pieces of beef. He scooped up potato in one last desperate bid to finish the meal while Kent put his jacket back on. They wound their way through the tables of chatting ladies back out into the late afternoon breeze.

A car pulled away behind them and Kent started at the squeal of tires, then stopped dead in his tracks as a tan Studebaker passed them at a good rate of speed. Callaghan, chatting animatedly, bumped into him hard, jolting him forward.

"Jesus and Mary, Callaghan, what the hell!"

"Sorry, Sir," Callaghan blurted adjusting his glasses. "I just could not anticipate that you would stop suddenly in the middle of the sidewalk."

"Dammit Callaghan for the last time call me Riley!"

The man on the passenger side of the tan Studebaker was familiar, the profile of the face, the jaw, the long dark hair. Kent knew that face. He shook his head. There was no way Flynn Dolan could get into Canada. It simply wasn't possible.

CHAPTER EIGHT

"I think he saw you, Flynn!"

"Of course he didn't. No one can be that aware, not even Kent Riley." He glanced back at the quickly retreating restaurant. "No, Not even Kenny."

Liam shook his head.

Flynn smiled slightly. "He's looking well, isn't he?"

After a few more miles were between them and Kent, Liam pulled the Studebaker over to the side of the road and turned off the engine. "He's looking strong enough and fast enough if that's what you're meaning, Flynn. What about the boy with him?"

"That boy would be the wiring genius, Constable Michael Callaghan, youngest member to ever work Special I. He's the one who'll be developing the remote."

"On his own?"

"No, with his father's help. I can make the bomb, Liam, but I can't work the remote without that boy and his father."

"Do you want to go back to Dan's house now?" Liam asked, starting the Studebaker back up.

"I can't imagine why Kent was eating in that place." Flynn lit a cigarette and rolled down the window. "It looked like a restaurant for old ladies, not at all the kind of place that Kent would like."

"I said, are we going to Dan's now?" Liam stared straight ahead.

"Yes, yes." Flynn waved his hand dismissively as Liam pulled away from the curb.

"That bespectacled constable doesn't look like much of a challenge," observed Liam. "He looks to be about twelve years old."

"But he's smart," Flynn countered.

"So?"

"You wouldn't know it, Liam, but smart is much more dangerous than strong."

"What's that supposed to mean then?"

"It means nothing. Let's get back to Dan's house. I want to know if he's found the guard assigned to the Queen at the hotel yet."

At the house, Constable Dan Smythe sat sweating at the kitchen table with a stack of papers covered in names and numbers. He looked like he'd rather burn the lot than study them a minute longer.

Flynn didn't say a word as he leaned casually up against the counter.

Crumpling the top sheet, Dan threw it on the floor. "Flynn, there's just no way to track down who's been assigned to guard the Queen. There's no talk of it at the Detachment and everyone I've checked in with has no idea. I'm not even sure the Staff Sergeant's been told."

Flynn remained silent.

"Look, I have to be careful. I could get in a lot of trouble from the Staff Sergeant for speaking to Cervide – let alone snooping around the hotel arrangements. I can't be seen asking too many questions."

Paul O'Rourke strode into the kitchen. "Gentlemen."

Liam nodded at his cousin but didn't break the tension of Flynn's silence. Paul washed his hands, then took bread from the box on the counter and put a couple of slices into the toaster. He surveyed the men without speaking further.

Dan resumed his work, crossing out names, jotting down others. Paul buttered the toast right on the counter so it left a mess of crumbs.

"Ah, I was hungry," Paul announced to no one in particular.

His casual comment was swallowed in the cool silence, but he bit into his toast all the same. It was Constable Dan Smythe's head on the chopping block, after all. He'd had days to pin down the security details at the Empress.

But it *had* been Dan who'd found out that a decoy was going to Government House, not the Queen herself. Flynn cracked out the *Bushmills* that night and they had a roaring time of it. But then there was talk of some Ladies-in-Waiting being at the hotel, and Flynn's joy turned to doubt. What was the point of knowing the Queen was being secured at the Empress for the night when they couldn't pin down where.

Paul put two more slices into the toaster.

"Use a plate, Paul," Dan growled. "You can butter your damn toast on a plate."

Paul looked around in surprise. "There's no reason to talk like that, Dan. What's eating you up anyhow?"

"Listen," Dan said to Flynn. "I can't find them. Three quarters of the staff in the damn hotel are Brits. I've been at this for days. It could be anyone! Maybe the guards are with her now in Washington and will accompany her on board their ship."

Liam crossed his arms with a sigh. "Calm down and think, Dan."

"I mean I've tried every single contact and no one can give me anything else. It's a mystery. Somebody always knows something about somebody, but no one knows who's guarding her or where she's staying for certain. If they have a contact stationed in the hotel, I can't find him."

Getting up, Dan wet the rag hanging over the spout of the sink. He wiped up Paul's crumbs and pulled a plate from the cupboard and slammed it onto the counter. He threw the rag into the sink and stared out the window.

Speaking with his back to Flynn, he explained: "I've already done three security sweeps at the Empress in anticipation of the Queen's arrival. I thought for sure I could get the inside track then."

Flynn remained silent.

Dan spun around. "You think I'm not trying hard enough?"

Flynn didn't reply.

"Look, I've gone through the lists. I've checked all leads. I've talked to everyone I could without drawing any attention to myself. I've also done two twelve hour shifts at the hotel watching people go in and out around the clock, but I still don't know who her guards might be or in which suite she and the Prince will be staying."

Flynn went over to the pile of Dan's papers without speaking. He looked through it. Many pages had names crossed out while other names had notes by them or stars in the margin. Not even Paul moved now. The butter sitting on the counter was getting soft. Paul didn't look at Dan or even at Liam.

Flynn said into the suffocated space of the kitchen. "I'll be going down to the Empress Hotel to find the Queen's guard myself."

"But—" spluttered Dan.

"Months of planning," Flynn could barely control his fury, "every inch of ground she will walk on has been thought about, every door she opens and every minute she spends in that hotel will have been orchestrated."

"You won't be able to find him."

Flynn slammed his hands down on the counter and the butter dish crashed to the floor.

"I *have* to know who's been doing the planning or she might just slip through our fingers."

No one breathed.

Flynn would find the Queen's guard if it was the last thing he did.

CHAPTER NINE

Kent drove while Callaghan navigated, which evidently required a constant stream of 'out loud' thinking. Kent thought sadly of those first moments when they'd met at the Detachment and Callaghan had seemed so taciturn and quiet. He never should have engaged him in even slightly personal conversation at the restaurant. It opened the floodgates and Callaghan was on a roll.

"Ah let's see, it must be here." Callaghan squinted ahead. "Now what does that sign say? Is it 4040? Yes that's it, on the right. Here we are! The Crawfords."

The Plymouth wound down a curving drive that seemed to lead into the heart of a forest more than to a house. The trees were so different from the ones Kent was used to seeing back east. There weren't any maples. Here the trees had gnarled branches with dark green leaves that seemed to curl in on themselves. Other trees had peeling reddish bark and huge limbs with waxy leaves. They pulled up at a low ranch-style house with angular lines. It was more horizontal than vertical and only steps from a rocky shore and the ocean beyond. Riley knocked on the door while Callaghan hopped from one foot to the other, until Kent told him to stop it.

"Sorry, Sir, I'm a bit nervous."

The door opened a crack and stopped on the chain. A woman peered through the narrow space.

"Hello? Can I help you?"

"Mrs. Crawford, I presume? Investigator Riley, and Constable Callaghan, RCMP, we'd like to talk to you and your husband." Kent put his badge up so that she could get a good look at it. Unlatching the chain, she opened the door and ushered them in. "I'm sorry, Investigator Riley and—"

"Constable Callaghan," the boy announced and then he reached over and shook the woman's hand! What was he thinking?

"Well, do come in, gentlemen. Charlie, my husband, is in his studio." She was wearing a purple dress in an Asian style with a high collar. She wore a slender watch on her right hand and a sapphire ring surrounded by diamonds. Her blonde hair, swept up with silver hair clips had the faintest streaks of silver through it. "Come and sit here in the living room and I'll get us some coffee."

They descended two steps that led down to a large carpeted room that had an entire wall of windows that looked out onto the sea. Several huge paintings with black tar and monumental figures in white outline dominated the other walls. Kent thought that the white forms were somehow familiar. And then it hit him. They were like the chalk sketches they drew around dead bodies in the movies. It created a strange, haunting effect. The furniture was low-lying and boxy. There was a notable absence of any clutter in the space – everything seemed to have its place. The room felt full of air and energy. Even Callaghan seemed at a loss for words, an unanticipated blessing. Kent paused in front of the window. The coastline curved off to the right so that he could see other houses perched along the rocky shore.

He sensed the arrival of Charlie Crawford before he saw him, a rugged, older man dressed in gray trousers and a white t-shirt stained with paint of various colours and shades. His eyes were intense. He was fit and strong with great shoulders and long legs. He looked like he was from Texas.

"Investigator Riley," boomed Crawford and walked over to Kent and shook his hand forcefully. "Finally, someone who knows what they're doing."

Crawford looked over at Callaghan. "And who might you be?"

The boy perked up and announced, "Constable Callaghan at your service."

Kent had never met a man who said things like 'dandy' and 'at your service.'

Mrs. Crawford returned with a tray balancing a sleek silver coffee pot and several cups and set it down on a nearby end table. "How do you find Victoria, Mr. Riley?" She asked.

"Breezy."

"I imagine after the heat and humidity of Toronto in July, you'd like a little breeze." She poured coffee into a cup. "Do you take cream or sugar?"

"No thank you, black is fine."

"I'll have cream and sugar," piped up Callaghan.

Kent went over and took the offered cup from her and stared out the window at the grounds surrounding the rancher. The painter took a cup of coffee from his wife. He put his hand on her arm and gave it a little squeeze.

"Where were you when the robbery took place, Mrs. Crawford?" Kent asked.

"I was visiting my sister in Vancouver," Mrs. Crawford answered.

"Do you visit her often?"

"Not as much as I'd like to. Charlie and I usually go together, but he was in the throes of inspiration and couldn't bear to leave his work." She smiled over at her husband, but the smile only affected her mouth. It was absent from her eyes. Kent sat down on the couch and pulled out his notebook. Crawford had placed himself in an immense black leather chair. He was sprawling rather than sitting.

"When did you first realize there were intruders, Mr. Crawford?" Kent bowed his head as if to write, but kept his lowered eyes on the wife's face. She looked appropriately upset, Kent thought, but something was off.

"I was in the studio," Crawford said, "it's on the far side of the house. It was close to midnight. I never heard a sound. Nothing. And then I looked up and there were two men standing in the doorway, one tall, and the other about medium height. Both had guns."

"Tall?" Kent felt a prickling at the base of his neck. "Did you see his face?"

"No, both men wore dark green masks that covered their faces completely except for the eyes."

"Green? Are you sure?"

"I know my colours, Investigator Riley."

Kent wished he hadn't said dark green masks. He had begun worrying when the Deputy Commissioner first told him that the thieves had only taken one piece of art. Then there was the 'constable' that had spoken about his wife with Chisholm in Ottawa. Then that feeling of being watched back at the Empress. A Royal Visit. The dark hair he glimpsed in the tan Studebaker and now dark green masks. Flynn? Flynn Dolan. Dammit all to hell! But it couldn't be. There was no way he could get past the border. The RCMP would have simply returned him to Ireland and he would have gone back to prison where he belonged.

Callaghan rattled his cup and saucer as he placed them on the low table in front of the couch. He looked over at Kent. "Is it alright if I look around a little?"

Kent nodded his approval.

Mrs. Crawford got up. "I'll take you through the house, Mr. Um—"

"It's Constable Callaghan," he said warmly, rising and joining Mrs. Crawford as she led him down the hallway to the left. He said over his shoulder to Kent as he exited. "I'll do an inventory of the house's layout, Sir."

Inventory? Layout? Kent looked over to the painter, pushing down his frustration and hoping the Crawfords didn't lose all faith in the RCMP.

"Okay, so the two men appeared in the doorway. Did either of them speak to you or say anything?" Kent asked.

"No, I was so shocked when I saw them that I froze for a moment. I think I may have asked 'who are you?' or something like that and there was no reply. The tall man stepped to the side and the shorter one trained his gun on me."

"What kind of gun was it?"

"I didn't see the make." Crawford crossed his legs and ran his hands up and down the sides of the chair.

Kent didn't think he was lying. He seemed embarrassed.

"There was nothing I could do." Mr. Crawford said heatedly. He sat up in his chair and rested on the edge leaning in closer to Kent. "Thank God Susan wasn't here."

Kent watched him. The man looked more angry than afraid.

"The tall guy—" Crawford began, but Kent interrupted.

"What about the other one. He was shorter?"

"Yeah, average size I guess. He moved like a shadow, always holding the gun trained on my head, circling around me."

"Okay, so the tall man—" Kent got up and tried to visualize the moment.

"He motioned for me to sit on a straight-backed chair I have in the studio."

"Can we go to the studio now while we're talking about this, Mr. Crawford? I want to try to piece together what happened."

"Yes, it's down the hall." They deposited their cups onto the low table and Kent followed the painter up the steps and then down the hall to the right.

"Do you remember exactly what you said when you called the police?"

"I told them that there were men with guns robbing my house. Not that it helped. They sent two blunderers, one who managed to get shot, rather than save my Brancusi."

"Are you sure you told the dispatcher that the men had weapons."

"Am I sure?" Crawford's voice edged up a notch. "Yes, I'm Goddamn sure."

The studio had wide glass doors that opened out to a patio that dropped off to the sea below. There were several boats plying the calm blue waters. The studio was absolute chaos, pots of paint and brushes stacked everywhere, three or four canvases in mid-process up on walls, some of the smaller ones positioned on big easels. A large painting of a horse outlined in white loomed over a table. There were tins of different coloured paints, a small pot of what looked like tar and a narrow table with tools on it, knives and spatulas, paintbrushes and wires. Kent couldn't figure how the thieves made their way through the mess. He closed his eyes and tried to imagine

Charlie Crawford facing his canvas at midnight, but instead he got a sudden memory of Sarah, her hands gripping his shoulders. Kent shook the memory away and squelched the sickening sense of just how absent she was.

"There are two straight-backed chairs." Crawford explained. "So the tall one gets this chair here and motions for me to sit."

"And what were his movements like?"

"Movements? I don't know. Smooth, almost like he was enjoying himself. He wasn't in any kind of a rush. He was a Goddamn professional and what does the RCMP do? They send a couple of rookies!"

Kent's mouth felt dry. "Would you say he had a certain formality to his movements or is that going too far?"

"No, it's dead on." Crawford looked at Kent with a tinge of new respect. "He moved elegantly like he was a charming host at a party showing me to a choice seat."

"So you're sitting down then."

"Yes, I had to. The other guy had a gun in my face."

"Of course you had to be sitting, Mr. Crawford." Kent appeased him. "Can you show me where the chair was."

"Right here," the painter picked up one of the chairs and, stepping carefully over the pots of paint, he put it in the middle of the room. Kent picked his way through the jars and pots and brushes and sat in the chair.

"So were you facing this way then?"

"Yeah, I think so, definitely away from the window."

Kent got up from the chair and moved to the side. "Can you sit on the chair for me and sit exactly the way you were when they tied you up?"

The painter thought for a moment and then approached the chair. He sat down and pulled his hands behind him so that they were entwined tightly behind his back. He stifled a low angry animal sound.

"Are you alright then, Mr. Crawford?" Kent asked. The painter did not reply.

"If you are able, and this isn't too much to ask, could you show me – try and imagine you are tied up – show me how you reached your knife and cut through the rope."

Kent watched the man's long fingers twist slowly up, a tiny bit at a time, until they fiddled with the waistband of his trousers. The left hand pushed up from below a knife that he manipulated into the fingers of the right hand that would have found purchase on the rope because it was taut against his hands. At least this part of the story was true.

Kent came over and put his hand out. "Is this the actual knife you were using?"

It was a thin blade, but sharp, sharp enough to sever a rope, even a tightly wound one.

"Yes," Crawford took the knife back and slipped it back into his trouser waistband. "I carry it with me always. I paint with it. They tried to take it as evidence." Crawford leapt up off the chair, his face red and blotchy. "Those bastards. Cowards with their hooded faces and their guns while they go through my house and steal my Brancusi!" He slammed one fist onto the chair back, sending it and several paint cans flying. At the sound of the crash, Kent heard Susan Crawford's anxious voice.

"Charlie? Is everything alright in there?"

The painter came up close to Kent and said in a low voice. "Listen to me, Investigator, I want my Brancusi back. I don't care what you do or how you do it. I need it back! I want those thieves to pay for this."

He set the chair right and Riley hastened to pick up the toppled paint tins. Mrs. Crawford appeared at the door with Callaghan right behind her, trying to peek over her shoulder, and Kent felt like he'd been caught doing something wrong. He straightened up and waited for a cue from Charlie Crawford who replied with a sarcastic drawl.

"Sure darling, everything's just fine." His mouth twisted. "I've lost my Brancusi and everything's just fine."

Kent smiled up at the wife in an attempt to smooth over the moment. Trying to include her, he asked, "Could you take me to the room where the head – I mean the sculpture, was taken?"

Before she could reply, Crawford gestured to the left, "This way," he snarled. Mrs. Crawford and Callaghan moved aside allowing the two men to pass. The child prodigy's eyes fluttered behind his glasses. Kent resisted the urge to tell him to stop it. Charlie Crawford's jaw was clenched and Kent imagined that he could hear his teeth grinding together.

They entered a long narrow room that opened up to a vista of the sea at one end. It was full of natural light from windows interspersed with paintings and sculptures. Kent went over to what was clearly the pedestal that had until recently held the Brancusi. It stood empty like a bird's nest except that instead of twigs and feathers, the base was surrounded by spiky shards of glass. There were two other pedestals with glass enclosed sculptures – a marble face with stylized eyes and a tall polished bronze piece that looked like a quill.

"Why do you think they just took the one piece?" Kent asked.

"My *Sleeping Muse*. Why take only that one?" The painter's voice was pained. "They took it because it's priceless!"

Kent walked down to one end of the room and back. Crawford was brooding quietly, still looking at the empty pedestal, his hand jammed deep in his pockets. His features were caught somewhere between rage and despair.

"What does the sculpture mean to you?" asked Kent.

The painter put his hand over the sharp glass nest on the empty pillar. Kent almost reached out thinking the painter was going to rub his hand on the glass shards. Instead, Charlie Crawford moved his hands like a potter shaping clay.

"She was my inspiration. I would go to her at night when I couldn't sleep and take her from the case, putting my hands on the cool bronze of her eyes and lips and hair. I was able to see what I needed to paint."

Kent nodded, stepping away to give Crawford time to gather himself. He waited at the window. Crawford's wife hovered in the doorway with Callaghan right behind her. Kent wanted to shoo them away.

Crawford cleared his throat and Kent resumed.

"So while you're tied up down the hall, the thieves come in here, smash the case, take the sculpture, and exit out the front door."

Charlie Crawford nodded. "Yes, I suppose that's what happened." I was too busy trying to get my hands free to hear exactly what they were up to. I didn't wait to find out once I cut the rope."

Kent added the details to his notes. He went over to the case. They must have smashed the case when Crawford was already at the neighbours or at least on his way there. If they went out the front door, what door did Crawford take to escape? "Mr. Crawford, how do we get from this room into the master bedroom?" Kent asked.

"It's through here." The painter approached the window that looked onto the sea and opened a door on the right. "Straight through here."

They entered a room that was pale blue with French doors that opened onto the flagstone patio. Against the far wall was a bed covered with white linens and pillows. There were several dresses laid out on the bed. Sleek mirrored tables were on either side and books were scattered here and there. One of Crawford's paintings dominated the near wall and Kent found himself drawn to it. It was about four feet by five. There were birds outlined in white in one corner and two sheep-like figures grazing over the middle. The colours were much more vivid, tawny orange, mossy shades, and sharp blue accents. So different from the other ones he had seen in the gallery that had so much black. This one was gentler. There was a male figure in another quadrant of the canvas and he gestured as if reaching out for something.

Kent had never been to an art gallery before he met Sarah. 'Teach me what the paintings mean,' he'd asked her.

She'd smiled up at him. 'No one can teach you. You just need an eye for detail. Notice the details and the painting will tell you its story.'

Kent could see them together that day in the Tate. He'd put his arm around her waist. 'Teach me,' he'd insisted.

She'd laughed, tilting her face up at him. 'Learn to read paintings. It will make you a better detective.'

They walked for hours in silence sometimes, holding hands, stopping before works that intrigued them. Kent reached his hand out, but she was not there. It would be two years this Friday that she'd gone.

The Royals would arrive on Saturday.

Time was quickly slipping away.

"Are there steps leading down to the sea from the patio?" Kent inquired. "A dock maybe?"

"Right this way," said the painter as he unlatched the French doors in the blue room and strode out to the patio.

"There are steps that lead down to a small beach, but there isn't a dock." The painter hadn't entirely lost the surly tone he had used with his wife moments ago.

"But a boat could pull up to the beach and push off from the shore?"

"Yes," then Crawford added, "why didn't the cops think of that on the night they took my *Muse*? Doesn't help us much now does it?"

"I'm thinking that's how your thieves arrived and left, by boat. They would have been apprehended by responding patrol cars on Seaview or even Cadboro Bay Road if they'd left in a vehicle. The dogs would have picked up their scent if they went through the forest. It had to have been by boat. Are we able to go down there and look around?" Kent gestured to the stone steps.

What didn't make sense was that if they were escaping by boat, why did the thieves come back to the front of the house? They came back for something else, maybe more artwork?

The painter was gazing into his studio to the right of the bedroom. "Just a moment." He went back into the room and looked closely at one of his paintings. He moved it slightly so that the light hit it differently. Kent wondered if he was, in all honesty, thinking about his painting or if he was worrying about what might be discovered at the beach. Kent started down the stairs. He held his hands out on either side, noting that the walkway down was actually quite narrow. Crawford shuffled down behind him.

"How long were you tied up for, all together?"

"Hard to tell, maybe twenty minutes, half an hour?"

The beach was more like a shelf; it was narrow and full of crushed shells and rocks. There was a wet, rocky ledge that rose up behind it with trees and moss clinging to the top and draping down.

"So they left you in the studio then?"

"Yes and turned out the lights."

"And you didn't see them again before you escaped."

"No. Once I was free, I went out the side door and across to the neighbours to call the police."

"That means they must have brought the sculpture through the bedroom down to the boat here."

But why did the thieves go back to the house? Crawford was tied up as far as they knew. They had what they wanted or did they?

"Did you hear anything?" Kent asked.

"You won't believe this, but I did not hear a sound," admitted Crawford. "Not until they fired the gun."

"How many shots did they fire?"

"Only one that I remember."

Kent looked at him and felt the lid shift off the well of feelings he'd lived with for the last two years. There were few men who could shoot a police officer in the dark and not kill him, with one signature shot to the head.

Flynn Dolan.

CHAPTER TEN

Flynn's pace increased. How heavenly to be unencumbered, alone. He walked rapidly down Government Street toward the Empress Hotel. He breathed in the sea salt on the air. Joyce's *heaventree of stars* rustling softly in his mind. He missed Kent. He never should have involved Sarah, never should have threatened her. Her neck taut beneath his hands, the glinting drops, not even drops, just a blood red line, a necklace. It was a brothers' pact and Kent got it all wrong, misinterpreted Flynn's grand gesture.

Slowly mounting the steps of the hotel, Flynn glanced up at the windows, thinking that Kent was staying in one of the rooms above. It was too risky to walk the hallways. Kent would not be ready to talk yet. Everything had to be exactly in place before they met again. He knew he could win him over. Now that Sarah was dead, he would be able to talk reason with Kent. Remind him of where his heart truly lay, remind him of what he owed to his father, what he owed to the men and women at home, his people. Ireland.

Flynn settled into a silky chair in the Empress lobby, the air stuffy after being out in the fresh sea-salted breeze. Angling the chair so that the service elevator was in his sight lines, he set about watching for the right girl. He kept his cap and coat on just in case Kent came through. Twenty minutes stretched into half an hour. Maybe it was too late for the maids to be working. Perhaps they had already cleaned rooms and served tea. Then out of the service elevator came a young, brown-haired girl carrying a large oval tray full of dirty dishes. Perfect. Flynn hastily crossed the lounge area to follow her. At the far wall she struggled to balance her tray while opening a large door. Her tray pitched at a dangerous angle.

The girl looked up at him gratefully as he propped the door open with his foot. Beyond, Flynn could see steps leading down to what had to be the kitchens in the basement.

"Thank you very kindly, Mister."

Her words betrayed that she was Scottish. He need go no further. He removed his hat and his tousled hair fell into place. The girl's eyes brightened.

"What's a lovely girl like you doing with a door like this?" Flynn smiled down at her.

The girl blushed and paused. Her hair was pulled up on her head, a mass of curls, and her white cap was slightly askew. She had to be about eighteen. Her eyes looked tired for someone so young, but they gleamed like antique wood under Flynn's gaze. He felt depressed by her servant's uniform and her aged, hungry eyes. He could tell by the way she was standing that her legs ached.

"Can I be helping you with the tray, Miss?"

"Oh, no I can manage, thank you Mister."

"You're looking tired."

"It's been a long shift."

"Could I ask you a quick question?"

"Of course, are you looking for work?"

"No, I'm trying to find a friend of mine who's working for the hotel."

"Oh, and who might that be then?"

Flynn took the heavy tray from her, set it on a stand at the top of the stairs, and let the door shut behind them. The girl's face was shadowed and hopeful. Flynn felt her yearning and swallowed his disgust.

"I'm going to have you guess his name."

She smiled quizzically at him. "A game?"

"What's *your* name?"

"Emily Campbell."

"Emily now that's a lovely, old fashioned name. Well Emily, you'll be having to guess who my friend is from my description. I'll tell you only three things. First he's got an Ox-Bridge accent."

She started to smile.

"Second clue, he's a terrible snob." Her smile grew wider. "And last, he doesn't have a minute for anyone."

She grinned at him conspiratorially. "I know exactly your man! It's Mr. Chisholm. He's too fancy for the likes of me, you can believe that."

"Ah ha! So he is here. Now here's the rest of the game. I want to surprise him after the weekend's done. So, you'll be needing to keep our talk a secret and then maybe—"

"Maybe what?" She leaned toward him and he caught the scent of her fatigue, her hours of serving food and clearing dishes.

"Maybe you would do me the honour of taking tea with me one of these days? We could surprise Mr. Chisholm."

"I would like that very much! But you haven't told me your name."

"Jamie Finnington."

"Jamie." She said his name like he might be a hearth at which she could rest.

"Tell me Emily, how does Mr. Chisholm look? I've not seen him since the War."

"Oh, you were at the War together. Is that how you know him then?"

"Yes, we're both survivors, he and I. We were in hospital together, but I was well enough to be sent home before him and we lost touch. It took me all these years to track him down."

"Mr. Chisholm's older than you I'd say. He's tall, as you know, but maybe what's different is his stoop. His hands are badly damaged, must've happened in the War. It's not something you'd talk about."

"Are there burns?"

"He does have a burn, but he's also missing nails on the right and—"

"What's the matter, Emily?" Flynn spoke gently.

"Well, I don't know if you know, but he's missing his thumb."

Flynn pulled on his own fingers until they clicked back into place. He couldn't get out of this gloom fast enough. "Has he ever told you his first name?"

She laughed. "Ah, yes. The manager said it one morning at check-in and we all had a good laugh." She put on a posh accent. "Mr. Fenwick Chisholm, if you please."

"What mother would call her son such a thing?" Grinning, Flynn gave a mock bow. He opened the door a crack and locked eyes with the girl.

"Emily, I'd love to leave him a message in his room. Surprise him, but you're a busy girl and I wouldn't want to—"

"No, no, Jamie, I've got time. I love surprises and I've seen him go into a room on the seventh floor. It's a restricted floor where the rest of us maids aren't allowed to go!"

"Restricted? Whatever for?"

"They've been doing renovations on the seventh floor. We thought it was for the Royals. Of course you know the Queen is coming to visit and while she'll be staying with the Lieutenant Governor, two of her Ladies-in-Waiting will be staying with us at the Empress! Everyone's so excited! But they'll be on the floor below in the Vice-Regal Suite."

"I hadn't heard that. It's not been in the papers."

"Oh no, you mustn't tell anyone, Jamie. I could lose my job for telling."

Your secret's safe with me, my dear," Flynn whispered. "But you say that Chisholm has access then to the floor where the Ladies-in-Waiting will be staying?" Flynn pressed gently for a bit more information.

"No, I saw him one floor up where the work's being done. I can't say for sure, but one afternoon last week, Louise and I ran out of top sheets and we were in such a rush and would've been in so much trouble for being behind schedule cleaning the rooms. So I quickly dashed upstairs to grab some fresh sheets from the seventh floor linen cupboard and there was Mr. Chisholm letting himself out of the turret room!"

"Turret?"

"It's actually room 708, I believe, but we all call it the turret room. You can see it from the outside of the hotel, if you look way up, there are little circular rooms at each corner of the hotel where normally our guests are allowed to stay. They are very popular because of the view, but until the renovations are done, no one's allowed to stay up there. The entire floor is off-limits."

"Were you seen?"

The girl began to laugh. "No, no he didn't because I was so frightened, I hid in the linen cupboard until he passed, grabbed my sheets all the same and went back downstairs. I didn't even tell Louise!"

"I believe, Emily, without a doubt that this is my old pal Fenwick. A secret between you and me, he's rather a bit of a war hero." Flynn straightened the crease in his trousers. "There's a chance the hotel will be employing him to keep an eye on Her Majesty's Ladies. Wouldn't it be grand if we could sneak into his room tomorrow or the next day and leave him a message?"

"Then after the Queen's visit, you could introduce us!" Emily's eyes sparkled. She placed her hand on Flynn's arm and he resisted the temptation to pull away. Instead, he leaned in to the girl. "What time will you be finished then tomorrow, Emily?"

"I don't have a moment tomorrow because I must cover an extra shift for Louise. But on Friday, my shift is done at two." She put her hand on his arm again. "Oh Jamie, I can feel my heart about to burst with excitement. I won't tell a soul. My mother's always said that I can be a silly girl at times, but I am like an old woman when it comes to keeping a secret."

"Until Friday then, my dear."

Emily smiled and blushed all at once. "Good-bye Jamie, until Friday indeed."

He hoisted the heavy tray back off the stand and handed it to her. For a moment, he considered taking it down the stairs for her, but it was too risky. He couldn't afford any questions or introductions. He pushed the door open, but turned for a moment to watch her descend the dark stairs below.

Flynn put his cap back on and slipped out the heavy door. Keeping his eyes down, he exited the lobby and back onto Government Street. He had found the Queen's guard. Dan Smythe be damned. Fenwick Chisholm, the Queen's guard, with his Oxford accent, privileged life and his damaged hands.

Flynn walked to the corner of the block and then turned and looked up at the hotel. Rows of great windows traversed the brick façade in straight lines reaching a rather fanciful rounded turret on each corner. He hadn't noticed before just how much the Empress Hotel was constructed like an English castle.

CHAPTER ELEVEN

After skipping hard in the hotel weight room, and going at the punching bag like it was an enemy bent on taking his life, Kent still felt compelled to take a walk to tame his demons. Leaving Callaghan in his room, he grabbed a light jacket to offset the wind. Along Dallas Road, the ocean rustled at the shore and the wind sculpted the trees of a park on the other side. He tried to clear his mind. He felt drained and needed to be sharp for the interviews with the dispatchers in a little over an hour.

Charlie Crawford seemed legitimate. His story added up.

The wife might be having an affair, according to Callaghan, which could be relevant. Kent had to admit the boy's eye for detail wasn't bad. 'She had two outfits on the bed. She's been trying on clothes. She's bought new make-up and the boxes are in the bathroom garbage bin.' Kent had started to laugh and Callaghan had puffed out his chest, 'Sir, I don't know much about women, but I recognize someone who's lonely and looking for romance.' Good God, how did the boy ever survive Depot – twice?

It was possible the wife wanted to move some of the artwork out of the house prior to some kind of divorce settlement. Maybe she was jealous of the *Muse's* power to inspire her husband.

Kent couldn't believe he had given Callaghan a key to his hotel room. He hated sharing information, let alone sharing access to his room. Ah well, if Callaghan wanted to get in, he could probably find a way, key or no key. The early evening sun was still bright, but the heat was not oppressive like in Toronto. The constant wind off the ocean made it perpetually crisp.

A woman passed him with a baby carriage and he imagined Sarah walking like that proud mother. She would wear a headband like the white one she had that pulled the hair off her face and showed off her hazel eyes. She would reach down and check to see that the baby was sleeping. For a moment, fear gripped Kent. He couldn't indulge in these fanciful thoughts.

Sarah was gone, gone two long years now. He walked fast and hard back to the hotel. He ran up the hotel's backstairs two at a time, anything to clear his head.

He let himself into his sixth-floor room. Callaghan was up on a ladder and he spun around, training a large squat gun on Kent's face. Kent's hand went automatically to his holster, but the boy smiled and Kent realized Callaghan was holding an electric drill.

"Jesus and Mary, Callaghan, what is it you're doing?"

"Sorry, Sir, I'm almost done. I was going to try and look at the telephone wire from here just to make sure there were no bugs. The phone itself is clear. I'll do a final check to see if there are any extra wires inserted into the line between the switchboard and rooms to be safe."

A bead of sweat trickled down Kent's face. Brushing it aside, he pulled off his jacket. He'd best not reply to Callaghan at this time. Going into the bathroom, he sat down on the edge of the tub and unlaced his shoes. He pulled off his sweaty shirt and dropped it to the floor. His muscles ached in a way that felt good. He wallowed in the rare luxury of a shower in this fancy hotel. Scalding hot water would hopefully clear him of the desire to throttle Callaghan. He dried off and wrapped a towel around his waist. Pulling out the electric razor his dad had given him for his birthday, he plugged it into the wall outlet. He turned the machine on, pushing away the awful thought that it would slice into his cheeks. He touched the shiny screens covering the whirring metal blades below with his fingers. Although he'd used it a number of times, it was still unnerving to take something with whirling blades and buzzing with electricity and put it directly on his skin.

The door opened a crack and there was Callaghan! Kent clicked the machine off. "What is it!?"

"Nothing, Sir, I just wanted to see your electric razor."

"Damn it Callaghan."

"Is that a Philishave?"

"Can't a man have a shower and shave in privacy?"

"I've never used one of those before. My father has just begun stocking the Philishave razor and they're flying off the shelves." Callaghan eased the door open and looked with admiration at the machine in Kent's hand. The boy glanced up at Kent with a shy smile, but when he caught sight of Kent's face, he quickly retreated and shut the door.

"For the love of Mary," Kent said to his reflection in the mirror.

Kent finished shaving, muttering curses all the while against his hapless partner. Going into the bedroom, he paused. Callaghan was back up on the ladder plastering the hole where he had checked the telephone lines to the room. Marching into the bedroom and firmly closing the door behind him, Kent grabbed clothes from the closet, dressed quickly and returned to the sitting room.

"Callaghan." Kent went right up to the ladder and stood at its feet.

"Sorry about that, Sir." Callaghan was still plastering as if his life depended on it.

"I gave you a key to this hotel room because we're partners, right?" Kent looked up at him trying to keep his face impassive and his tone neutral.

"Right, Sir."

"But when I'm in the bathroom or the bedroom, could you give me a little privacy then?"

"Yes, Sir, sorry, Sir." Callaghan pressed around the hole, smoothing the plaster.

"I'm calling room service," Kent picked up the receiver. "What do you want to eat?"

The boy paused in his work. "Can I get a chicken sandwich and something to drink? Tea would be dandy. I would like pickles on the side and please ask them to hold the mustard. I like butter on only one of the slices of bread. Oh, and milk with the tea please, not cream. I would prefer the bread be lightly toasted if possible."

Kent called room service. "Hello, it's Room 602. Yes. Two ham sandwiches and two coffees, please."

"How long will it take you to make sure there hasn't been any tampering with the outside phone lines tonight?" Kent asked.

"Not long. I just need to get up the pole and take a quick look."

"Are you almost done here?"

"Yes, Sir," Callaghan tapped the plastered area with his fingers. "It needs to dry a bit and I'll sand and paint it."

"I want to listen to the dispatch tape," Kent said, "and I want you to hear it too, before we meet with Sylvia James."

"Yes, Sir."

Callaghan's fiddling with the phone receiver and the two reel-to-reel recorders required far too much fussing for Kent's liking. He could barely concentrate on the file.

"You just have to push this button here to activate the machine, Sir."

Kent looked over and made a mental note of the switch. "Alright."

"This little gem is modeled on the type 88 – a microphone," Callaghan announced. "It's utterly brilliant. The diaphragm velocity remains essentially constant for a constant sound pressure over the frequency range of 60-10,000—"

Kent rattled the file, but put it down when Callaghan turned on the reel-to-reel. They sat there listening to the events that had unfolded during the night of the shooting – it was as if they were right there in Dispatch. The nearly dead deer, the call from Crawford at the neighbour's house, panicked and angry. Dispatch sending out commands. The response from Car 12.

Constable Marcel Chasseur becoming more and more frantic as the robbery spun out of control. There was a knock at the door. Kent scrambled to stop the tape, when Callaghan deftly snapped it off.

"That's okay, Sir, it's just this button right here."

Kent went to the door. "Who's there?"

"Room service," a woman's voice replied, muffled by the door. Kent kept the door slightly ajar behind him and took the tray from the server, handing her a few coins. While Callaghan transferred the plates and cups off the tray and onto the table, Kent listened several times to Crawford's call. "It seems wrong, Callaghan."

The child prodigy took a bite of his sandwich and poured coffee out of a little white pot first into Kent's cup and then into his own. He looked like an old lady having a bite to eat before a game of bridge. He opened up his sandwich and scraped off the mustard with a teaspoon.

Picking up his sandwich, Kent turned the reel-to-reel back on. They listened again to Dispatch call Car 12 and route the two constables from Arbutus Road to the Crawford's house on Telegraph Bay, no mention of 10-82, even though Crawford clearly stated the men were armed. The dispatcher even specified "no sirens," although it was faint. Constable Chasseur's voice crackled on the tape: "Dispatch, Car 12, 10-23."

Kent clicked off the machine and put his sandwich down without taking a bite.

"Why didn't Dispatch tell them 10-82? That makes no sense."

"It sounds to me like she says "no sirens," Callaghan chipped in.

"Dispatch would have known the thieves had guns from Crawford's telephone call." Kent couldn't wrap his mind around it. "Write that down, Callaghan."

Callaghan kept hold of his sandwich in one hand and slipped a pen out from under the pile of papers with the other. He added this detail to the growing list in his notepad. Kent switched the reel-to-reel back on.

Chasseur was speaking urgently, but it seemed as if it were from a distance. "Dispatch, Car 12. 10-32. I repeat 10-32." He must have tried to reach Vittorio Cervide. From far away, but still distinct was a gunshot.

"Car 12 to Dispatch, we've got a 10-40," cried Chasseur.

And then screaming. Bloodcurdling screams – that must have been after Constable Cervide's ear was blown off.

"Car 12 to Dispatch," Chasseur's voice was raised. He was almost shouting. "It's a 10-41. I repeat a 10-41," he sounded desperate. "Vittorio's been hit. Car 12 to Dispatch," Chasseur cried. "Vittorio's down. We've got a 10-33! Send all units! 10-64, 10-64." It was an eerie repetition of what he had said in the psych ward.

The dispatcher's voice had come through, urging him to calm down, advising him that an ambulance was on its way, but she didn't respond to the call for backup.

"Where's the reply from Dispatch on backup? Is this the only tape?"

"This is the only reel that Staff Sergeant Jones gave us, Sir. Could you play that again?" Callaghan gestured with his half-eaten sandwich.

"Right after Constable Chasseur calls for backup?" asked Kent.

"Yes, right there."

Kent reversed and played the section of tape again.

"Now listen," Callaghan said. "There! Did you hear that? Do you hear the faintest gap, or am I hearing things?"

Kent listened again to Chasseur's cry for assistance and then there was the slightest of – pauses – it was probably just the tape moving through the machine. "Is that what you wanted me to hear?" he asked Callaghan and reversed, then played that part over again.

The boy nodded, his mouth full. He swallowed. "Someone edited that tape, I think. You can hear it even though it's just a fraction of a second. They might not have cut the tape on enough of an angle, or not glued it carefully enough, maybe they were hurrying, Sir."

"Are you saying this tape has been doctored, Callaghan?"

"I'm not positive, Sir. That gap on the tape just doesn't sound right. I think this is a re-recording of two different tapes spliced together."

"Do you think the dispatchers are covering something up?"

"I do, Sir."

Kent clicked off the dispatch tape. He'd lost his appetite. Pushing his chair back, he watched Callaghan take thoughtful bites of his sandwich. The boy put a little milk in his coffee and tried it. He added a little spoonful of sugar and tried it again. Then he put in just a pinch of sugar using his fingertips. Kent was mesmerized.

Sylvia James arrived ten minutes late in a fluster. She had blonde curly hair swept up in the latest fashion. Her eyes were sparkly and full of exuberance. She was the kind of woman that most seriously bored Kent.

She gushed as she met Kent at the door, "Oh Investigator Riley, I'm so sorry I'm late." She gave him an appraising look and Kent would not have been surprised if she'd let loose a low whistle. If Sarah personified 'still waters run deep', this girl was proof that babbling brooks ran shallow – very, very shallow.

Callaghan stepped forward and helped take her light raincoat. "Good-evening, Miss James, we've met before, I think, or at least spoken through Dispatch, Mick Callaghan. Constable Callaghan." He tacked on an awkward, little laugh. Sylvia James didn't seem to hear him, or for that matter even see him. She was solely focussed on Investigator Kent Riley.

"I had to walk five blocks and these heels are new. I think I have blisters." She kicked up one of her silk-clad legs and glanced at her foot, smiling all the while. Her most notable feature was plush lips painted carefully with a plum-coloured lipstick. It made her look as if she was pouting. Callaghan apparently couldn't take his eyes off those lips and Kent considered slapping him to break the spell.

"Why don't you come over here and sit at the table, Miss James. Can I get you a glass of water or anything then?" Kent asked, locating his notepad and pen.

"No, I'm fine, thank you. Do you mind if I smoke?"

"Of course we don't," Callaghan replied, rushing off to get her an ashtray, evidently delighted with the idea that those pouty plum lips would soon be pursed around a cigarette.

"I'm going to turn on the recorder," Kent said. "This is standard protocol in these matters. I'm sure you won't mind."

Miss James looked startled for a moment, but regained her composure, settled in the seat across from Kent and pulled out a worn cigarette case. She wore a dark flared dress that had seen two seasons too many. It flattered her plump feminine look.

"So Miss James, could you tell me about the night of the shooting. Start from the beginning and try to remember as much detail as possible."

Inhaling, she paused before speaking. "I had to do the nightshift because Simon Boyer was out of town and we got a call in that George Murphy and two of the other regular dispatchers were down with flu. They've been extremely sick." She crossed her legs and took a long draw on her cigarette. The pungent smoke wafted into a bluish-white cloud around her.

"Gwen and I do the day shifts with a rotation of four others. Weekdays are quieter. We usually get a higher volume of calls on the weekend." She waited for him to speak and then continued when he remained silent. "So we'd already both worked a full dayshift Monday and we were both beat – but I asked Gwen to be on shift with me because I didn't want to work with someone I didn't know in Dispatch at night. Gwen and I always work together."

"Surely Dispatch is the safest place you could possibly be in this city," Callaghan said, and the woman smiled and relaxed even more. Kent could see the advantage of having a boyish presence saying things like 'dandy' and 'at your service' while conducting an interrogation. Kent made women edgy and guarded. Sylvia James crumpled her cigarette into a cut crystal ashtray Callaghan had placed on the table.

"Well yes, in my head I know it's safe, but late at night, when the precinct is quiet and calls are coming in? I only wanted Gwen to be with me. She's such a good kid. So, it was around eleven or so, maybe a bit later, when a man called in to say that a deer had been hit and was blocking the road out Ten Mile Point way."

"What was the name of the caller?" Kent asked.

"Um, I don't remember."

"Who took that call, you or Miss Heller?"

"I did." Miss James straightened up in her chair. "Is there a problem with that, Investigator Riley?"

"No, no problem at all, but we need to know the sequence of events as precisely as possible," Kent assured her. "You understand that don't you, Miss James?"

"I understand, but I also know that Gwen and I didn't do anything wrong. We did everything by the book and I'm sorry that Constable Cervide got shot." Her eyes misted over and the pout became even bigger. Callaghan practically fell out of his chair rushing to get her a handkerchief from God knows where. She dabbed her eyes.

Kent didn't say a word, he just watched her. "Would you like to talk about something else for a moment, Miss James?"

"Yes, please could we? It's all been so difficult. Gwen cried herself to sleep last night."

"You and Gwen are great friends, I imagine. In fact, I understand you live together." Kent relaxed his pose in the chair. He pushed away the notepad and pen and reached for the cigarette case. "May I?"

Callaghan slapped his knees. "And I thought that you and I were the last two men on earth who didn't smoke!"

Kent felt his revolver pressing against the side of his chest and he imagined whipping it out and plugging Callaghan on the spot. Miss James' generous look became slightly more sceptical, but she opened the case and offered a cigarette to Kent.

"Yes, Gwen and I are very close, and we look out for one another."

"So how do you and Gwen spend your days off?"

Kent would not be surprised if this part of the interview would be when Callaghan started taking copious and very detailed notes.

"We love to walk along the harbour and go to the shops. Sometimes we see a movie at the Tillicum Drive-In or go for ice-cream at Ian's Diner over on Richmond Avenue."

Lighting the cigarette, Kent breathed in the fragrant burnt aroma. "Do you girls ever get short with one another, considering you not only work together, but also live together?"

Sylvia James smiled, "Gwen is the little sister I never had. I can honestly say I adore her." She fiddled with the cigarette case and then put it back in her purse. "Nothing Gwen does ever could make me cross. You'll see when you meet her. She's the sweetest, smartest girl."

"Do you feel a need to protect her?"

"A need to protect her?" Sylvia James moistened her lips and tapped the matchbox up and down on the table. "Yes, I think we look out for each other."

Callaghan went over to the wet bar and returned with three tall glasses of water. Sylvia James smiled her thanks and took a small sip.

"What or who do you need to protect one another from?" Kent asked, leaving his water untouched.

Callaghan spilled a bit of his water on the rich carpet and up he got to grab a cloth. The man was a jack-in-the-bloody-box.

"We protect each other from unwelcome advances."

"Do you or Gwen have a boyfriend or someone special, Miss James?"

"Not at the present," she laughed, but Kent could hear an underlying strain. Her eyes flicked away from his. "This is an absolutely gorgeous room. I have only ever been in the Bengal Lounge for drinks, but this room is – I don't have the words."

"What does your family think about you living and working in Victoria on your own, Miss James?"

She fiddled again with the clasp on her purse. "My parents are very proud of the work I do, Investigator Riley."

Callaghan interjected warmly. "I bet they are."

"Where does your family live then?"

"My mother and father live in Vancouver. They run a little bakeshop in Kerrisdale."

"Do you have any brothers or sisters?"

"No, I had a sister named Virginia, but she died when I was thirteen."

"I'm sorry to hear that. That must have been terribly difficult for you and your family." Kent got up. "Come look out at the view of the harbour, Miss James. It really is spectacular."

"When I look out at the harbour, Investigator Riley, all I can think about is the arrival of the Queen." She swivelled toward him.

Callaghan called out from the table. "Three more days!"

"She's coming in three more days!" Miss James let out a little squeal of excitement, while Kent's mind suddenly conjured images of kidnappings, beatings, broken bones and the jolt of bodies riddled by bullets. Royalty should stay home in the safety of their castles and not roam about as wartime mechanics, lounge on yachts anchored in foreign harbours, or stay in fancy hotels.

"Miss James, just a few more minutes of your time. I am hoping to get back to the night of the robbery."

Her face clouded over as she returned to the table and Callaghan gave her a sympathetic look. She pulled her purse onto her lap and ran her fingers over the clasp.

"I understand that Constable Cervide got out of the vehicle to kill the deer and get it off the road. Is that correct then, Miss James?"

"Yes, but after, it's all a bit of a rush. Gwen took the call about the injured deer on Arbutus Road. She was talking to Constable Chasseur, about the deer when I cut in with the robbery in progress at 4040 Telegraph Bay Road I believe it was." Miss James clicked the clasp open and shut quietly while she talked.

"The boys had some trouble finding the road in the dark. It's pretty rugged out there. More forest than houses, and it's not well lit. When Car 12 arrived at the house Constable Chasseur radioed in. Next thing we heard was a voice shouting 'Police–don't move! Drop your weapons. I repeat—' then the shot rang out. We heard the bang, then the screaming." Miss James talked like she was in a trance.

"How many shots did you hear then, Miss James?"

"I don't remember, but I think there were a number of them. We could hear them. Marcel started shouting for backup. We didn't think the thieves were armed, but Gwen issued a 10-82 and 10-30. Our policy is to be safe rather than sorry." She looked at them both apologetically. "Gwen called in backup and—"

"In the initial call from Mr. Crawford then, was there no mention of the thieves being armed and dangerous?" Kent asked.

"Not that I remember," Sylvia James faltered.

"It *is* normal to be confused after such an upsetting experience," Callaghan chimed in.

Kent glared at him and then watched Miss James' face. She was clearly trying to remember exactly what happened that night.

"So you called in backup?" pressed Kent.

"Yes, well no, I mean we did, Gwen did. I think. She called an ambulance."

"But *police* backup never arrived," Kent pushed her to confirm.

"No, no it didn't."

"Why not?" Kent insisted.

"I don't know," Miss James' brow creased with concentration. "Something went terribly wrong. We were bombarded after Constable Cervide was shot. Constable Chasseur was hysterical. I was keeping him calm, keeping him on the radio talking. Gwen was calling an ambulance in response to the 10-64. We didn't know where the thieves were. We didn't know if Constable Cervide was—" Miss James was on the verge of tears again. Callaghan took her hand.

"It's okay, Miss James, it's okay. We're almost done."

Kent continued in a neutral tone. "You do know Miss James that we have a record of exactly what transpired in Dispatch that night."

She raised her eyebrows. "Oh, I see. So that's what the prototype's for. It's so that you can sit around after we do our job and point out what we did wrong."

"No, that's not—" Kent began.

"Not at all!" Callaghan said emphatically, while Kent swallowed his fury at being interrupted yet again.

Miss James looked from one man to the other. "Have *you* ever had to deal with information being transmitted from someone who's frantic, but you aren't there and can't see what's happening? Have you ever felt completely desperate – hearing someone you see nearly every day screaming in pain?" Her voice rose. "I doubt it," she answered her own question. "And yet you think you can suggest to me with your silly tape – your 'prototype' recording of my performance that *we* weren't doing our job properly."

Kent tried to keep his tone gentle. "What I meant was simply that the recording of Gwen Heller's exchanges with Constable Chasseur do not accurately reflect what you remember from that night." Kent shifted his gaze when he saw Callaghan nodding his head up and down. He focused on Sylvia James. "On the tape, Miss Heller said no sirens. She issued a 10-83."

"Not 10-82? That isn't possible. She said it. I remember she said 10-82 and advised them of the danger and to proceed with caution. Honestly, it's what I remember. Gwen called an ambulance and surely she called for backup. She called—" Miss James leapt to her feet. "Hold on a minute! Are you accusing me of lying, Investigator?"

Kent stood while Callaghan remained seated, which for some reason added a layer of affectation to the standoff between Kent and Miss James. Taking a deep breath, Kent clung to his sense of calm. "We need to find out what went wrong, Miss James," he said deliberately. "Therefore, your *full* co-operation would be *greatly* appreciated."

Holding her purse tightly, Sylvia James took her seat cautiously and Kent also sat. Callaghan inexplicably stood up and gripped his chair back as if it had somehow misbehaved and he needed to keep a hold of it for everyone's mutual protection.

Kent motioned at him to sit down again. "Do you know Constable Cervide and Constable Chasseur outside of work, Miss James?"

Again, her eyes flicked away. Then she met his gaze squarely. When she spoke, she blushed slightly and sat up. Her pout increased. "Constable Cervide is married and has a small child and does not really spend time out with anyone from the Detachment. Marcel joins us on an occasional outing." She opened her purse and put her cigarettes and matches away.

"*Marcel* joins you and Miss Heller?" asked Kent.

"Yes," was the terse reply.

"On what kinds of occasions?" he pressed.

"Oh, just casual get-togethers, you know. We go out for coffee and the like."

Kent closed his notebook. "Thank you very much for your time, Miss James. I know you've been put through a very difficult time."

"Do you want me to stay while you talk to Gwen?" she inquired, with an appealing glance at Callaghan who was gazing at her with doe eyes further enlarged by his round glasses. For a moment, her usual brash manner gave way as she blundered on. "Gwen's not well, she's got a flu or something and maybe it would help if —" She looked over at Callaghan. Her plum lips were slightly open as if she might blow him a kiss.

"I'm sure that—" the boy began.

Kent cut Callaghan off. "No, no that'll be fine. I think that will be all for tonight. We really need your assistance, Miss James. I'll be contacting you tomorrow if I have any further questions."

"I want to help. I want you to catch the thieves that wounded Constable Cervide."

Kent gave her a formal nod. He looked over at Callaghan who took the cue for once and saw her to the door. Kent went into the bathroom and splashed water on his face. He could hear a slight giggle and then the door shut. Wiping his face with a towel, he walked back into the room. Callaghan returned from the door. Kent sat back down at the table.

"Did you notice that she called him 'Marcel' that time then? I'm getting the feeling that Miss James knows him better than she's letting on, perhaps even *intimately*," Kent mused.

"Why didn't you ask if anyone had had access to the tape during the night?" asked Callaghan fiddling with the smaller reel-to-reel that they used to record the interview with Sylvia James. He rewound it while pulling on headphones.

"I want to ask them about it tomorrow morning when Staff Sergeant Jones is present. In my file, it says that the only people who were in Dispatch until the tape was secured in the morning were Gwen Heller and Sylvia James. Callaghan was working the smaller reel-to-reel and not listening to a word Kent had said. Kent waited impatiently. The boy pulled the headphones off and smiled. "Worked like a hot damn. Here, you should listen. It's such a break-through and all thanks to Jack Mullin."

Kent took the proffered headphones. "Who's that then?"

"What? You don't know Jack Mullin? Come on, Sir, he's U.S. Army, Signal Corps. He's the guy that figured out that by applying a high frequency bias current to the recording head, he could—"

Kent slipped the headphones over his ears to save himself from Callaghan.

Sylvia James' voice came in perfectly clear. It was amazing. It sounded like she was right there in the room. He slipped the headphones off and clicked off the machine. Callaghan was still talking.

"I loved the shade of Miss James' lipstick. I just asked her now what it was called and she said the name is 'Summer Harvest.' I'm going to pick some up for my girlfriend, Courtney, as a gift. Have I told you about Courtney?"

Kent slipped the headphones back on. When he saw Callaghan's mouth finally close, he removed them and handed them back.

Callaghan unplugged the headphones and rewound to the place where Miss James called Constable Chasseur, 'Marcel'. He listened to it twice.

"There's a pause when she's talking about multiple shots, but I can't be sure." He put the headphones back on and then gave them to Kent.

He listened, but couldn't detect any sound or pause or anything. He removed the headphones and shook his head. "I can't hear anything."

"It's almost as if she begins to say something else," Callaghan suggested.

"I'm not able to tell," admitted Kent.

"I think you're right about Sylvia James knowing Constable Chasseur better than she wanted to let on," Callaghan acknowledged.

Kent sat down at the desk again, reflecting on what Sylvia James had said. He wondered how Gwen Heller would react when confronted with the same recording. He was glad that Callaghan had lost that dreamy look; it suggested he had stopped thinking about Sylvia James' lipstick and had instead decided to analyze the tape. Sketching the head of a buffalo next to the scribbles in his notebook, Kent tried to get the facts straight. "Charlie Crawford said he only heard one shot, but Sylvia James remembers a number of shots being fired. What do you make of her being so upset? Were you thinking that was a bit of a show then?"

The boy took his time. Kent could see him mentally going over the conversation.

"I don't know. I need to listen to the tape again. She seems protective. Maybe Gwen Heller was the one that made the mistake, and now Miss James is trying to cover up for her."

"Let's see this Gwen Heller before we decide what to do, but I'm thinking that driving a wedge between them will be the key to getting to the truth about what happened on Monday night." Kent stretched his stiff back by reaching upwards and rolling his shoulders. His legs ached from skipping and his neck was tense. There was a tentative knock at the door.

Kent opened the heavy hotel door. He almost gasped at the sight of the young woman before him. She looked utterly foreign, but at the same time he could swear he'd known her all his life.

"Hello, I'm Gwen Heller, and you must be Investigator Riley." She peeked past Kent and smiled gently, "Constable Callaghan, good to see you."

She had almond-coloured eyes and dark hair streaked with auburn, a most unusual look. Her skin was olive toned. She was the sort of woman men would fight a dragon for. Kent was still standing and looking at her framed in the doorway. He shook himself to break the trance. "Nice to meet you Miss Heller. Please come and sit down."

Callaghan pulled out a chair for her and took her coat over one arm. She was wearing a pale brown blouse un-tucked over a blue skirt. The blouse had tiny stitched strawberries in black thread around the collar and cuffs. Gwen's neck was long and her hair was in a ponytail that made her look both young and modern. When she spoke, she tilted her head like an animal listening for a sound in the forest.

"May I have some water please?"

Callaghan was off like a shot.

"This is an exquisite room, Investigator Riley." She looked around. "It's much nicer to meet here than at the Detachment."

"Do you mind if I record our conversation, Miss Heller?"

"Why would you need to record it? If you don't mind me asking."

"It's standard protocol in these kinds of investigations."

"Am I under investigation?"

"We're just trying to figure out what went wrong on Monday night given that an officer was grievously wounded. Surely you can see the importance of following protocol, Miss Heller."

"Yes, well yes, I do."

"Where are you from then, Miss Heller?"

Callaghan returned from the kitchenette with a glass of water for her. He removed Sylvia James' glass and then settled, or at least Kent fervently hoped so, at the table.

"I'm originally from Montréal."

"And is that where your family is living then?"

"No, I was orphaned at the age of seven and was raised at Mont Providence. It's a house for girls run by the Catholics."

Callaghan clucked sympathetically and Kent clenched his jaw.

"How was it that you came to Victoria?"

"The priest at Mont Providence has a sister who lives here and she wanted assistance with house-keeping." Gwen took a sip of her water and then drank several gulps more. She seemed unusually thirsty, perhaps nervous.

"I moved here when I was eighteen and I worked for her for three years before she passed away. Then I needed a job. I didn't have enough money for a ticket back to Montréal and I saw an advert in the paper for secretary work at the Detachment. I applied for the position and the Staff Sergeant hired me and then an opening came for a position in Dispatch. None of the officers wanted it – they'd much rather be out walking a beat or doing other fieldwork, not answering phones and sending radio calls." She finished her water and Callaghan bounced off to get her another glass. She smiled at him.

"Can you tell me what was happening then on Monday night?"

"You mean with Sylvia and me or the events themselves?"

"In Dispatch, tell me what happened."

"I think I'm to blame," she sighed. "Sylvia would never let you know. She's like a sister to me, but I think – I mean it was an accident – I was trying to call in backup and I needed to get an ambulance there and it all happened so quickly." She licked her lips and took a sip of water. Her hands slid down onto her lap and she leaned back slightly in the chair.

"When you took the initial call from Mr. Crawford, did he tell you the thieves were armed?"

"The call from Mr. Crawford? No, I don't think so." She knit her brow. "There was no mention of guns that I remember. He was frantic, actually very angry. They had tied him up and he was very distraught."

"Upset about what?"

"He was less upset about being tied up. It was that the thieves were there to steal his art." She looked up at Kent with the slight tilt to her eyes and then she inclined her head just slightly. Kent said nothing. Callaghan was about to speak, but then Gwen continued reflectively. "Mr. Crawford called from the neighbour's. He said he'd escaped out onto his patio and crossed through the forest to their house. He said two men were robbing him. He said to send everything we had. That's what I remember."

"So you did not inform Constable Cervide or Constable Chasseur that the thieves were armed," said Kent. "You told them to go without sirens."

"I didn't know. It seemed more like a straightforward B & E. Armed thieves are rare, but a B & E? We get those here, maybe once a week. Still I called a 10-82 to be on the safe side. The officers would have gone sirens on. I distinctly remember issuing a 10-30—"

Kent interrupted her. "No, no you didn't because you specifically said not to put sirens on and you didn't advise them 'danger, caution.' We have it all on tape."

"No, I am sure that—"

"Here, listen to the recording, Miss Heller."

"No sirens?" Gwen Heller leaned in apparently surprised.

Kent played the section of the tape and her voice emerged from the machine: "Car Twelve, we've got at 10-83 at 4040 Telegraph Bay Road. Thieves may be present, the homeowner is safe at neighbour's house. No sirens required."

Gwen's hands dropped to her lap and she interlaced her fingers slightly. She looked puzzled. "It's always strange to hear your voice on tape. It sounds so hollow almost like it's someone else's." She lifted her hands back up to the table and shook her head. "Sounds like I did issue a B & E protocol, but I could have sworn I called a 10-82 – I'm sorry about saying no sirens. Sylvia and I were so exhausted and I guess I was thinking not to wake the neighbourhood or something. The thieves seemed, from what I understood from Mr. Crawford, to be simply robbing what was now an empty house. Mr. Crawford's wife—" Her voice trailed off. Suddenly looking strained and pale, Gwen Heller stood up. "I really should go," she said abruptly, "do you need anything more from me?"

"I just have one last question," Kent stood as well. "How well do you know Constable Cervide?"

"I wouldn't say we're friends. We have a nice working relationship. I know him to see him. He has a small boy, Antonio. He's four." She looked distressed and closed her eyes. "I'm sorry. I'm really not feeling very well."

"And Constable Chasseur then?"

Callaghan fetched her coat. Kent strolled over to the door with her. Her colour rose slightly and she pulled down her blouse over the waistband of her skirt.

"I used to date Constable Chasseur. Everyone at the Detachment knew about us."

Callaghan stopped in his tracks. "I didn't!"

She directed a sweet look at him. "You don't go out for drinks with us and you don't gossip, Michael." She turned back to Kent. "We were together for almost a year, but we broke up a while back."

"Sorry, when was that you broke up then?"

"A while back."

"How long, Miss Heller, could you try to be a little more precise?"

She was now looking very pale. "A week ago." She was practically whispering, her almond coloured eyes welling up with tears. "Anything else?"

"No, you're free to go." Kent's voice was cold. He had pulled out of his reverie. He gave her a hard look. "We'll talk more," he paused, "when you're feeling better."

She turned back from the door, a little unsteadily. "Do you actually believe that I would ever want to see any of our officers hurt? I take full responsibility for—"

Her eyes filled with a look he couldn't account for. Her sadness suddenly struck Kent as enormous enough to fill the room and spill out to blanket the harbour.

There was still something she hadn't told them.

Callaghan looked absolutely horrified.

"You don't believe—" she began with a shaky voice.

"Miss Heller, it's alright then. I believe you, but sometimes situations can be clouded by feelings."

Once again, she turned to Kent just outside the door and asked intensely. "Will I lose my job, Investigator Riley?"

"That's not what this is about, Miss Heller. There are some issues in Dispatch we need to clear up and if it means anything, it'll simply be more training." He paused and took a step back from her. "Considering there was almost an officer fatality, we need to know exactly what took place."

"Absolutely," Callaghan added stepping in front of Kent who had to restrain himself from kicking him. Kent was caught right behind him and was therefore forced backward, feeling usurped and childish all at once. The boy called out brightly.

"Good-evening, Miss Heller! Hope you are feeling better soon. Would you like me to walk you down to the elevator? No? Alright then, good-night."

Callaghan closed the door loudly and then one heart-beat later opened it a tiny crack and peered out. After a few moments, he shut it again very softly and turned to Kent who had resumed his former place. The boy was practically forced to rest his chin on Kent's chest he was standing so close. Kent refused to move from the position he had held when Callaghan walked in between him and Gwen Heller.

Callaghan moved back towards the door. "Sorry to cut you off like that, Sir, I just wanted to watch what she did when she left." He studied Kent's scowling features and babbled on. "She grabbed something from her purse. It looked like food of some kind, a biscuit maybe?"

"Yes, she didn't seem overly well." Kent's anger collapsed as Callaghan had made an interesting observation. He was so irritating, but smart, and Kent liked intelligent people. The boy continued. "I think she may have an ulcer or something. She kept putting her hands on her stomach."

"Maybe it's the stress of the job. I mean she's just a young girl then, no family, no support. It can't be easy, and to be living with that tart."

"You mean Miss James? I thought she was lovely."

Kent rolled his eyes. "Do me a favour, Callaghan, listen to what you've got on the reel from the interviews and then listen to the dispatch tape. Compare the voices. I want you to tell me if it was in fact Gwen Heller who called the 10-83 and specified 'no sirens.' I've got a hunch that it might be Sylvia James on that tape."

Callaghan busied himself with the two recorders. He placed the prototype machine on the table beside the other reel-to-reel. Kent paced for a moment. "I've got to phone the Deputy Commissioner and report in," he said. "We need to get the phone line secured. I'll spot for you."

"Yes, Sir."

The phone rang.

"That'll be Deputy Commissioner Tepoorten now." Kent went over and took a breath before picking up. "Kent Riley here."

The voice on the other line came surging out of the past.

"*Ah Kenny, it's so good to be hearing your voice.*"

Kent's stomach lurched. Callaghan was listening to one of the reels. He was stopping and starting. Rewinding. The light had gone from the room and all Kent could see was the darkening harbour.

"What is it you're wanting Dolan?" Kent's threatening tone made Callaghan turn with a quizzical look.

"I want to inspire you," said the keenly familiar voice on the line. Kent put his hand over his eyes and replied, trying to keep his voice calm. "Leave me alone."

"I think you're sleeping and I want to wake you up." The voice was elegantly playful. The line went dead.

"Was it the Deputy Commissioner?" asked Callaghan.

"No. It was nobody."

"You look like you've seen a ghost." Callaghan's face creased with concern.

"Like I said, it was nobody."

Callaghan stopped both reel-to-reels "Another woman issued the 10-83 to Constables Cervide and Chasseur," he announced. "Not Miss James *or* Miss Heller."

Kent struggled to process what he was saying. "How can you be sure?"

"I'm good with voices and there's something with the tape that's not right as I said before. I'm thinking somebody spliced in a new section or erased a few minutes and re-recorded it."

"How hard is that to do?" Kent asked.

"Why would she do that?" Callaghan implored. "Why would Gwen Heller let us think that it was her? That she was the one who issued the 10-83 and said no sirens. I don't get it."

Kent's breathing was shallow. His mind was roaring. All he could hear was Flynn Dolan's silky voice, "*Kenny, I want to wake you up.*"

CHAPTER TWELVE

Flynn pulled gently on his fingers and the bones slid into position with a satisfying pop in the joints. He watched as Liam glanced down the hospital corridor for the hundredth time. Removing a small flask from his jacket, Liam took a sip of whiskey. Marcel Chasseur took the flask from Liam. He was flushed. The nurse might see that he'd been drinking. Liam never should have given him the first sip.

"When are they going to release me, Flynn?" Marcel's voice sounded husky like his throat was burning. "I can't stay much longer or I really will lose my mind."

"I don't know. Dan said the doctor told the Sergeant that he's pleased with 'your progress,' but that he wants to be sure you'll not be a hazard to yourself or anyone else. You've being overdoing it, Marcel my boy."

Liam started to laugh, his high-pitched voice going higher. Flynn glared at him and he stopped abruptly. "Sorry, sorry. It's just—"

"You'll be watching the door, Liam, and keeping quiet." Flynn took the flask from Marcel as he was raising it to his lips. Ignoring Marcel's protests, he handed the flask to Liam and pulled out a folded up floor plan of the Empress Hotel from his jacket pocket.

"So, here's the Vice-Regal suite on the sixth floor. There will be at least two men positioned at the door and by the stairwells around the clock," said Flynn.

"Everyone at the Detachment said she's going to Government House," countered Marcel.

"Dan's found out that a decoy's going to Government House."

"Why wasn't I told?" Marcel asked.

"Flynn's got to keep it quiet, Marcel, you know that," said Liam.

"If Kent has a room at the Empress," said Flynn, "then that's where the Queen will spend the night. I wasn't sure Dan had it right until I found out Kent's stationed at the Empress."

Marcel reached for the flask, but Liam moved it out of reach, patted Marcel on the knee, and gestured at Flynn's floor plan.

"Look here," Flynn pointed to the far corner of the hotel. "According to my source, this is where the Queen's man Chisholm has set up his base. He's using the turret room on the north corner of the seventh floor. All access to that floor is blocked until after the Queen leaves," explained Flynn.

"How will she get to the Empress without anyone knowing?" Marcel interjected.

"I don't know," Flynn admitted, "but the cover story is the Queen's two Ladies-in-Waiting will be in the Vice-Regal Suite on the sixth floor."

Liam's jaw dropped. "No – you don't think."

"I do. It's the Queen herself who will be in that room on Saturday night."

"Who's going to get rid of the Queen's guard?" Marcel asked.

"Rooke." Flynn spoke the name as if it was hard to pronounce. "He's one of Henry's men. Cold fish that one. He showed us the Queen's new quarters this morning."

"How can we trust him? He's slow and heavy. He can barely speak English," argued Liam.

"Look, Henry's picked him for the job and that's good enough for me. Besides, I don't care if he can speak. I'll be needing him to get rid of Chisholm, not chat with him." Flynn's patience was waning. The weight of it all hammered in his head, repeated blows from a blunt weapon.

"What about Kent?" Marcel fingered the gold cross at his neck.

"I need to talk to Kent." Flynn's mood suddenly shifted.

"But when?"

Marcel's whining had to stop.

"Tonight," Flynn informed him. "I'll call him tonight. I'll let him hear my voice. You can't be rushing Kent. He's the fastest man at a sprint, but you can't be rushing him on this job." He could hear Kent's voice from his 'wake up' call. He could hardly wait to call again.

Liam laughed his scratchy laugh.

"Jesus and Mary, you're sounding like one of the inmates, Liam," said Flynn.

"Yeah, so talk to Kent tonight, Flynn," said Marcel. "We need him on side."

"I thought first we'd be going for the boy from Special I, *then* Kent," Liam reminded him.

"The boy might pose a problem," Flynn countered. "He's smart. They're saying he's a genius."

"So?" Marcel queried.

"So, those geniuses are hard to anticipate." Flynn spoke slowly. "You can't be predicting how they'll move or what they'll say because they're thinking differently than everybody else."

"Aw come on, you're building him up," Marcel said. "I've seen him around. He's just a kid, wet behind the ears. He's the least of our worries." Marcel stood, but there was nowhere to go. "Look, I need to get out of here. You need to deal with the Queen's guard and get Kent on-side."

"I'll be sending someone tomorrow to see you. Maybe we can use Dan to get you out."

"Okay, you'd better leave now," Marcel advised. "The next nursing shift starts soon."

Liam pulled the door open for Flynn and gave Marcel a firm clap to the shoulder to shore him up.

About halfway down the hallway, Liam spoke. "Why didn't you tell Marcel that you'd already called Kent?" he asked. "What was it that you said to him then?"

"I simply told Kent that we needed him," Flynn replied. "I wanted him to know that we need to have him back with us, right?"

"Absolutely, Flynn that's right, that's exactly right," Liam said.

CHAPTER THIRTEEN

Kent pulled on a dark sweater. Callaghan grabbed his tools and they went to the lift.

"Sir, Staff Sergeant Jones told me that your wife—"

"My wife died in a car accident, Callaghan. I'm not wanting to talk about it."

"I'm sorry to hear that. What was her name?"

"Her name was Sarah."

"How did you meet?"

"I don't want to talk about it."

"Was she from Ireland too?"

"Callaghan I'm telling you, I don't want to talk about it right now or *ever.*"

"Okay, sorry."

The lift arrived. There was a formidable lady holding the hand of a small girl dressed in a light blue coat. Kent got an immediate sense of what he and Callaghan must look like, dressed in black, carrying a metal toolbox. Apparently though, Callaghan did not think that casually chatting about love affairs was in any way inappropriate in these circumstances, or any circumstances for that matter.

"I'm dating a girl that I met at a dance. Her name is Courtney Hayworth."

Kent remained silent, praying Callaghan would stop, but to no avail.

"She has the prettiest brown eyes I've ever seen."

As the door opened into the lobby, the lady and girl hurried out. Kent and Callaghan exited out a side door into a rose garden which put them on a path leading to the back of the hotel. Kent looked for the telephone pole the hotel manager had directed them to use. The night wind was now cool, almost cold, as it sifted through Kent's cropped hair. Callaghan got what he needed from the kit and climbed up the rough ladder of metal hooks embedded in either side of the pole.

Kent wished he could write Sarah a letter, but fear, far colder than the wind, swirled around him. He wandered around the back area of the hotel. This was clearly where the work took place. No fancy gardens here. There were large shipping bays, large garbage containers and oversized laundry hampers with numbers on them.

Callaghan was high up on the electrical pole. The hotel windows glinted beyond him. He was fiddling with tools he was drawing from his pocket, pulling clips out and something that looked like a wrench. Kent called up quietly. "Are you alright up there, Callaghan? Everything going okay?"

"Just fine, Sir! I'm almost done."

Less than a minute later, he started down the pole.

"It's all clear," the child prodigy called down. When he got to the bottom, Callaghan rubbed his hands on his trousers. Kent had a sense this was something he often did, clearing his fingers of electricity and wires.

"Let's go for a walk," Kent said. "I want to talk to you. Stowe your kit here, next to that hamper, no one will touch it. We'll pick it up later." Callaghan stifled a yawn and Kent felt his own fatigue. It had been a very long day, preceded by a very long flight.

Kent crossed Government Street with Callaghan beside him. He went down stone steps to the lower part of the path along the harbour and then down a ramp to the boats bobbing in the black water below. Halyards clanked against masts in the slight breeze, boats creaked up against their moorings. The city hummed above and behind them. Kent walked down to the end of one of the docks and looked around. There wasn't anyone to be seen. He looked out over the water.

"Callaghan, we can *never* talk about the pending Visit while we're in the hotel room."

"Yes, Sir."

"I know you checked, but I'm still worried about some kind of listening device."

"What? I didn't see anything."

"It's just that the call—"

"You mean the one you said was 'nobody.'"

Water lapped lightly against the hulls of the boats. People were laughing as they paraded along the darkening street above. Kent decided just then to leave the call out of it.

"Forget it, Callaghan, the only place you and I will ever say anything about the Visit is when we're surrounded by noise or in a remote place where we can be sure we can't be overheard."

"Yes, Sir."

"Call me Riley."

Callaghan stifled another yawn.

"Let's call it a night," Kent said.

They walked back behind the hotel in silence and grabbed the toolkit from behind the laundry hamper where Callaghan had stowed it. Crossing over to the parking area, Kent noticed a man, with his hat pulled low, leaning against a wall by an alley behind them. There was something about his build that was familiar.

"What are you looking at, Sir? Do you know that fellow over there?"

The man disappeared down the alley. Must have been a trick of the light, but Kent didn't like it. The elegance of the way the man carried himself was striking and far too familiar. There was no way Flynn could actually be here, but the fact that Kent was feeling his presence, seeing his shadowy form, was a sign of how badly Dolan's call had shaken him. And that, he knew, was exactly what Flynn had meant to do.

He pulled the car keys from his pocket and tossed them to the boy. "You take the Plymouth and pick me up here tomorrow at zero nine hundred."

"Sir, I'll pick you up at eight. We need to get into the girls' apartment and see about tapping their phone – if we need to have someone listening, it's at least installed. Won't take me long, but you said you wanted that done."

"Yes, you're right, zero eight hundred then. We have to see Dr. Mason at ten and we should go over what we're planning to say in the interview with Constable Chasseur beforehand."

"I have some ideas," said Callaghan, with what Kent hoped fervently was *not* a wink.

"Well don't be telling me now."

Callaghan smiled up at him. Kent strode back towards the hotel lobby. He felt tired, but edgy. Please, God, let it not be Flynn who had stolen the sculpted head. Why would he have, anyway? Was it worth that much to someone? That was possible. It all seemed too coincidental, but that was exactly how Flynn worked. He was disturbingly patient. He would have spent months planning the heist.

But he couldn't be here, couldn't get into the country, and that's why he phoned, to rattle Kent. If Flynn were in Victoria, he would come and see him in person. Still, the phone call suggested Flynn was in fact up to something, and that alone was enough to make Kent's blood run cold. Then there was the face in the passing car, and now the man in the alleyway.

He found himself standing in front of the Bengal Lounge. The sound of violins and cellos rose above the murmurs lending an air of elegance to the shadowy room. Kent walked in and threw himself into a deep leather chair. He had to admit he liked the dark of this place. There were tall tropical plants that gave privacy to the polished tables. A fire burned brightly against a wall where a tiger skin stretched taut above it making one feel as if the day had been adventurous and triumphant. People were laughing and chatting. One couple was knee to knee and the man's hand was part way up the girl's thigh.

How ironic, drinking in a bar that was an homage to colonial Britain. Only in Canada would political oppression be celebrated as if it was a safe place to lounge.

A waiter in a crisp white tunic approached "Good evening Sir, what can I bring for you this evening?"

"A glass of your dark please."

"Right away."

Kent could almost feel what it would be like to have Sarah beside him. She would be telling him about her mother's latest scandal. The outrageous thing she said at Lady Whomever's luncheon to raise money for so and so and Sarah would be in affectionate hysterics about the absurdity of it all. Kent would shift toward her and slide his hand along her thigh beneath her skirt. He would feel the taut place where her stocking ended.

A man walked up to the table. "Ah – hello – Investigator Riley?"

Kent froze. The man seemed extremely nervous and he waited with his hands clasped behind his back. He was holding something. Kent stood slowly and his hand slid under his jacket.

"No need for that, Investigator Riley," the man said, looking even more nervous. "I work at the RCMP Detachment." He extended his hand with his badge nestled in it. Kent pulled his hand over and angled it so he could read the badge in better light.

"Constable John Feiring," the man mumbled.

"Sit yourself down then Constable." Kent threw himself back into the seat. It had been too long of a day. Maybe this was the man he saw at the edge of the alley. The man that he thought was the shadow of Flynn. The waiter appeared with his beer and asked after the other man.

"He'll have the same," Kent said looking over at this anxious cop who seemed like he might jump to his feet and run out the door at a second's notice.

"I've been waiting for you," Constable Feiring said, "I was going to talk to you before in the lobby, but I lost my nerve." He swallowed. "What I have tell you must be kept quiet." He glanced around the lounge.

The waiter returned with the man's beer and Feiring did not touch it. Kent decided that an uncomfortable silence was the best policy. The man was maybe late twenties. He was fit, but not solid, more on the skittish side. His hair was almost black, and his eyes were a muddy blue. Out of uniform, he seemed dressed to blend in rather than stand out and his clothes were neat. He did not wear a watch or a wedding ring. A soft leather satchel sat at his feet.

"I saw something that may be relevant to Vittorio Cervide's shooting."

Kent sat up straight.

"But first, I need to know that you won't turn me in."

"Turn you in? Turn you in for what exactly?" Kent eased back in the lounge chair so as to appear less threatening.

"The way I got the information is part of something that's not good."

"Do you mean not legal?"

"Uh, sort of."

Kent drank his beer and thought about it. The man watched him closely from across the small marble-topped table between them. He let one of his hands stray down to the satchel, beside him.

"Do you have evidence?"

"Yes."

"You'll have to leave it with me."

"I have evidence," Feiring choked out, "but you *have* to keep me out of it. They'll *kill* me."

"Who will?"

"I can't tell you."

"Alright then. I'll do my best to see your name and what you're involved in is kept quiet."

How bad could it be? Kent would have to decide afterwards just what he would do with this so-called cop, John Feiring. But he needed the information and if a white lie for the greater good was a means to an end, so be it.

Feiring placed his glass carefully on the table. "After hours, I work at a place downtown—"

"Where?"

"I get paid to take pictures of people when they're in the private rooms. The establishment sells the photographs back to the gentlemen afterwards and they pay a lot to get them."

"A brothel."

"Not exactly, it's an after-hours club with three private rooms and some *advantages* like the one I just, uh, mentioned."

"What's it called?"

"I can't say."

"Just so I'm clear, *Constable*, you take photos of people in compromising circumstances, without their knowledge, which are then used for extortion or blackmail. Do I have this right?"

"Yes." The constable looked miserable and rightly so. Jesus, what next? Kent waited for him to continue. He took a sip of his beer.

Kent scanned the lounge to be sure that what followed was not overheard. The buzz of conversation, the violins and cellos were enough.

"A month or so before Cervide got shot," Feiring began, "and this is why I never said anything to anyone, I mean it wasn't my business and I would have destroyed the photographs, but I didn't. I don't know why. It sort of felt like I was abandoning her, but it was also like I was accusing her."

Kent struggled to keep the details straight in his head as Feiring babbled on.

"In May, a guy came into the club with Gwen Heller."

"Gwen Heller, the dispatcher who was engaged to Constable Marcel Chasseur – that Gwen Heller?"

"Yes, that's the thing. They were planning to get married. Everybody knew about it. Now no one will talk about it, especially not to you." Feiring fiddled anxiously with the clasp on the satchel. He pulled out a file folder and handed it to Kent who opened it up to find a number of enlarged photographs.

"So this big guy, goes into one of the rooms with Gwen Heller. I don't know it's her until after when I was developing the shots. I wasn't really watching, I was clicking away and not really, uh, paying attention, but when I developed the pictures." Feiring's voice died out.

The top picture was a dimly lit room. Kent couldn't tell for sure that it was Gwen Heller because the photograph was blurry and the woman's back was to the camera. The waiter materialized at the table and Kent quickly closed the file folder.

"Another round, gentlemen? Would you like to see our late night menu?"

"No thanks, we just need the bill."

Kent opened the folder again after a quick look around. He shuffled to the next black and white photo in the pile – this one clearly showed it was Gwen Heller. Without a doubt. The man in the image had his shirt off and was removing Gwen's clothes – it looked like she was protesting. In the next shot, she was naked. The pictures were graphic. So graphic they sent Kent's head spinning.

The room was all in burgundy tones, patterned carpet, a big square mirror on one side and lewd paintings on another. Against the wall was a stripped down bed. The man in the picture was imposing, with a muscled back and powerful arms. Initially, he was stripped to the waist with his belt undone. Gwen was now on the bed – she had the most exquisite legs and her breasts were those of a young, fresh girl. Her arms were pushing up against the man and her legs were splayed out beneath her. The heat began to rise in Kent from his feet up. In the next image, the man was over top of her. Kent hurried through the final photographs – but stopped suddenly and studied the final one. It was the first time he could see Gwen's face. He looked at the next one and the next in rapid succession and muttered under his breath, "Oh my God."

In one photograph, Gwen's face was turned aside as the man's arm was lifted above her. In the next picture, his hand struck her face. In another shot, her nails gouged his shoulder and in the next he gripped and twisted her arm. She was screaming. Constable Feiring studied his face and looked as though he might be sick.

"You see. You see why I had to talk to you."

"Why didn't you do something!?"

"I didn't realize. The music's loud in the club. No one would have heard her. I see pretty crazy stuff in those rooms and have learned to get my pictures done, get out and not look too closely."

Gwen's face looked like it was being torn apart. Her mouth was a gash of pain and terror. Kent studied the other man.

"Who's the man then?"

"I don't know."

John Feiring reached for the folder, but Kent pulled it back. "You'll be leaving these with me. I'll keep you out of it, but I need these."

"What are you going to do with them?"

"*Who's the man?*" Kent asked again. He was done with Feiring who would be smart to leave quickly.

"His name's Paul O'Rourke. He's based over at Naden. He's a Navy man."

"Does he use those rooms often then?"

"Yes."

Kent put some coins on the table and stood. He looked at the constable who remained slumped in his seat. "I recommend, *Constable* , that you never return to that establishment – find another way to make extra cash."

"You'll keep me out of it?"

"I'll do my best."

"I'm telling you if they find out, I'm a dead man."

"If *who* finds out?"

"I can't tell you."

"Then you make it hard for me to protect you."

"You don't know what you're dealing with here." Feiring stood, his head bowed.

Kent was about to leave, but then paused. "It took courage to bring these pictures to me. You're not the kind of man to be working in a place like that."

Feiring lifted his head. "Thank you, Investigator Riley."

Kent walked out of the lounge and went to the lift. He pressed the button and stood watching the descending numbers of the car. Paul

O'Rourke could be anybody. He was not going to worry until he had something specific to worry about, something factual, as opposed to fear. Fear caused errors. Flynn Dolan was an ocean away, phone call or not. Dolan could plan and direct robberies from overseas, but lesser men would have to be carrying out his orders. Kent could handle lesser men. Flynn Dolan would not risk trying to enter Canada, even if the Queen herself was coming here.

He would definitely not risk going back to Crumlin Gaol.

THURSDAY

.

CHAPTER FOURTEEN

The morning was grey and cool. Kent lifted weights, skipped hard, punched the bag until his shoulders ached. He ran the stairs and only then did he feel clear enough to phone Deputy Commissioner Tepoorten. He sat on the hotel room bed and dialled the Deputy's direct line. Like Kent, Tepoorten was an earlier riser and would already be at his office even at this hour.

"Richard Tepoorten."

"Deputy Commissioner, Investigator Riley."

He could hear the Deputy sit down. Kent looked over his notes. After he briefed Tepoorten, he would try and find the words to explain about Flynn Dolan and what was at stake if in fact he had commanded the theft or worse, was planning some kind of move against the Queen and Prince. The Deputy Commissioner needed to know that the Royals could be in jeopardy, but how to explain his own involvement? Kent hoped the words would come.

"Good morning, Riley. Do we have anything to be worried about?"

"I'll tell what I know so far. The Crawfords were cooperative. It seems most likely that the thieves escaped with the Brancusi by boat."

"By boat?"

"Their house is situated above a small beach. There are stairs that lead straight down from the house. They could have easily left a boat pulled up and then slipped away without detection."

"Excellent work, I'll put out an alert to the Coast Guard."

"What I don't understand," Kent said, "is why the thieves circled around to the front of the house and shot Constable Cervide."

"I agree that is unusual. Keep working on that."

"We consulted with Constable Cervide—"

"He was well enough to speak to you?"

"Yes, I interviewed him yesterday at the hospital. He can't remember Constable Chasseur's position when the shooting happened. He remembers seeing the two men though."

"Any identifying features?"

"No, they had masks on and hoods, besides it was dark."

"Do you have any doubts about Constable Chasseur?"

"I spoke with him directly after meeting with Cervide. Chasseur *appears* to be in some form of post-incident shock. My instincts say he's not as traumatized as he appears."

"Interview him again. Take a more hard-line approach. Break him if you need too."

"Yes, it's what I hoped you'd say. Callaghan and I are due back at the Jubilee for a meeting with Dr. Mason at ten hundred hours." Kent took a breath. "I interviewed the dispatchers Sylvia James and Gwen Heller last evening. Both Callaghan and I believe James appears to be protecting Heller. Reasons unknown at this time."

"You listened to the prototype?"

"Callaghan is of the belief that the tape has been tampered with. He's identified a part of the tape that he thinks may have been recorded over or maybe even spliced with another tape and re-recorded."

"Have you informed the Staff Sergeant of this?" Tepoorten sounded furious.

"Not yet. I'm not fully confident in the Staff Sergeant," Kent hoped this wouldn't infuriate him further. "We will be doing further questioning of him and the dispatchers this morning."

"Keep me informed. Why do you think Miss James is protecting the other dispatcher?"

"Miss Heller seems to be unwell."

"Really? This is a problem."

"I'm very sorry to inform you," Kent struggled to find the right words, "that about a month ago, it appears she was raped."

"Who was raped!?" Tepoorten demanded.

"Gwen Heller."

"The dispatcher?"

"Yes, it was at some sort of bar or club. I'll see what I can find out about it. A Constable John Feiring brought this matter to my attention last evening. He had incriminating photographs. That evidence is now in my possession."

"I don't know Feiring."

"He's very worried for his safety. Should we put a man on him – for his own good?"

"You've got the evidence. Let him stay on the outside for now. He could be useful. Did he know the rapist?"

"He identified him as Paul O'Rouke, a Master Seaman, based at Naden."

"Ugly business," the Deputy Commissioner still sounded furious. "The Staff Sergeant should be informed immediately."

"I worry it is connected somehow," Kent ventured. "Can you have someone do a background check on O'Rourke, and Callaghan and I will pay him a visit today if he's still at Naden."

"Yes, good idea. I'll make sure the military police know you're coming. I know their Detachment commander." There was a pause. "I'll give Lieutenant Commander Coles a call. We liaised over security for the Visit."

"Thank you, Deputy. I believe the rape may have a connection to the robbery and the mix-up in Dispatch."

"That certainly seems like a stretch, but I agree with you these issues are most concerning."

"Turns out the dispatcher, Gwen Heller was engaged to Constable Chausseur and *he* broke it off."

"Did the Staff Sergeant know of this? That is against all rules. Was this before the rape?"

"No, after."

"Well then, we may well be looking at a lovers' triangle – unlikely to have any bearing on the Visit, which is our primary concern. But rest assured, I will be having Staff Sergeant Jones and his Detachment thoroughly investigated."

"Alright, I still think we should do a routine check in with Paul O'Rourke over at Naden – then hit Constable Marcel Chasseur hard to see what shakes loose."

"How's the constable from Special I working out?"

"Constable Callaghan? He looks about fourteen years-old, but he's got a keen eye for details and his technical skills are as good as we were told." Kent could hear another phone ringing in the background."

"Riley, London on the other line. Call me back later." The line went dead.

Kent hadn't told him about Flynn. A surge of frustration overwhelmed Kent and he slammed the phone down hard, and then smashed it one more time for good measure.

He turned around to see Callaghan standing in the doorway with his eyes wide behind his spectacles. The boy stuttered cautiously. "Good, good morning, Sir."

"Morning, Callaghan, *for the love of God*, call me Riley. And would you *please* do me the courtesy of *knocking* on the door before waltzing in here. The room key is for when I'm *not* here."

"Yes. Sorry about that, Sir." He coughed awkwardly. "How was your night?"

"Restless. I have new information and we have a busy day ahead of us to say the least. Let's go." Kent grabbed Constable Feiring's file folder off the table and put it into his briefcase. He patted his pocket to make sure he had his wallet. He put his revolver into his holster and took one last glance around the room. He looked at the phone for a moment. He knew he was missing something. "Are you able to drive us over to Naden this morning? How long will it take?"

"About twenty minutes." Callaghan replied with a puzzled look. "Why do we need to go there?"

"You install the bug on the dispatchers' phone, then we'll go to Naden. I'll explain in the car what we're dealing with."

Callaghan navigated the Plymouth out of downtown and past the manicured grounds of what to Kent's eye looked like a convent. The black wrought iron sign read *St. Anne's Academy*. Gwen Heller had been raised in an orphanage out east. She hadn't had much of a life.

Kent filled Callaghan in on the unexpected visit from John Feiring. He thought it better not to show the photographs of Paul O'Rourke raping Gwen Heller. Callaghan paled at Kent's description. He didn't say a word, but he gripped the steering wheel all the more tightly. They reached the dispatchers' apartment. Gwen and Sylvia lived on the main floor of a wooden house on Moss Street. The houses were fronted with lush green lawns and the street was lined with Chestnut trees. Callaghan parked down the block a ways and then began to regale Kent as if he were addressing a prospective home-buyer.

"This neighbourhood is called Fairfield. It's bounded by Dallas Road to the south and the Strait of Juan de Fuca," he gestured the two or so blocks to the expanse of blue water opening up at the end of the street, "and the shops of downtown," he pointed off to the right, "and yet it's really a wonderful little community unto itself. Oak Bay's to the north," he pivoted slowly, "and Beacon Hill Park is just there to the west!"

Kent had just told Callaghan about a brutal rape and here he was chattering about a delightful little collection of Victorian homes in a quaint neighbourhood. Maybe it was because he refused to look at the photographs. Smart boy.

"Okay, Sir. I'll get to work and you make sure no one sees me. Miss Heller and Miss James should be on their way to the Detachment for their meeting with the Staff Sergeant by now." He set his tool kit down on the porch and rifled through it while fiddling with the doorknob. Kent felt his heart rate increase and he started scanning the street. "Callaghan, if I see anyone approach, I'll give a low whistle. Do you have that?"

"Yes, Sir."

Kent couldn't see anyone. There was a car up the street, but it turned at the corner. There was an elderly lady posting a letter at a mailbox, but she was too far down the street to worry about. He strolled along the side of the house, and out of habit scoped the ingress and egress points. When he got back to the front of the house, Callaghan was already inside. The boy was the fastest picklock Kent had ever known. He relaxed slightly now that Callaghan was not on display to the houses on the other side of Moss Street.

Kent studied the neighbourhood. The houses had porches to the side, bay windows, many with designs at the top that were jewel-toned in the sunlight. Kent looked back down at the ocean glinting improbably at the base of the street. He imagined walking down to the sea with Sarah. She'd be holding her hat and pulling at a white skirt that the wind would ruffle. Kent could almost hear her laughing.

"Sir, it's done."

"What?"

"The phone's all set. Should we take a look around?"

"We don't have time. We need to get to Naden and find O'Rourke. Close that door and let's be on our way."

Callaghan drove the Plymouth down Moss and turned right onto Dallas Road. They traveled past stately homes on one side and on the other the steep tree-lined cliffs overlooking the Strait. They entered a park full of tall grasses and crinkled trees and then through the busy shops of Victoria's downtown. Leaving the shopping district in the rear view mirror, Callaghan navigated through drab warehouses, harbour side docks and then past Chinese groceries and restaurants with roasted ducks turning in the windows. Kent was suddenly hungry. As they approached a large blue metal bridge, bright lights started flashing and a bar came down like the ones at train crossings. Callaghan braked to a stop as the bridge slowly pulled apart, a massive cement block lowered, and the whole road seemed to open up and lift so that a tug pulling a barge stacked high with metal containers could make its way through.

"Sir, is it true that you were brought in to deal with the faction causing trouble in Québec because you were an Irish nationalist?" Callaghan asked out of the blue.

Kent almost choked. "Nationalist?"

"Uh, the, you know, the IRA? I mean *that's* ridiculous, but that is what people say."

"You think I'm with the IRA, Callaghan?" Kent put his hands into a prayer position and angled them at the windshield, "Jesus and Mary, Mother of God and all the Saints."

Callaghan laughed anxiously. "I knew it was a silly rumour, but you are rather famous for preventing the kidnapping because they say you could *think* like the terrorist cell in Montréal."

"Callaghan, I was born in Northern Ireland. I know the suffering and desperation that fuels resistance. I know how rebels think and it's the same whether it's in Ireland's Ulster or Canada's Laurentians."

The bridge started to sink slowly back down into place. The bar lifted and they crossed over the narrow body of water that linked the inner-harbour of the city presided over by the Empress Hotel and the Parliament Buildings with what must be the working harbour with its docks, tugs, barges and loading bays. Kent shivered at the thought that the bridge would not fully close and they would fall through the metal decking. They passed a series of industrial tanks squatting beside a small shipyard, then wound up Esquimalt Road.

"I did my degree at University College Dublin, Callaghan," Kent said. "That's where I learned how to be an investigator."

"What did you study?"

"Politics. I learned how to be reading beneath and behind the story." The boy nodded as if this made perfect sense. Kent continued, suddenly wanting Callaghan to know something about him, something personal. "I policed first to pay for school, but then when it became more about solving problems, finding out motivations, and less about manhandling people, I began policing for myself."

Callaghan laughed. "I fixed lamps and radios and telephones to pay for university so I could join the force. My dad still wishes I would come back and take over the shop."

"And you're not wanting to?"

"No, I'm like you, I have too much imagination."

Kent couldn't believe that the Canadian Pacific fleet was somehow going to materialize out of the trees that leaned out over the roadway. The air had a tangy salty smell. Two Indians walked along the side of the road. One was pushing a bicycle. A man at the hotel told him that the Indians used to own the whole harbour and the English took it from them. How typically British. He shook his head to free his mind.

The trees soon gave way to a new suburb of fresh, post-War homes, the sight of a protected harbour disappeared for only a few moments before the Plymouth coasted down a gentle hill toward the base. HMCS Naden loomed up grey and forbidding. Destroyers and patrol craft rested against the docks, their iron gray paint highlighted against the light blue sky and darker blue water.

They pulled up to the security gate and Callaghan passed both of their badges to the MP guarding the gate. After looking over their ID and making a phone call he lifted the gate.

"Do you know where we could find Master Seaman O'Rourke?" Callaghan asked, pocketing his ID.

The MP looked down at his watch. "At this time of the day, most everyone is at the mess hall for coffee. The Junior Mess is to your right." He came out of the booth and pointed. "See that tall, grey, square building? It's in there."

Parking in front of the building, Kent strode up the steps into what was probably the main barracks of the base. Directly across the main foyer were doors that led to the Junior Mess Hall. Callaghan held one of the doors open for him and they entered the large, humid room full of uniformed men drinking from mugs and talking loudly.

"Can you recognize him from the photographs, Sir?"

"No." Kent scanned the tables. Callaghan leaned down and asked a man to identify him. The man half-rose and pointed out several tables over the now unmistakable Paul O'Rourke. He looked up at the two men with a scowl. Callaghan seemed about to give a little wave when Kent caught his arm and pulled it back down.

O'Rourke continued to casually drink his coffee. He had the hunch of a rugby player with a powerful, thick neck. His jaw was square. He looked like the kind of man that would start a fight just for the pleasure of spilling some blood. Now studiously ignoring them, O'Rourke got up slowly from the table, picked up his tray and walked over to the clearing station. Kent could feel Callaghan bristling at his side, but he stood in silence and watched their quarry.

Sure enough, O'Rourke approached them, with a slight smile as if he'd been expecting them. "A couple of suits like you must be looking for somebody."

"Investigator Kent Riley. Constable Callaghan. Is there a private place where we could speak with you, Mr. O'Rourke?" Kent asked.

"It's Master Seaman O'Rourke. And does the place have to be private?"

"No, I could bring you into the Detachment if you'd prefer," Kent replied.

O'Rourke raised his eyebrows slightly, his condescending smile unwavering. "This way," he pointed.

He went through the mess hall door and led them to a chilly room on the other side of the foyer. There was a table for about eight people and a chart table with a map of Esquimalt Harbour in one corner. He closed the door and gestured that the other two take seats. Callaghan sat while Kent remained standing. There was something oddly familiar about O'Rourke's face. Some detail in the way he moved his jaw. Kent could imagine him leaning over the gunwale of a boat, his face dark over the ocean. It was eerily familiar.

"Sit, Master Seaman O'Rourke, I have some pictures I want you to see."

He threw the file folder down in front of him and flipped it open. The sailor's face remained completely neutral as he went through the photos. Near the end, when Gwen's facial expression was visible, he winced ever so slightly. It was just a slight compression of the lips. He closed the folder and looked up.

"What do you want to know?"

"What would you like to tell me?"

O'Rourke grinned. "I met a girl, we had sex, end of story."

"That's not a girl O'Rourke. That's Gwen Heller." Kent's voice expanded. "That's not sex, O'Rourke. That's rape." He leaned right in the face of O'Rourke, slamming his hands on the table. "Now what is the Godamned story!?"

Callaghan nearly leapt out of his skin, but O'Rourke did not move a muscle. Kent lifted his hands from the table and stared down at him, daring the sailor to take a swing at him.

"How was I supposed to know she was a virgin?" O'Rourke said. "Besides, she came with me to the club. We were together. We had a few drinks. She came willingly enough into the room with me. It's not like I dragged her. Ask anyone." O'Rourke stood, as if they had taken up more than enough of his time. His smile was like an oil slick. "Now, how is that rape, Investigator?" He gave Callaghan a knowing look. "If the girl changes her mind mid-thrust, what's a guy to do?" Kent collected the folder and Callaghan stumbled to his feet.

"Is there anything else I can be doing for you suits?"

Meeting O'Rourke's eyes and again getting the flashback to the gunwale of a boat and a rough, dark sea, Kent said simply, "We're done. For now."

As they pulled up at the security gate, Callaghan slowed. Kent got out and walked over to the guard, showing his badge. "Get me Lieutenant Commander Coles."

The MP's eyebrows shot up. He dialled immediately, spoke briefly, and then handed the phone to Kent.

"Good morning, Lieutenant Commander Coles, Investigator Kent Riley, RCMP here."

"Deputy Commissioner Tepoorten told me you'd be checking in with me at some point. Everything is in order for the Royal Visit. I can assure you that—"

"My concern is related to the Royal Visit."

"Yes?" the Lieutenant Commander's voice sharpened.

"I would like Master Seaman Paul O'Rourke confined until after the Visit. He is presently under investigation in a related matter and I want him secured."

"What has he done?"

"Rape."

There was a long silence. The Lieutenant Commander cleared his throat. "And this is a threat to the Visit?"

"I believe so."

"I assume you have evidence to support the charges?"

"That I do."

"Consider it done. It'll be D26 for O'Rourke. Keep me apprised of your investigation."

"I will. Thank you." Kent hung up, nodded to the MP and got back into the car. Imprisoned in D26 couldn't be a pretty thing, but charged with rape would be a whole lot worse. Kent would ensure O'Rourke was charged if it was the last thing he did. Trying to breathe calmly, Kent concentrated so that the knot of molten rage eased in his chest. Gratefully, Callaghan knew enough to keep his mouth shut. The kid was learning.

CHAPTER FIFTEEN

Liam and Flynn walked down Douglas Street in the hazy morning light, looking for *Electrolife*. The Hudson's Bay Company department store loomed on one corner while shops full of life's necessities lined the other side of the busy thoroughfare. There was a fabric store, a houseware shop full of pots and pans, a cobbler and the hardware store where Flynn had bought materials for the bomb. Liam stopped at a two-storey building with a life-sized placard in the window of a housewife vacuuming a floor. She wore a white apron and an expansive smile as if her Hoover vacuum was a gift from God.

A small bell jangled as Flynn pushed the door to *Electrolife* open. Behind the counter were shelves full of appliances of all kinds. Lined against a wall was every style of radio imaginable – each with a carefully numbered tag hanging from a dial or knob. A cash register dominated one side of the long wooden counter. On the glass shelves to the right appeared to be the latest toasters, blenders and mixers with small rectangular placards singing their praise. A balding man stuck his head out from the back workroom, just as feet clattered downstairs somewhere else within the building.

A woman's voice called out as she bustled forward into the shop. "I've got it, Jeremy." A little breathless, she approached the counter to greet her newest customers.

"Good morning, gentlemen. How can I help you?" She was wearing a flowered apron over a dark blue dress and she twisted and tucked in wisps of dark brown hair, streaked with grey, back into her bun.

"Hello, ma'am, might we be speaking with your husband as well?"

She gave them an anxious look, taking in their suits, hats and Liam's briefcase.

"Just a moment please, I'll fetch him from the workshop."

She'd be in her early fifties, Flynn figured. Liam hadn't said a word in his high-pitched voice. He hated this kind of thing. He was not a great liar. Good for jobs, good to get things done, tasks, but he was not a good liar. Liam went over to the row of vacuums and proceeded to examine each one carefully as if he were planning to purchase one. The woman returned, followed by her husband whose hands were stained with black grease. He was heavy-set and had large square fingers. It was hard to imagine him working with slender wires and delicate tools.

"Good morning Mr. Callaghan," Flynn smiled warmly. "My colleague and I are working with West Coast Insurance and we've been establishing policies with businesses along Douglas Street and our records show that you don't have any coverage with us at all."

"Well, yes that's quite true, Mister—?"

"Mr. Cadwell and my partner here is Mr. Lorimor." Liam came over to the counter and shook Mr. Callaghan's hand.

"You've been building up quite a store here, Mr. Callaghan, quite a store, and you and the wife have a fine reputation in the business community."

Mr. Callaghan smiled proudly and his wife seemed to relax a little. "We're lucky to be part of such a fine downtown, Mr. Cadwell." He glanced over at his wife. "I'm not really sure about insuring the place though. We have just finally moved from renting to owning and—"

"Excuse my interruption, Mr. Callaghan, but am I right in assuming that your living quarters are above the shop."

"Yes, that's true, but—"

"Well, it's forward thinking. It's planning ahead to always be secure in your business and your home. For a very reasonable monthly amount, we'll be offering you full coverage, a safety net against theft, vandalism, fire, flood, if you know what I mean, something that helps a fellow sleep more soundly at night."

Mrs. Callaghan seemed about to speak, but her husband put his hand on her arm. "Listen, gentlemen, it's a tempting offer and to be honest, it's something we've considered. It's just that—"

"Well, I don't want to be imposing, but perhaps we could leave you some literature on the policies and simply take a quick tour now, do some measurements, that kind of a thing and draw up a detailed quote in case you change your mind."

Liam busied himself with his briefcase, pulling out some papers and a measuring tape. The woman started to sputter and Flynn jumped in quickly.

"Now, now, it's only to give you a sense of the cost. There are no promises being made today. Nothing is being agreed to. It just would be so much easier for us to outline your small monthly contributions if we actually knew the size and contents of the business and the home being insured."

Callaghan senior went over to the counter end and lifted up the flap to allow the men to enter.

His wife's exasperation evaporated. She became all hostess. "Well, my heavens, Jeremy. I am just going to dash upstairs right now to tidy up and put on some tea. I had no idea we were to have visitors today!"

The doorbell jangled and a woman entered with a freckled boy who looked like he'd just walked into a toy store. He went right over to the glass shelves and gazed up at the shiny machines.

"Don't you dare touch a thing, Matthew! Good morning, gentlemen. Mr. Callaghan, have you had time to see to my radio?"

Flynn slid through the open counter followed more slowly by Liam.

"You fellows can take your measurements and gather your information. I'll join you in a minute after I see to Mrs. Jacobs and my favourite customer." He went over to a beautiful wooden radio against the wall with Mrs. Jacobs in tow. Flynn could still hear him as he walked up the stairs.

"Now Matthew, why don't you come around and see if you can find my box of candies!"

CHAPTER SIXTEEN

After driving in silence for exactly ninety seconds, which must have posed a significant challenge, Callaghan asked, "Do you want to stop for coffee, Sir? We still have half an hour before we need to go to the hospital to meet with Dr. Mason."

"I want to quickly stop by the Detachment and talk to Gwen Heller."

"Are you sure we have time, Sir?" Callaghan turned to look at Kent and almost drove into an oncoming car.

"We're on a tight schedule, Callaghan. There are only two days left before the Visit and we need to have this whole Dispatch situation cleared up and, right now it's a bloody mess. So yes, we'll be needing to confer with Miss Heller, even if we're pressed for time."

At the Detachment, Kent sat in an empty interrogation room, dreading the discussion with Gwen Heller. He felt clammy and his stomach was churning. He had the bitter taste of coffee in his mouth. Callaghan tapped lightly at the door.

"Miss Heller is here, Sir."

She came in quietly. Callaghan gave Kent a searching look and then bowed out, the door clicking closed behind him. Kent resisted the impulse to go over with him, one more time, *exactly* what Callaghan was supposed to communicate to the Staff Sergeant. Kent didn't have time to update Jones himself.

"Miss Heller, please sit down. How are you feeling?"

"Better, Investigator Riley." She did not look well. "The Staff Sergeant says it's likely that Sylvia and I will be suspended without pay until further notice." Her eyes filled with tears.

"I'm sorry to hear that. I'm sure that this will all get sorted out soon enough."

Her olive skin was pale and looked waxy like that of a mannequin. She seemed to be holding herself awkwardly in the steel chair across from Kent.

"Miss Heller, do you know a Master Seaman Paul O'Rourke?"

Her face changed slightly. A thin, but impenetrable wall slid down over her features. It was like a safe house, Kent thought and then his mind went to Sarah with a terrible lurch. He pushed those thoughts away and focused on Gwen Heller.

"No, I do not know him. Why do you ask?"

"I understand that you know him rather well, perhaps even romantically."

"I don't see how my personal life is relevant to your case, Investigator Riley." She looked even more strained if that was possible.

"Your relationship with Mr. O'Rourke is relevant because you were engaged to Constable Marcel Chasseur and had things gone differently, *he* might have been killed on Sunday night. Instead, Vittorio Cervide nearly ended up dead. And I'm trying to understand why."

A couple of tears slid down her face that she did not bother to wipe away. She seemed to writhe slightly in her seat like she was in pain.

Kent hated himself, but continued. "And Chasseur and Constable Cervide were endangered due to problems in Dispatch – problems you were intimately involved in. Therefore, Miss Heller, your personal life is in fact *highly relevant*."

"Will I go to jail?"

"That depends on you, Miss Heller. Your cooperation is imperative. I need you to tell me everything about O'Rourke."

Her face was strained with something more than the tension of their conversation, but Kent couldn't figure out what. "Mr. O'Rourke is a friend of, of Marcel's. They were in the Navy together." Gwen started to sway slightly in her seat. "A little more than a month ago, we all went out for dinner." She licked her lips and Kent handed her a glass of water. She went to drink from it, but then her face tensed up again and she put it down on the table her hand trembling.

"Are you alright, Miss Heller?"

She glanced up at him and then looked back down at the table. Her face crumpled again with tension. This had to be a tough story to tell. Her voice was so quiet Kent had to strain to hear her.

"I'm not feeling very well, I'm sorry."

"Take your time, Miss Heller."

"Marcel had to work. He was on night-shift so he asked Paul to take me home." Kent slumped slightly in his seat so that he could watch her downcast face that creased again as if the emotional pain she was feeling was rushing through her body.

"He took me to a club." She spoke almost with a groan. "He said we'd just have one more drink together to talk about Marcel. I wanted to hear because they'd been friends for years. I had already had quite a bit to drink. I wasn't really thinking straight."

Her face was twisting with pain. It seemed cruel to make her go on, but he needed a formal statement. She didn't have a chance against O'Rourke. A judge would throw the charges out of court with her story about going to the club, drinking and then claiming she didn't know what she was doing. But Kent needed to know and Marcel Chasseur most definitely needed to know. She was starting to take in great breaths as if she couldn't get enough air. Her skin seemed to have gone a sickening yellowish hue.

Kent stood. "Miss Heller? Are you alright?"

He started to move toward her as he saw her eyes rolling back in her head. Her head began to make slow, widening circles as if she was fighting to stay conscious. Kent lunged forward, knocking his chair aside and grabbing her as she collapsed and fell towards the polished concrete floor. She moaned as he caught her in his arms. When he lifted her, he felt warmth all over his hands. He glanced down at her chair as he rushed to the door and stopped. The seat was dripping. He looked down at his hands cradling her, and his fingers too, were covered in blood.

"Callaghan!"

Callaghan burst into the room.

"Call an ambulance," Kent directed. "Tell them to meet me in the parking bay. *Now!*"

Kent carried Gwen down the back corridor. "You'll be okay, Miss Heller, just hang on there. You're going to be fine."

The ambulance couldn't come fast enough. Kent kept talking, but he was losing her. The amount of blood was staggering. An ambulance roared into the parking bay. A tall, thin paramedic jumped out of the driver's seat while his partner flew out the passenger side and they launched into action. They had Gwen Heller on a stretcher and hooked up to an IV in what seemed like seconds.

"Please stay in the back with her and try to keep her conscious," said the thin paramedic as Kent hopped into the ambulance without any hesitation. He steadied himself against the stretcher as the ambulance jolted through the streets siren wailing and lights flashing. He thought woozily about how he wouldn't be late to see Marcel Chasseur at the hospital because that was exactly where they were going – to the Royal Jubilee. He reached out and grabbed the paramedic's arm. The man passed him a round plastic container and Kent vomited. He caught the man's eye. "Sorry, I'm feeling a little shaken."

"It's alright, happens all the time. Don't worry too much mister. She'll be okay." He looked over at one of his instruments and checked the reading. "She's young and strong." He reached up and flicked the bag of fluid hooked up to her arm. "There's a clotting agent in the IV. She'll get to the doctor in just a minute." The man put his rough hand on Gwen's pale forehead. She started writhing up on the stretcher and moaning.

"Can you tell me what's wrong?" Kent asked.

"I'm not allowed to diagnose, that's up to the doctor, but unofficially, it looks like she's having a miscarriage." The paramedic looked up, suddenly startled. "You're not the father are you?"

"No, no I'm not. She and I work together."

The ambulance careened to a halt in front a large red and white Emergency sign at the hospital entrance. The paramedic leapt back into action, unclipping the stretcher as the driver came around back and threw open the double doors. Kent tried to push against the vehicle's side to be out of the way.

"Miscarriage," the paramedic informed the triage nurse as he wheeled the stretcher into the Jubilee at a run. "She's haemorrhaging."

Callaghan came running up alongside the ambulance. He glanced at Kent. "I'm going to go in with Miss Heller to take care of – to do the paper work, Sir." He pulled out the Plymouth keys and tossed them to Kent. "Sir, you should go back to the hotel and change."

Kent looked down and saw that his suit was ruined with blood. He looked at his watch. "But I'm late for Dr. Mason."

The boy's face was tense. "I'll just go and have them call Dr. Mason and tell him what happened." Hurrying into the Emergency room, he called over his shoulder. "I'll meet you at the Psych Ward or come back here to collect me." Callaghan actually looked angry. Kent's wanted to wash his hands. He shoved them in his pockets. "I'll be back as soon as I can – take care of her," Kent said in a low voice, but Callaghan was already gone.

• • •

Striding quickly across the Empress lobby, Kent scanned for his RCMP contact at reception. He waited in line for agonizing moments then finally got to the desk.

"I need a large plastic bag," he said quietly. "Get someone to bring it to me in 602."

"Are you alright Mr. Hatfield?" Macdonald's face was impassive.

"Yes, not my blood."

People were staring at him.

"I'll send up someone in a moment." Macdonald said.

Rising up in the lift, Kent had a feeling he was not alone. When he got into his room, he quickly searched it, hand on gun. He stripped down. His suit was soaked with blood and it had seeped through his shirt and onto his skin. His gorge rose and he forced himself to swallow. He went into the shower, turned the water as hot as he could bear and scrubbed with his nails and soap and the flat of his hand to get the smell off. He was pulling on a fresh pair of trousers when the phone rang.

"Kent Riley."

"How was your visit with Paul O'Rourke? Was it nice to see an old friend?" The high-pitched voice scratched into his mind.

"Who is this?" Kent demanded.

"Isn't he a bloody charmer?" The playful tone was maddening. The phone line went dead.

"Hello? Hello!"

Goddammit. He should have pressed that button Callaghan showed him. What was the point of having the reel-to-reel if he didn't record the conversation? He grabbed his belt from the bed and pulled a jacket out of the closet. Such an idiot – so careless.

Still, he knew that voice. It was not Flynn Dolan, but the man was Irish. The voice was high-pitched and familiar in a strange way. Kent's anxiety felt like needles on the surface of his skin. How could Flynn and his crew know about O'Rourke? Then again, Flynn's latest specialization was torturing women. Kent searched the room again. There was something amiss. He was losing track of something.

He stuffed his bloodied clothes into the bag Macdonald had sent up from reception and tossed it into the bathtub.

CHAPTER SEVENTEEN

Drawing on his cigarette, Flynn watched as Paul O'Rourke showed his cousin Liam how to operate the boat's controls. His voice sounded stern like a father teaching a son how to drive. Paul pressed the starter and the boat roared to life. Flynn got up from the cockpit and looked back at the powerful twin motors as they churned up the dark green sea.

Much as he hated him, Flynn was impressed with Paul O'Rourke's ability to plan ahead. Not many men would go toe to toe with the likes of Kent Riley and still have the wherewithal to make a smart escape. Not many men would slip into the ocean in the very heart of the Pacific Fleet and swim for hours to evade being put in the brig. And unlike his cousin Liam, Paul didn't complain. He was blue and shivering uncontrollably when he stumbled through Dan's kitchen door.

Coming down the boat's port side, Liam joined him. "She'll be a powerful one won't she?"

Flynn threw his cigarette butt into the water, figuring such a comment did not deserve a response. "Liam, you'll be on the boat then with Paul and the Prince."

"What? I thought you were wanting me to stay with you and the Queen."

"No, Kent and I—"

"You don't know if Kent's going to come with us."

"Well, let's suppose he does. Kent and I will be escorting the Queen to Henry's and you and Paul will be taking the Prince on the boat."

"We'll leave him at the buoy then?"

"No, you'll be leaving him *on* the boat. Paul is taking us to the drop off point now. We'll be leaving the boat completely concealed. I figure it'll take the police about two days to find it. With 'Constable Dan Smythe helping' them it might even take longer."

"Where'll Paul and I be going then?" Liam asked.

"Paul is getting a man to pick you up. No questions asked. Don't be even speaking to him about it. He'll drop you at the harbour. You'll bring Paul to the hotel, tie him up, and leave him hidden somewhere in the basement of the Empress Hotel to be found. You'll go to Marcel's and basically disappear until I get word to you."

"Disappear?"

"Liam, it'll be only for a short while," Flynn assured him.

"Why won't I be staying with you at Henry's?" Liam asked. "Kent can take the Prince."

"I can only have *you* do it because you're the only one I totally trust. Kent will be a wildcard, Liam, you were saying so yourself just a moment ago. I'll be needing to watch him at all times."

Liam patted his arm and rasped out against the wind. "You can trust me, Flynn. I'd do anything for you, anything to see your plan work. We owe it to so many people, Flynn, so many people."

Paul yelled for Liam to cast off. Rushing over to undo the ropes from the dock, Liam released the boat. Paul had Liam steer, but he gave him pointers each step of the way. Easing the boat away from the dock and out of the inner-harbour, Liam let the engines idle for a moment then gunned the boat and they skimmed over the green water, away from the city, past the Ogden Point breakwater into the open sea. Flynn looked down at his watch and started timing.

CHAPTER EIGHTEEN

Callaghan was sitting in Emergency just staring out the window when Kent entered. He stood when he saw Kent walk through the glass doors.

"How is she?" Kent asked.

"They've stopped the bleeding. They're taking her through the miscarriage." Callaghan looked down at the floor blushing and then cleared his throat and straightened up. "She's no longer in danger, the doctor said, but she'll be weak from blood-loss. He thinks she can leave in two or three days."

"Thank God for that," Kent said, already looking around at the hospital signs that would get them to the Psych Ward. "Did you reschedule the meeting with Dr. Mason?"

"He might be able to meet us later, but said to check with the nurses," said Callaghan falling into stride with him. "Sir?"

"What the hell is it, Callaghan?"

"Just an idea—"

Kent felt fury rising in him. Yet, strangely, Callaghan's aggravating ways were making him feel less scattered.

Kent found the sign and set off for the Psych Ward with a vengeance. He couldn't give a damn how traumatized Marcel Chasseur might be. Today was the day for answers if it meant he had to extract them with—

"Sir?"

"What, Callaghan?"

The child prodigy took in a deep breath. "I personally believe, and this is my own opinion, that it would be beneficial if you let me talk to Constable Chasseur first."

"*Forget it.*" Kent found the corridor and could see the nurses' station down at the end.

Callaghan tried again. "I think that Chasseur will tell me more if I act like his friend." He slipped his glasses off and polished them with the cuff of his suit. "He's scared. And if you make him feel even more scared, he'll get all worked up like last time and we won't find out if he's hiding something."

"We're here at the request of Dr. Mason," Kent told the nurse. "Do you have to contact him?"

The nurse indicated the sign in sheet and then opened the door for them. "Dr. Mason has authorized your visit, Investigator."

He marched into the quiet hallway and he could feel Callaghan tensing in case there was more screaming, like last time, and he wanted to be ready.

"I don't trust Constable Chasseur either, Sir. I hate that he's somehow involved in Miss Heller's situation. But I still think—"

"Okay," Kent interjected. "I'll give you five minutes and if you're getting nowhere then we'll be doing it my way."

"Yes, Sir." Callaghan had the gall to smile.

The boy went in first and Kent followed. Constable Chasseur was sitting in the same chair looking out the window. He did not seem surprised to see the two men. Kent walked to the far wall and leaned back against its smooth cool surface. Callaghan sat on the bed and faced Chasseur.

"Marcel, how are you?"

"Better," he replied fiddling with a little golden cross hanging from the chain around his neck. Kent imagined pulling that gold chain tight across his throat while he watched Chasseur's face turn a satisfying shade of blue.

"Good," Callaghan said. "Everyone down at the Detachment is worried about you and asking how you're feeling."

"I feel badly for Vittorio. The nurse took me down today to visit him. He smiled at me and took my hand." Chasseur's eyes filled with tears and Kent had to resist the temptation to slam his fist through the white plaster wall. Callaghan glanced at him and turned back to Chasseur, making those clucking noises that were his specialty. Kent's teeth clenched and he concentrated on relaxing his jaw.

"He thinks I tried to save him," Chasseur said.

Callaghan went with it. "You did try to save him."

"He doesn't know that it's actually my fault."

Kent stood a little straighter against the wall. Now they were getting somewhere.

Callaghan got up from the bed and lightly rested his hand on Chasseur's shoulder. He leaned down to him. "Come on Marcel. It's no one's fault. Things go wrong in our line of work. Things happen fast."

Chasseur started shaking his head and then he started rocking. Kent imagined pinning Chasseur up against the wall and banging his head into it.

Callaghan glanced back at him and his eyes seemed to be flashing, but it was hard to tell for the reflection of his glasses.

"Why is it your fault, Marcel?" Callaghan asked. "You'll feel better if we talk it through."

"I broke off the engagement. It's me Gwen wanted to hurt, not Vittorio."

"Not Vittorio, not Vittorio – I understand." Callaghan patted his hand and Chasseur actually became a little calmer. He only rocked slightly and he seemed as if some of the burden had shifted. Callaghan sat and waited. Kent's anger began to ease.

"Gwen was unfaithful," Chasseur explained. "She cheated on me."

Callaghan looked appropriately upset. "That's terrible, but she seemed so in love with you. You two seemed really happy together."

"But she was unfaithful and so I asked for my ring back. I told her we couldn't—" He trailed off into silence.

"Couldn't marry?" Callaghan prompted. "How did you find out she was unfaithful?"

Chasseur got abruptly to his feet and sent the chair skittering back. Now his face was suffused with disgust. He raised his voice. "How do I know? How do I know? Because it was with my friend!"

Callaghan rose as well, matching Chasseur's passion. "That's even worse!"

Kent tried to fade into the wall, not exist in the room. He tried to clear out any emotional presence and let the story come.

"Women can't be trusted," encouraged Callaghan.

"Not Gwen, not her. She wants me to marry her because she's pregnant!" Chasseur spit. "A whore is bad enough, a pregnant whore is sickening."

"She got pregnant with your friend?" Callaghan asked. "Why would she think you'd marry her?"

"She said she loved me. Can you *believe* that?"

"That's not love. Maybe she was trying to make you jealous?"

"No, it's worse than that. She says he raped her! My friend would never do that. He's not that kind of man, and he would never touch the woman I was engaged to marry."

"Is he a childhood friend?"

"No, we met in the Navy. He's still in." Chasseur was up and pacing frantically in the constrained space. "He's the best friend a fellow could ever have. He was driving her home. She threw herself at him. She told him it was over between us and she wanted to be with him." Chasseur sat back down in his seat and folded his hands on his lap. "My friend got confused. Gwen seduced him. I can never speak to him again."

"What's his name?"

"It doesn't matter. We're not friends now."

Callaghan looked at Kent as if to say, enough? Kent came forward and pulled the folder of photographs out of his bag. "Could you please identify the two individuals in these pictures, Constable Chasseur?"

Chasseur looked startled. He took the folder, but didn't open it. He looked at the two men.

"Open it," Kent ordered, his voice hardening.

Chasseur opened it and went through the photographs. The colour rose on his face and he stopped when he came to the first one showing Gwen's terrified, pain-filled face. He glanced up at Callaghan and Kent searching their faces. Then he let out a scream. Callaghan leapt to his feet and almost flew to the door. Kent reached forward and slammed his hand over Chasseur's mouth.

"Shut up."

It was too late. A nurse came swooping into the room. Gathering up the photographs, Kent took a step back from Chasseur and said to him under his breath.

"We're not done yet."

Chasseur started banging his head against the wall.

The nurse rounded on Kent. "What have you done?! You've ruined days of good work here. Now I must ask you to leave!"

Kent looked over at Chasseur and said again more loudly so that he could hear him. "We're not done yet, Constable Chasseur. We'll be back." The nurse pushed them out the door.

Kent and Callaghan stopped at the nurses' station.

"Dr. Mason is in another meeting," said an older nurse, "and he won't be able to see you until tomorrow afternoon. Shall I make an appointment?"

"No. We don't need to see him." Kent felt out of control. There was too much going on.

Callaghan steered him down a series of hallways while his mind went into overdrive. The boy sat him down and bustled away. Kent looked around and realized Callaghan had led him to the hospital cafeteria. Callaghan sat down across from him and placed a sugar-dusted bun and cup of black coffee before him. Kent stared blankly at the wall while his mind did an inventory of the details that were starting to generate two patterns: one narrated by Marcel Chasseur and another one that lay beneath, just out of sight.

Callaghan again surprised him by not asking any stupid questions. Kent needed the silence in order to see the two narratives and the ways in which they did not add up. He could barely stand the thought of eating, but couldn't afford not to. The bun was perfect because it had no taste. He finished it and Callaghan popped up and soon appeared with another one and set it down in front of Kent. Still he did not speak.

Kent drank the last of his coffee. "There's something wrong with Chasseur's 'trauma.' His story doesn't add up."

Callaghan brought his sugary fingertips up to his mouth. Kent braced himself, but the boy wisely chose to wipe his hands on a napkin.

"If Chasseur is truly emotionally deranged," Kent continued, "he should be reverting to his native tongue. But we've not heard so much as a French curse out of him."

Callaghan sat up excitedly. "You're right! You're absolutely right. But why would he fake it and then tell us everything today. I mean he basically confessed his romantic involvement with Gwen."

"He wasn't confessing," Kent shook his head. "He told us exactly what he wanted us to know – nothing more, nothing less."

"You mean about what happened to Gwen?"

"Yes, don't you see, Callaghan? He's telling a convenient revenge story – Gwen gets raped and then jilted. Now, she's pregnant so she tries to get revenge. She uses her position in Dispatch to put Chasseur and Cervide in harm's way."

"So you don't believe that Gwen's guilty?" Callaghan asked, his face exuding relief.

"No, I don't. Gwen is being used by Marcel Chasseur to distract us from what's really going on." Kent's mind circled around the false version of events, but couldn't seem to get to the heart of it quite yet.

"It's so cruel," muttered Callaghan.

"There's something else going on that Chasseur is wanting to keep hidden, but what?"

"I don't fully understand, Sir."

"Use your imagination, Callaghan, and call me *Riley*."

Kent got up from the table and Callaghan scrambled to follow. He walked down the hospital corridor and into the main foyer. Callaghan was jogging along at his side. They exited into the fresh air and Kent paused at the Plymouth, searching his pocket for the keys. He got into the driver's seat. Mixed up police codes, single bullet to the head of the wrong guy, art heist, sleeping muse and wake-up call, the broken girl, Québec and Ireland.

Callaghan started to say something, but then stopped abruptly.

Kent pulled rapidly out of the hospital parking lot and turned right onto Fort Street. He felt like he was being chased. He looked over and the boy was gripping the armrest as if they were about to hurtle into space. Kent glanced at the Plymouth's speedometer and slowed down. His thoughts were a jumble. Callaghan unclenched his hands, released his death grip on the armrest and colour slowly returned his face.

"It's too neat, too tidy," said Kent. "Sylvia James and Gwen Heller don't strike me as capable of doctoring the Dispatch tape; they barely know how to use it, never mind having the time to make the switch."

"But who—" interjected Callaghan.

"So someone else did it, but that someone else is keeping us focused on the girls and what they might be covering up."

"Wait how—"

"Then that someone gives us the motivation for Constable Cervide getting shot, because the bullet was actually meant for Marcel Chasseur."

"Really?! And so—"

"Gwen was violently raped and pregnant. Her fiancé has abandoned her in her time of need and so she wants revenge."

"But that means—"

"Someone wants us to be pointing the finger at Gwen Heller."

"Yes, who would—"

"And that someone wants us to be seeing Sylvia James as the sweet friend trying to cover it up. It's just all too tidy."

"Definitely too tidy!"

CHAPTER NINETEEN

Even though hours had passed, Flynn still felt the ocean's cold and the boat's rocking motion, but the plan was coming together. In the smoky shadows of the Matador, Paul sat hunched over the table with the other men. Cards were scattered about the table, but no one was playing. Liam picked up odd cards and looked at them as if they held answers to his deepest questions. Paul drank from his near empty glass. Flynn saw something flicker across Paul's face as he noticed one of Henry's men standing and staring at him from the shadows. Could it be fear? Paul squinted through the smoke at the henchman staring at him and shuddered ever so slightly. Flynn suspected he was remembering the cold ocean he immersed himself in to avoid the brig.

Constable Feiring was the fool he had expected him to be. Flynn had no patience for divided men, but the young constable had served his purpose. On the one hand, he bucked authority with his side job at the Matador. But on the other hand, he wanted to play the hero and save the girl. What a man like that could never understand was that sacrificing Gwen Heller was nothing when weighed against the deprivation caused by the British to the mothers and children back home. The heat of his cigarette began burning his fingertips as he stubbed it out in the ashtray.

Even Henry was predictable, enough that he would kill Feiring so that Flynn didn't have to do it. He was sure Henry would agree to dump the body at the painter's house, for the right price. It was important to capture Kent's imagination. He wouldn't work with just anyone. He would only return to Flynn if he could impress him with the beauty and elegance of the plan to restore equality and justice. That required *imagination*.

Flynn caught O'Rourke's eye and purposefully shifted his gaze to the heavy-set man in the corner playing the piano with the woman singing beside him. Paul said this would be the perfect woman to seduce Kent –

who had lived like a monk for the last two years as far as Flynn could tell. Surely Kent was ready for a little comfort from a great beauty like her. Lexie had on a black velvet dress decorated with rhinestones. Her auburn hair was piled high with tendrils curling down softly about her neck. She must be about thirty or so. Her full figure and low voice sang the siren song of experience.

Flynn watched her closely.

"So what do you think about Lexie for the job?" Paul asked him quietly.

"She'll do," Flynn replied. "How much does she want?"

"We haven't talked money yet."

"What did you tell her?"

"I told her the job was to catch Kent's attention at the Bengal Lounge and get him to come up to her room for a drink. I said we'd get her a room at the Empress for a couple of nights. She's pleased about that."

"Can she do it?"

"She's never failed before." Paul grinned. "I'll wait for them in Lexie's room. I'll meet them and then bring Kent to you. One way or another."

"No. No one will be meeting Kent, but me," said Flynn. "I'll be waiting in the girl's room." He lit a cigarette. "You can introduce us tonight. Can she swim?"

"What?"

"I asked you – can she swim?"

CHAPTER TWENTY

"Will Miss Heller go to jail?" asked Callaghan clutching a napkin he must have brought from the hospital cafeteria.

Kent shook his head. "No, but we were wasting our time bugging the girls' phone. It's not the girls we need to be worried about. This isn't a crime of passion. There's somebody pulling the strings in E-Division and I'm more convinced than ever this can only be about the Visit."

"The Visit? I'm not sure I completely understand, Sir."

Kent's mind was humming. Maybe he was going to have to talk to Callaghan about Flynn Dolan. He had to face it. He hadn't even told the Deputy Commissioner yet. But Callaghan had a right to know.

They walked through the lobby of the Empress Hotel and Kent snatched the napkin from Callaghan's clenched fist and threw it in the garbage can by the lift. The floor slipped away as the car ascended. He and Callaghan got off on the sixth floor, then quietly went up the stairwell to the seventh floor and approached Fenwick Chisholm's turret room. Kent knocked on the door once.

"Yes?"

"Riley."

Chisholm opened the door to the little round room. There were charts all over the wall and an army cot in one corner. A pink marble tub was off to one side and seemed utterly out of place in what was clearly a strategic base of operations. The views of the harbour from the corner room were remarkable.

"Constable Michael Callaghan, this is Officer Fenwick Chisholm, the Queen's personal guard."

Chisholm shook Callaghan's hand and Kent was pleased to see the boy hold his own showing zero reaction to the missing thumb or burned skin.

"An honour to meet you, Officer Chisholm!"

Chisholm studied Callaghan's face as if he found something lacking in it. Kent resisted the impulse to compensate for the boy's portly bearing by explaining how clever he was.

"Sit here," Chisholm commanded, gesturing to two plain wooden chairs that must have replaced the cozy reading chairs the hotel would have had for their guests. Swallowing his desire to ignore the order, Kent sat, as did Callaghan.

"Why don't we just talk in the suite?" The boy asked in a loud whisper, his knees almost touching Kent's.

"With hotel staff roaming about, even if they have no business being on this floor, we can't risk anyone seeing us going in and out of that room, Callaghan." Kent used a severe tone that would hopefully indicate a need for intelligence and formality.

Fenwick Chisholm stood ramrod straight. "Status report, Investigator Riley."

Kent avoided formal police terms just to be aggravating. "It's not good. Have *you* seen or heard anything, Chisholm?"

"The hotel staff have now been briefed about Her Majesty's Ladies-in-Waiting staying in the Vice-Regal Suite on the sixth floor. The staff are delighted and proud. I have not noted anything amiss in their reaction. However, what I'd—"

"What's that smell?" Callaghan asked suddenly.

Both Kent and Fenwick Chisholm immediately took deep breaths of air in through their noses. Was it gas? Poison?

Kent spoke curtly. "I don't smell anything but lilac soap."

"That's it!" Callaghan said brightly like he had just figured out the one mystery that vexed them all. He popped up from his chair and went over to the tub where he picked up a pale violet package with a purple ribbon that must contain a bar of luxury bath soap.

"My mom used to—" Callaghan began to explain, but Kent's burning gaze incinerated the end of his sentence which fell into ashy silence at his feet.

Chisholm's eyebrow rose on one side as Callaghan replaced the fragrant package onto the edge of the marble tub and retook his seat. "Sorry, Sir, you were saying?"

Kent wished he could pace, but the room was too narrow. "I have nothing definitive to report either, Chisholm. We've made some progress unravelling the mix up in Dispatch and the art theft, but I have a hunch that there is something else unfolding that involves the Visit."

"A hunch, Investigator Riley?" Chisholm asked as if he'd never heard the word, let alone used it.

"While investigating the Crawford robbery and issues at Dispatch, we've uncovered events that I believe may point to a larger plot which could be linked to the Visit.

"What events?" asked Chisholm.

"Small details at the Crawfords that don't make sense. The thieves escaped by way of a small beach below the main house where they must have had a boat waiting. Why then did they return to the front of the house and risk everything by shooting at the two constables?"

"Anything more?" Chisholm asked. "You mentioned Dispatch."

"Callaghan believes that the reel-to-reel was likely tampered with and the original replaced with an altered version."

"Is Dispatch trying to cover up errors made or—"

"No, I don't think so," Kent said. "It's all a little too obvious. Even the tampering with the tape wasn't that hard to spot."

"I don't follow," stated Chisholm.

"It appears that a story of revenge is being carefully spun by—"

"Miss Heller miscarried," interjected Callaghan in a strained voice. "Sorry, sorry to interrupt." He blushed causing Chisholm's brow to rise once again in apparent disbelief.

"At present," said Kent, "I still think we need to proceed as planned, as soon as there are any changes that may require us to abort the Visit, I will inform you immediately."

"Did you find out who the constable was that spoke to me about your wife?" Chisholm asked.

"No, but the Deputy Commissioner is looking into it and Callaghan has been quietly investigating the men at the Detachment in case there's a leak."

Callaghan was about to speak, but clamped his mouth shut at the look on Kent's face.

"We've learned that Gwen Heller, one of the dispatchers, was raped about six weeks ago," Kent explained. Her attacker was a RCN Master Seaman."

Chisholm's face hardened.

"Miss Heller was engaged to Constable Chasseur, one of the two officers shot at during the Crawford robbery."

"Marcel Chasseur, the officer that has been hospitalized for trauma? Are you sure?" Chisholm asked as if it could not possibly be true.

"She miscarried and it was just awful!" Callaghan blurted for the second time.

Kent was so thunderstruck at the boy's outburst that he lost his train of thought.

"Miscarried?" Echoed Chisholm, his voice rising. Callaghan nodded emphatically.

"Regardless," Kent spoke firmly trying to re-establish control, "we're meant to believe that the robbery, the tampering with the reel-to-reel, the shooting, Chasseur's trauma and even the rape revolve around Chasseur and Heller's failed romance." Kent hesitated, "but I think this is merely a diversion and I worry the Queen may be at risk."

Chisholm's face remained still, as he processed Kent's pronouncement. "What other information do you have that suggests a threat to Her Majesty?" he asked.

Kent had to tell him about Flynn Dolan's call, but couldn't find the way to do it without compromising himself. Chisholm was looking expectantly at him.

"Marcel Chasseur knew the rapist, Master Seaman Paul O'Rourke, but this afternoon I had him confined to D26, the naval prison until further notice."

The phone rang. Chisholm excused himself and reached for the receiver. "Chisholm here."

Kent leaned over and was about to tell Callaghan to shut up and let Kent do the talking when Chisholm spoke again, "O'Rourke? Yes, yes Investigator Riley is here. Yes, I will tell him."

"That was the military police from the Navy base. Macdonald is on the front desk and put him through. Paul O'Rourke is not confined to D26. He's AWOL."

Kent felt like he had just taken a blow to the temple. "How is that possible?"

"There is a search on for him as we speak. Lieutenant Commander Coles believes it's only a matter of time before he is apprehended. Riley, explain to me how this ties into the Queen's Visit."

"I can't prove anything definitive. It just seems as if—"

"I need specifics. I can't operate on hunches and 'things that seem like other things'. Why don't we meet again tomorrow before eleven hundred. I will see what I can find out. I need facts and I need them quickly. If we are going to cancel or postpone the Visit, it requires almost as much red tape as establishing it in the first place."

"Of course, however—" Kent tried.

Ignoring him, Chisholm continued. "It is fundamental at all times that the Queen is the one who is in control of international tours and appearances." Chisholm stood up. "I am under very strict orders, not just here in Canada, but all over the world to secure the necessary conditions so that Queen is never put in the position of cancelling or seen to be cowering, if you understand my dilemma, Investigator Riley."

"Chisholm, I understand perfectly, it's just that—"

"Facts, that's all I need. If you can give me reason to cancel, you can rest assured that that is exactly what I will do and my orders will be obeyed. Her Majesty's safety is paramount above all else."

"Thank you, Chisholm. We'll do our best to get you the information you need."

Kent checked the corridor was empty, unlocked 702 and ushered Callaghan inside. "This is where we'll be stationed on Saturday night. The Prince and the Queen will be in 704 between Chisholm and us." Kent took his jacket off and threw it on a chair and sat down at the table. Why didn't he tell Chisholm about Flynn Dolan? He had to tell him.

Callaghan went to the window, opened the door into the bedroom, glanced in, then joined Kent at the table. "I have a bad feeling about O'Rourke, Sir. I'm glad that no one in E-Division or anyone else knows where the Queen will be staying."

"O'Rourke is smarter and more slippery than I gave him credit for. That was a serious mistake on my part."

"I really like Officer Chisholm," said Callaghan. "He is so worldly and intelligent. You can tell that he knows what he is talking about with every word he says."

Kent chose to ignore this inane comment. He wished he could put the reel-to-reel headphones back on and think in peace. Instead, he threw himself onto the couch. He had to clear his head for a minute. He'd best move his things into 702 before the police were set up outside the Vice-Regal suite. He got up and started pacing. How could they have let Paul O'Rourke escape?

"Check this place for bugs, Callaghan. I feel like we're not the only ones who are listening in."

"Yes, Sir."

It was reassuring to see Callaghan scrutinize light switches, paintings, the edge of the carpet.

"I'll have to bring the ladder up, Sir, so I can check the ceiling tiles."

Kent stared out the window. Two serious errors. He hadn't told Chisholm about Dolan and he'd blundered the containment of Paul O'Rourke. The caller suggested he knew O'Rourke and that nagging sense of having seen his face before returned. After a time, Callaghan came into the sitting room and sat gingerly on the couch beside him.

"It's all clear, Sir. This place is clean."

"Are you sure?"

"I can honestly say that it's absolutely free of bugs. I'm good at this, I really am."

"Okay. Take notes. I need you to think this through with me. You need to know everything I do."

Callaghan loosened his tie then pulled out his rumpled notepad and hunted around for a pen.

"Sir?" Callaghan came up close to Kent's face. He almost reached out and touched his cheek, but seemed to think better of it. "Is the electric razor easier on your skin?"

"Callaghan! Can we talk about the razor later?"

"Yes, Sir." But Callaghan's eyes were still trained on his cheek. Kent took a deep breath and reminded himself that he needed to tell somebody about Flynn Dolan. A person not intimately connected to him. He needed someone who was not susceptible to Dolan's influences. Callaghan would have to do.

"When I went to Grosvenor—"

"High school, Sir?"

"Just let me tell the story, Callaghan, for God's sake!" Kent breathed deeply. "When I went to school, there was a boy by the name of Flynn Dolan. All the boys respected him and were afraid of him. His father, Richard Dolan, was a Fenian prisoner who was beaten to death in Portlaoise Prison."

"Beaten? By the other prisoners? Whatever for?"

"It wasn't the prisoners who killed him, Callaghan, it was the guards."

"Oh my God."

"At school, Flynn Dolan was a wiry kid. His father was seen as a hero, but Flynn could only think about taking down the system that killed his dad and then covered it up."

Callaghan jotted a few points down on his notepad.

"Flynn took a shine to me. He was a year older than me and acted for a long while like a big brother. He protected me, taught me how to box. He spent a great deal of time drawing me in until I did his bidding without question. It was easier than constantly coming up against his will."

The memories that surfaced constricted his breathing. Faces of kids getting smashed as his fists flew, their voices frightened and desperate; boys shaming themselves to get away and never meeting his eyes again. The things Flynn said he'd do, his patriotism made Kent believe that what happened was fated, unknown maybe, but scripted by a larger, more significant plan.

"My father got me a job with the Garda Síochána out of school."

Callaghan perked up. "Ah, the inheritors of the Royal Irish Constabulary, the very backbone of our Canadian force."

Kent figured if he just kept talking then he could ignore the remarkably aggravating and erroneous things Callaghan said.

"My father got me the job and it paid half-decent. I needed the money for university. Flynn assumed I'd work the system, supplying him with information, and I thought I would too. This was under Michael Kinnane, but the legacy of Ned Broy still lived on."

"Sorry Sir, who's Ned Broy? I've heard the name, I just—"

"Callaghan, when Ned Broy was Head of the Police, he supplied the Irish nationalists with names, information about his own men, about British constables. And then they were gunned down one by one."

It suddenly became important to Kent that the boy understood how things worked. "Trust me, Ned Broy's a hero in Ireland, but don't be forgetting that he betrayed the men who trusted him, plain and simple. Regardless of what side you're on, he betrayed his men."

"That's how you got the Scott medal isn't it, Sir?"

Kent never ceased to be amazed at all the things Callaghan knew about him. It was eerie. "I got it for stopping the murder of a farmer."

"But he was a British farmer," said Callaghan firmly.

The sound of the man's wife screaming suddenly hit Kent full force and he could feel his palms sweating as if it was yesterday. "They'd already near beaten him to death."

"They were Nationalists, but you wouldn't let them kill the farmer even then, would you, Sir? And the story goes you were unarmed, Sir, is it true you put three men in the hospital?"

"We're not talking about me, Callaghan. I did what I had to do. There are heroes on both sides and there's cruelty too, on both sides."

"I can well imagine!"

"I know IRA who are the most fearless and noble of any man you could meet," Kent resumed, "they're fighting against something so huge, something so hopeless. They're brave and they don't ever give up."

Kent's father, looking so tired, flashed before him. 'Kenny, we've got to be leaving Ireland. We've got to be leaving home. We can't stay here anymore. You'll be getting pulled in two different directions and you'll be torn apart. I've seen it happen to strong men, Kenny. I've seen it with my own eyes, too many times.'

For two years, Kent had kept a tight seal on these memories. To pull the lid off now and go back into that world made him feel like he was on the edge of a shoreline, up on a cliff and forces were advancing. He could see so clearly Sarah's quivering lip, Flynn's knife sliding along her throat like a pen underlining a sentence in a book. He shook off his rising anger and focused on Callaghan.

"All you're really needing to know, Callaghan, is that Flynn Dolan assumed, especially after I got into Intelligence—"

"Intelligence, Sir?" The boy repeated, pen poised, glasses sliding down his nose.

Kent felt that ricocheting sense that time was out of control. How many days until the Visit? Two.

When Kent was hired in Dublin for the job in Canada, they did not tell him he would have to swear allegiance to the Queen of England. On the day he was sworn into the RCMP, he found himself stuttering and the words came out choked almost as if his own throat found the promise impossible – but he swore his allegiance to her and he would keep his promise. Kent waited to see if Callaghan was actually considering interrupting him again and then silently praised Heaven above for the boy's choice to remain silent.

"When I got into Intelligence, I met men who were different. They lacked the cruelty that drove Flynn. They were patriots too, but they showed me another way of making change. Being with them, I looked back on what I had seen and done with Flynn and I found myself wondering, what had been achieved, if anything?" Callaghan let loose with some of his low level clucks and Kent got up and started to pace, in a desperate strategy to stifle the motherly sounds.

"All that misery, all those beaten bodies and broken boys and really nothing had ever come to fruition, no justice had ever been achieved. The realization shocked me, Callaghan. It was like I was pulling out of a drinking binge. As I sobered, I was finding Flynn's demands more and more revolting."

"Revolting," Callaghan echoed drawing out the 'e' for emphasis.

"Ultimately, Flynn went to prison."

"For assault?"

"Bomb-making. He was charged with terrorist acts. While he may have been released, he can no longer leave Ireland.

"Well, then why are you—"

"He has a network that he can control from afar."

"So you think that somehow he is involved in—"

Kent heard Callaghan speaking and asking questions, but he couldn't concentrate. The need to tell his story felt compulsive. No one knew what had happened.

"As Flynn's world got smaller, mine expanded. My father took me to London on business," Kent said. "He'd been hired to repair a special clock belonging to a very well-to-do family, and we stayed in the servants' quarters of the home for almost ten days. That's how I met my wife, Sarah."

'Have you been to London before?' Sarah had asked, smiling, and Kent's immediate reaction, which had originally been to lie and make himself appear more worldly, died on the spot. He sheepishly admitted to the young lady with slate blue eyes that no, he'd never been anywhere, but Ireland.

'Then I must show you around' Sarah had exclaimed. She pulled a black hat over her long dark hair and took his arm. 'I've been dying for an excuse to get out of the house all day, but my mother doesn't like me walking alone.' She didn't tell him until later that her mother burst into tears at the thought of her beautiful daughter walking the streets with an Irish man. If anyone who knew the family had spoken to them on their outing, her mother would have refused to leave the house for at least a month.

After they eloped, Sarah's family disowned her.

"She was the daughter of the family with the special clock?"

"Yes."

"So this is the wife that—"

"What you need to know Callaghan," Kent said sternly, "is that Flynn Dolan called me two nights ago."

"Was Sarah the same age as you?" Callaghan asked. "My girlfriend, Courtney, is three years older than I am."

"Flynn Dolan, Callaghan, called me."

"He called you from Ireland?! Did you get it on the reel-to-reel, Sir?"

"No. I got another call too."

"From Ireland?"

"I'm sorry, I wasn't thinking fast enough to record it, but the second caller had a high-pitched voice and taunted me about Paul O'Rourke. I don't know where he was calling from. But I'd bet the second call was local."

"What did he say?"

"Nothing really, it was just to provoke me. He asked 'did I like Paul O'Rourke' or something along those lines. This was right after Gwen Heller's miscarriage. It was as if he knew I'd be back at the hotel changing."

"And Flynn Dolan. What did he have to say?"

"He said he was wanting to 'wake me up' and to 'inspire me'."

"What does that mean, Sir?"

"I don't know, but my fear is that he might actually have gotten into Canada. The line was so clear it was as if he was in the room next door."

"But I thought you said—"

"I know. I thought for sure he'd be identified and stopped at the airport, but now I think he might have bloody well done it."

"How? By boat?"

"Possibly, but there is still a good chance he'd get stopped by the port authorities."

"Okay wait, let me think, let me work this one out!" Callaghan responded as if he had been given a riddle.

"If Flynn Dolan is in Canada, he may have come through Montréal," continued Kent ignoring Callaghan completely, "because there's no other way he could enter the country. He would have been stopped by RCMP anywhere else in Canada unless it was Dorval Airport. Maybe he slipped by the SQ."

"SQ, Sir? As in the Québécois police force – what are they called again?"

Kent felt a headache coming on. "Sûreté du Québec, Callaghan, for Christ's sake, and call me Riley for the hundredth time."

"Of course, sorry!"

"Didn't you work in Québec for a time?" Kent tried to keep his voice level.

"Indeed I did. It was part of the recruitment plan."

The only other person Kent knew who said 'indeed' was his long dead grandmother.

"I didn't work with the Sûreté at all really," Callaghan explained. "Shortly thereafter, I was sent to do a stint in Whitehorse and then Special-I here in B.C." The boy paused. "How would Flynn Dolan enter through Québec? Wouldn't he have needed someone inside SQ to get him in?"

"The Deputy Commissioner told me that Constable Chasseur is from Montréal." Kent rubbed his hands over his face. He wanted to look at Callaghan's notes so he could see Flynn Dolan contained on square pieces of paper, his power reduced to Callaghan's pen scratches on a page.

"I'm going swimming, Callaghan," Kent announced. "I need to clear my head."

"Swimming?" the boy yelped, which explained exactly why he flunked Depot the first time.

"The Crystal Gardens Pool is one of the great wonders of the *Empire*." Kent could not help but mock the word. "Besides, it's only a block from the hotel. Have been there?"

"No, I haven't, Sir. I'm not a fan of swimming, but Courtney loves it. Whenever she swims in the ocean, I just sit on the beach and watch."

Kent wanted more than life itself to go and change into his swimming trunks. When he had discovered the Crystal Gardens Pool, he'd bought himself a new pair at one of the fancy shops just off the hotel lobby. He had never been in an indoor pool. He would plunge into the water and swim so many lengths that he could finally rest his racing mind.

He'd never learned how to swim as a boy, but it had been one of Flynn's 'tests' when was older. Not only did Kent not drown, but he had discovered a kind of calm that only happened when he swam. It became a kind of joke between them. When Kent was angry or overwhelmed, he'd say to Flynn, 'I'm going swimming' and it meant 'leave me alone,' but they both knew, he'd also swim every chance he got.

Talking out loud had helped Kent see more clearly what needed to be done. They had to see Marcel Chasseur again and find out if he had ties to Sûreté and what his every move over the last two years had been. Every step he had taken, Kent wanted tracked. He'd have to get in touch with his colleagues in Québec and call in a few favours. The idea that there were ties between Flynn Dolan, Marcel Chasseur, and Paul O'Rourke was extremely worrying. Could O'Rourke have used his navy ties to facilitate Flynn's entry into Canada? It was possible – after all, Canada had thousands of miles of uninhabited, remote beaches where Flynn could have been put ashore without being seen.

Kent had no time to swim with the Visit less than forty-eight hours away, but if he didn't go, he knew he would never be able to fall asleep. He handed Callaghan the keys to the Plymouth and told him to get a good night's rest. And finally, the boy left.

Kent wandered along Belleville Street to Crystal Gardens Pool. He marvelled at the lush tropical greenery and glass atrium ceiling that spanned the entire length of the brick building. He swam up and down in the blue water, arms rhythmically pulling him forward and his legs kicking him into a deep restful state. There were few people at this late hour, but there was a very beautiful woman swimming lengths, almost in perfect sync with Kent. She had made it clear in so many ways that she would welcome a conversation and perhaps more.

· · ·

Kent had kept to himself at the pool, but now, sitting on the couch in the dark of his sixth floor room as the Parliament Buildings glimmered to the left and the few boats in the harbour rocked in the waters below – Kent thought about the woman's many glances and the water beading on her legs as she swung up the ladder. She had bent over, wiping the water from her thighs. She invited him with her gaze. He'd stood with the water up to his waist breathing hard after doing so many laps he'd lost count. He met her eyes and she rubbed the towel over her breasts and bent once again, this time facing him so that he could see the depth of her cleavage. She had dried first one foot and then the other. She swirled her wet hair up on her head and clipped it and flashed him a smile.

The phone rang and Kent snapped out of his reverie. He fumbled around to turn on the tape recorder.

"Kent Riley."

"Investigator Riley, Tepoorten here."

"Hello, Deputy Commissioner." Kent clicked off the tape machine and leaned back against the couch. The Deputy sounded exhausted.

"Have you met with Chisholm?" he asked.

"Yes," Kent replied. "Chisholm is confident in the hotel staff who have been informed that the Queen's Ladies-in-Waiting will be in the suite." He paused, searching for the right words. "There's certainly nothing concrete at this time to suggest security issues that might arise during her stay."

"And the internal problem at E-Division?" Tepoorten asked.

"In all honesty Deputy, I'm worried," Kent admitted.

"Details, Investigator Riley."

Kent clenched the phone receiver and took a deep breath. "Two nights ago, I received a call on this line from Flynn Dolan of the IRA."

"Flynn Dolan, the explosives expert? In my pre-briefings for the Visit, I was told he was serving an extended sentence at Crumlin Gaol."

"I heard from my father last year that some 'political bargaining' had gone on to do with Flynn. I worry he may have gotten time off in exchange for incarcerated British. As you know Deputy, this information is not always shared."

"Where did he call from?"

"I don't know, but I'm concerned he may have entered Canada."

"That's impossible. He could never get through our security."

"He could if he went through SQ at Dorval."

"Not damn likely, Riley!" Tepoorten actually raised his voice.

"I know, but it's the only way and it makes me wonder about Constable Chasseur and his possible involvement."

"Chasseur is from Montréal," the Deputy concurred, "still, I don't see how the Crawford robbery, a screw up in Dispatch and the rape of Gwen Heller here in Victoria can possibly connect back to Flynn Dolan in Ireland."

Kent was about to reply when the Deputy spoke again.

"Riley, does what you just told me have anything, and I mean anything to do with the Queen's arrival in two days?"

"That's why I'm worried. In my two days here, I've found a cop I think is pretending to be traumatized, uncovered a rape that links Constable Chasseur to a Navy seaman who should be locked up, but is now missing. I've had a provoking call from Flynn Dolan and I know I'm being watched."

"How do you know?"

"Because I got another call this afternoon—"

"From Flynn Dolan?!"

"No, another Irishman, mocking me over events that only took place hours earlier – it's as if my movements are being monitored." Kent shifted the receiver to his other hand. How could he explain to the Deputy that all of these seemingly unrelated details were quite likely part of a well-executed story that only Dolan could write and only Kent could read.

"I know you're Irish, Riley, but I still don't see why Flynn Dolan would call you of all people? He can't afford any RCMP attention, let alone from the likes of you."

Kent closed his eyes and willed himself to tell the truth. "I grew up with Flynn Dolan."

"What?!"

Kent pushed on. "And Flynn would have known that the Brancusi theft and shooting of Constable Cervide, combined with the error in Dispatch would be enough for you to bring me in."

"I don't believe it."

"I know, Deputy, it all sounds farfetched, but this is how Flynn Dolan works and I should know. The theft and everything Callaghan and I have uncovered so far have Dolan's name written all over it."

"I think you're giving Dolan too much credit, Riley."

Kent wondered if he was becoming paranoid. He paused listening to the Deputy's breathing through the tightly held receiver.

"So you think Dolan has come through Dorval?" Tepoorten asked with a sigh.

Kent's shoulders dropped with relief. He needed the Deputy to understand the complexity of the situation.

"Can you call one of your contacts in Québec, a person you trust, to provide a list of who has come through the airport in the last three to four months?" Kent asked. "Someone who can compel others to talk. You could try Jacques Lapointe. I'd trust him with my life."

"I will talk to Lapointe," the Deputy affirmed.

"Can your people find out everything there is to know about Marcel Chasseur?" Kent asked.

"Yes, I'll make some calls. In the meantime, detain Constable Chasseur until after the Visit. Does the Jubilee have a secure ward? I don't want any media attention."

"Can you get me paper work for that, Deputy? The hospital staff are rather protective of their patients – or at least this particular one. To avoid any attention, we should get a release from Dr. Mason who's the psychiatrist dealing with him."

"Give me a moment – I'm writing that down."

Kent continued slowly. "My other concern is – Lieutenant Commander Coles whose MPs failed to confine Paul O'Rourke in D26."

"That's not possible." The Deputy's voice rose again.

"It's possible that O'Rourke slipped over the side and swam to God knows where, but he's gone."

"Who knows about this?"

"Shortly thereafter, I got a call in my hotel room, the Irishman I told you about, insinuating that I knew Paul O'Rourke. And I must admit, there's something familiar about him. The name is common of course, but—"

"I don't like this, Riley. Frankly, I really don't like anything you've told me tonight. You'd better get hold of Chisholm *immediately*. If there is even a hint that the IRA is up to something, the Visit should be cancelled."

"I agree," Kent said. "There are too many unknowns right now and we're far too close to the Queen's arrival."

"I'll call Neville Heath to get his perspective on what you've told me. If the British still decide to go ahead, then at least we can say we apprised them about the potential danger."

"Yes, Deputy, I'm sorry about this."

"Call me tomorrow, Riley. I'll try and get you as much information about Chasseur and any persons of interest that may have crossed into Québec in the last twelve months or so."

Kent hung up the phone and went into the bedroom exhausted. Throwing the towel on the floor, he pulled on a t-shirt and boxers and went to the door. It was secure. On a whim, he unlocked the door and looked into the corridor. All seemed quiet. The Queen had put her trust in him to keep her safe. He had sworn allegiance to her in his final, terrible betrayal of those seeking justice at home. He would ensure she was not harmed. Relocking the door, Kent returned to the bedroom. He threw himself down on the bed.

If the Queen was at risk, even if it was by Flynn Dolan's hand, then Kent would die trying to save her. She was Second Subaltern Elizabeth Windsor, military driver and mechanic. Her family refused to leave London when it was being bombed.

Kent willed himself to think about the beautiful woman at the pool. No more thinking about the Visit, no thinking about Sarah. If he wanted sleep, he could not risk thinking about anyone that mattered.

CHAPTER TWENTY-ONE

Sitting in the dark, Flynn could hear the sounds of the Empress hotel. There was the low hum of a television in a nearby room. Down the hall, someone was knocking on a door. Out the window, lights flickered around the curve of the harbour. Then, there was a noise right outside the door. Flynn put out his cigarette. He remained seated although he felt like leaping to his feet. Now, he could hear the key rasping in the lock and he knew that the woman had brought Kent to him.

Flynn had thought for a long time about what he would say. If he was going to secure Kenny, make him come back, it had to be exactly the right words. He would let them come in and turn on a low light. He had given the singer from the Matador strict instructions.

And then he would stand slowly so he didn't startle Kent. He would just look at him. Let Kent fully see him and after that moment, he would say, 'Kenny, I'll be needing you to come back. Ireland is going to take its rightful place on the world stage – united and strong.'

Flynn would keep his voice steady, not yearning, just straightforward. He would simply tell the truth. Kenny always liked the truth. Then, he would take a step forward and that would be just enough to break the spell that held them apart, the sick spell caused by Flynn's miscalculation with Sarah. He would have to ask Kent to forgive him, but not right away.

The singer closed the door behind her.

Flynn remained seated as planned, but he could immediately tell it was all wrong, shouldn't the singer and Kent be talking softly or even laughing together at this sudden unplanned intimacy? But there was silence. Flynn sat up with a jolt. She was alone!

Lexie turned the light on. She wore a blue coat that made her face appear washed out despite its beauty. "I'm sorry, Mr. Dolan. He didn't take the bait," she reached out and then let her arms fall. "I almost had him, but then he just walked away. He did his fair share of watching, but then just turned on his heel and left like he had someplace better to be."

The woman sounded tired.

"Look, I really need the money. Maybe you and I could—"

Flynn leapt out of the chair as if to strike her. All of his feelings came rushing into his hands so that his fingers started to burn. He pulled gently on them, making the joints tense and then snapping them back into position. He couldn't speak to her. She'd failed. Then suddenly, he looked hard at her. Lexie took a step back. Flynn pushed past her and went to the door.

"Talk to Paul O'Rourke about your payment."

The woman sighed. Flynn closed the door behind him and walked rapidly down the hall. If Kent refused this woman, if he did not come back to the hotel with her after being so clearly invited by this pure beauty, then it meant one thing, and one thing only – Sarah was still alive. The car accident had been a lie. Flynn would have to find Sarah. Then Kent would have no choice but to come back into the fold.

Dan was already warming up the Studebaker when Flynn returned to the house. Liam came down the porch stairs and accosted him. "Where's Kent then. Did you get him?"

"No," Flynn replied. "Here, get in, Liam. You two are leaving late."

"Henry's wanting you to be at the warehouse at eleven to watch him deal with Constable Feiring," Liam said in a rush.

Flynn relished the thought. "Do you think it's too late for the boy, though?"

"No, he's been at his girlfriend's house. Paul called to say that he's just set off for home. Should take him about fifteen minutes, so we're right on time."

As they pulled to a stop on the deserted street, Flynn saw that Liam's estimate had been correct. Strolling happily down the sidewalk was a portly young man dressed in what looked like his father's suit. Flynn heard Liam's door open, and watched as he rounded the Studebaker to intercept their target. Constable Callaghan was just pulling his house key out when Liam dropped his hand onto the boy's shoulder. The other held a knife. Callaghan stiffened, but didn't turn around.

Flynn put the window down. "Get in the car, quietly. You don't want to be waking up your parents."

"Parents? What are you talking about?"

"Just get in the car," said Liam.

"No, leave me now and I won't wake the neighbourhood."

"Jeremy and the Missus would be so worried if they could see their baby boy now," Liam sneered. Callaghan stiffened, his hand reaching beneath his jacket. Dan turned the headlights on and Liam positioned his knife in the centre of the boy's back.

"Don't be reaching for your gun, Michael Callaghan, or you're as good as dead."

The boy dropped his hand. He'd probably never had to shoot anyone and had no idea what he was doing, but his sense of calm was impressive. He'd be ideal for detonating the bomb. Liam reached around and took the revolver from Callaghan's shoulder holster in a smooth, practiced motion. He removed the boy's glasses and put a blindfold over his eyes.

Callaghan let himself be steered around and into the car. He faltered for a brief moment, but then gave in. Liam shoved him into the seat beside Flynn.

"Good evening Constable Callaghan," Flynn said.

"Do I know you?" The boy's voice wavered slightly.

Dan eased the Studebaker away from the curb.

"My name is Flynn Dolan. I'm an old friend of Kent Riley, his oldest friend in the world, his truest friend. And you are Michael Callaghan. How do you like being Kent's new partner then?"

"Why do you ask?"

"I miss him," Flynn said.

Callaghan leaned back on the seat and did not respond.

"I'm wanting you to do a little job for me."

"What if I refuse?"

"Well then, you'd force me to burn your parents' store to the ground while they're sleeping in the apartment above." Flynn replied. "And I'm hating to think of what might happen to Courtney Hayworth. You two had such a lovely time tonight."

The boy swallowed visibly and wiped his hands on his thighs. "What do you want me to do? Not that I'll do it."

Dan swung the car into the laneway off Gordon Street. They pulled up outside the back of Henry's warehouse. The gravel of the laneway crunched under the tires and then under their feet as they exited the car. Flynn held the door for Callaghan. "Come and meet a friend. We have an idea, an offer to make you then." Liam took his arm and pulled him from the backseat.

"Offer? Offering what?" Callaghan asked, but no one replied.

When the warehouse door scraped open a crack, a cat jumped off a metal garbage can, knocking the lid onto the gravel. Callaghan gasped.

"It's alright lad, no one's going to hurt you," Flynn said. "I give you my word."

He put a hand on Callaghan's arm and steered him toward the entry. The door opened just wide enough for the three of them to enter single file. Scotty looked like he could do with a shave.

"Evening, Mr. Dolan."

They walked through the vast, dusty space of stacked boxes. Against the far wall, a line of green light glowed at the base of the office door. The Matador's music came faintly through the walls along with the thumping of dancing feet. Flynn couldn't make out the tune for the laughing and talking.

A distant glass shattered and Liam muttered. "Ah, they're having a real tie on tonight."

Henry was sitting behind his desk flanked by filing cabinets and his two men stood in the green shadows of the room's corners. Flynn sat Callaghan on a wooden chair in front of Henry's desk and sat down beside him. Liam remained at the door.

"This is Michael Callaghan, the electronics specialist," Flynn announced removing the boy's blindfold.

"Well, he doesn't look like much," Henry said. "Looks like he'd wet his pants at the very idea of a bomb – let alone rig one up."

"He doesn't need to be there. You don't understand how it works." Flynn turned to Callaghan. "Lad, you know how to build a remote control. You and your father have built one. Is that not so?"

"No," said Callaghan slowly, shaking his head. "A remote control? I don't know what you're talking about."

"Sure you do. Your father showed it to me yesterday. He talked at great length and with great pride about his genius son who has figured out how to set off explosives 'safely' using radio waves. Let me see – what exactly did he say?"

Henry looked doubtful. Flynn's voice echoed the father's way of speaking almost whispering as if he was telling Callaghan about a Christmas present that he could unwrap soon.

"Just think how it will save the lives of so many when dynamiting for roads and tunnels and bridges!" He raised his hands in an expansive gesture, just like Callaghan's father would do. "No longer will demolition crews have to risk life and limb to create the progress we all need to move into the future!"

Flynn sat back and let the boy think on it. Then he asked. "Remind you of anyone, Callaghan? Yes, we had quite the nice visit with your mum and dad, even had a tour of their upstairs apartment." He could see sweat trickle down the side of the boy's face.

"Do you care about your father and mother? Because if you do, you'll be working with me or like I said, they'll be going up in flames."

"No," the boy leaned forward in his seat. "I'll do it."

"We're wanting you to make a remote control to set off a bomb."

"A bomb where?"

"In the Empress Hotel."

The boy's eyebrows shot up. "Are you going to, to kill someone?" His voice was shaking.

151

"No, of course not." Flynn lied. "We're wanting the bomb merely for a diversion. No one's going to be getting hurt."

"Is it Kent Riley you're after?"

"No, we want the Queen." Flynn smiled.

Callaghan shook his head. "But she's being stationed at—"

"I know where she'll be Michael Callaghan. I know exactly where she'll be and I don't think you want to be lying to me."

"No, no I don't," Callaghan said in a rush.

"We're going to take her, and not harm her," Flynn tried to use a soothing tone, "but we'll be using her to get some changes made back home, changes that will help people who are suffering—"

"You want me to help you kidnap the Queen?"

"Well Michael, we cannot possibly get Her Majesty out of the Empress, past all that security, without a wee diversion," explained Flynn ignoring the question.

"What's the distance you need covered?" Callaghan asked.

"How much can you give us?" Flynn countered.

"I don't know for sure," Callaghan admitted. "I haven't fully tested the mechanism. It's a work in progress, and so using it is a bit risky."

"I'm trying to avoid deaths here, Callaghan."

"Avoid deaths? You might wound or even kill police, hotel workers." The boy said. "It puts the Queen herself at risk. What good is she to you if she's dead?"

The men in the room were completely silent. It was almost as if they weren't breathing.

"I have a bomb that creates a lot of noise," Dolan soothed. "It'll be making a lot of noise and a bit of dust and rubble, but won't extend as far as the Queen's room. Hopefully no one will get hurt."

"How much will you pay me?"

The men started breathing again. Flynn smiled slightly. "Ah, now we're getting somewhere, Michael."

"I can't help you do this and remain in Victoria. I need enough money for myself and for my parents and for Courtney," Callaghan said. "Enough to get out and re-start our lives elsewhere and new identities too."

"I have money enough," Flynn said. "We recently acquired some exquisite artwork that landed us a very nice take. I'll make sure you and your family have enough to disappear and start fresh."

"How will I know that your word is good?" Callaghan asked.

"You have no choice but to trust me."

"You're not in a very good position to negotiate," growled Henry, as the men in the greenish shadows both shifted slightly.

"What you need to believe," Flynn said gently, "is that I tell the truth and if you screw up, I will destroy your parents, then Courtney, then you."

Callaghan shoved his hands under his legs. "When do you need the remote?"

"Tomorrow. We'll come and collect you outside *Electrolife*."

Callaghan nodded. "What about Kent Riley?"

"He'll be joining me when he realizes the kind of change that is possible," Flynn said. "He's one of us from long ago Michael. But, if Kent doesn't cooperate, he'll have to be eliminated."

"I know that," Callaghan said blankly. "There will be no love lost there, at least."

"No love?"

"Riley despises me," Callaghan told the room.

"He just doesn't know how smart you are," Flynn offered. "I believe, I truly believe, that Kent will be joining us. He's hating the Empire as much as I do. He wants change and he wants to protect his loved ones just as much as you do."

Liam let out an almost inaudible whistle. Resting the flat of his palms on his desk, Henry leaned forward and pushed himself up. The meeting was done. The broad-shouldered men at his side stared straight ahead.

"Alright then, can we move on with the plan?" Flynn got up from his chair and took Callaghan's arm so that he was forced to do the same. He secured the blindfold back over his eyes.

"Bring the remote here with this boy tomorrow late afternoon," Henry said. "I want a trial run with the model before we set up at the Empress."

He addressed the silent man to his left, "Your job is to put Chisholm out of commission." The man did not speak. He locked eyes with Henry, nodded and then stared straight-ahead again.

"Chisholm's no fool," Liam interjected. "You're going to have to—"

"Just shut-up Liam," Flynn hissed, "for God's sake, shut-up."

"What?" Liam whined. "I'm trying to help a guy." He petered off.

Flynn took Callaghan's arm, gesturing him out. They walked in silence back to the Studebaker. Constable Dan Smythe started up the engine in the dark alley and drove them back to *Electrolife*. Lights were still on upstairs. Callaghan opened the car door and stumbled out.

"So lad, you've made the right decision," Flynn said warmly. "Sometimes there's pain and struggle involved in overcoming unlawful power."

Liam put Callaghan's glasses and gun on the door stoop while Flynn kept talking to distract him. "It's the only way to achieve fairness for all, not just for the ruling classes. I know you understand this because I know how smart you are."

Callaghan nodded. He started backing up towards his parents' storefront. He pulled off the blindfold. "Where are my glasses?" he asked anxiously.

"Tread carefully at the door my boy." Flynn advised as Dan pulled out from the curb.

"Dan, drive me back to Henry's."

"Now?" asked Liam. "It's too late Flynn. It's gone eleven now."

"He'll be attending to Constable Feiring and I don't want to miss it."

Neither Liam nor Dan spoke.

Back at the warehouse entrance, Flynn lifted his hand and rapped sharply. A moment later the door slid open just enough for him to enter.

"Henry's expecting you." Scotty gestured with his unshaven chin. "You know the way, Mr. Dolan."

Flynn walked through the boxes toward the greenish light pooling under the door of Henry's office. One of the henchmen was in position. He didn't move a muscle when Flynn entered. Henry looked up from papers on his desk and pushed back his chair. The throbbing sound of the Matador still filtered through the wall. There was male laughter and a woman's low singing. Someone called out a bar order.

Rooke brought in Feiring, who looked terrified. He sat him on the chair where less than half an hour ago Michael Callaghan had been seated.

"Where are the photographs?" demanded Henry.

"What ones? I've taken hundreds." Constable Feiring feigned innocence.

"The ones of Paul O'Rourke and Gwen Heller. You were there that night when he was in room three. The photos aren't in my files. Where are they?"

"I don't know. I must have missed that exact time. How long was he there for? Maybe someone else took them?"

"You were assigned to his room," Henry insisted.

"I must have gone off for a moment. I think I was changing my roll of film."

"He was in the room for half an hour. You must have gotten something."

"I swear to you. I don't have any pictures of him."

The silence that filled the room seemed to block out any sense of merriment from the Matador. Flynn tensed at the sense of doom closing in.

"How about I go home and take another look," Feiring suggested. "Maybe I have them, but didn't develop them right. It's possible the camera malfunctioned. I'll find out. I didn't know it was so important to you." His words were rushed.

Rooke slipped out a knife and held it between Feiring's shoulder blades. Flynn could smell his cologne. The other one walked slowly forward from the shadows.

Bathed in green light, Henry looked up at Feiring and spoke softly. "I can't have men like you working for me, men who don't know if they're with me or against me."

Feiring stood up abruptly. "I made a mistake is all, I—"

Henry continued right through Feiring's interruption. "It messes up my business plan, makes things unpredictable. Your mind wants one thing, but your heart wants another."

Flynn was concentrating so intensely on Henry's words, he didn't realize that Rooke was now pressing his blade to Feiring's throat, holding his arms securely behind him with a shovel-sized hand. Rooke twisted him toward the door and hauled him out of the office. Flynn leapt to his feet in time to see the knife plunge into Feiring's neck. What would have been a scream became a bloody gurgle swallowed up in the vast warehouse.

FRIDAY

CHAPTER TWENTY-TWO

Kent was dreaming that bells were ringing and he was quite sure they were wedding bells. It couldn't be *his* wedding because he and Sarah had eloped. There weren't any church bells, smiling parents or fluttering rose petals.

One misty Sunday during a walk in Hyde Park, Sarah tugged on his arm. She turned so that she was looking right up into his face. Her eyes were shining with mischief. "Kent, when are you going to ask me to marry you?"

Adopting a light tone, he said, "Your family would disown you."

Suddenly her eyes filled with tears. "I don't care." She said it so intensely and rose up on her tiptoes so that she was looking through his eyes right down into his very being.

He pulled her close to him. "Sarah, let's get out of here. Let's travel together away from all of this. My dad wants to emigrate to Canada."

She started to laugh. "I'm not any sort of a Nora Barnacle, Kent McGowan Riley. I'll only run away with you if you marry me first."

Then her father had said if she married Kent, she would no longer be a Flint-Rochester. She would be the wife of an Irishman and that was her choice. So she chose Kent and her father maintained a deadly silence, even though she tried over and over again to reach out, the letters and phone calls, the tears and gifts. It had been so painful to watch. Kent had walked around for more than a year in a straightjacket of anger and resentment. Then Sarah's mother had started calling and sending packages of beautiful clothes, always with the promise that Sarah's father would come around. Sarah had never said a word to Kent about regretting her decision, but he knew her proud heart had been wounded.

"You know, Kent, my father will regret this," she told him one day as they strolled through the art gallery on Dundas. "He's actually the most adoring of men, the most doting of fathers. He thinks I'm rejecting him!" Her voice rose at how preposterous this was. "He thinks I'm a 'rebel', because I didn't let him and mother choose the man I would marry from the chinless, spineless array." She put her arm in his and patted his hand. "He'll get over it, Kent, just you wait and see."

Kent shifted position in the hotel bed, wrapped in her voice, but there was that jangling sound interfering again.

There was no wedding. So the bells had to be an alarm. Kent's eyes flew open and he sat up. It was the phone. He put his hand on his revolver to calm himself. He opened the bedroom door to the sitting room. His eyes adjusted quickly and in the pre-dawn light from the harbour he could see the phone. He was about to walk toward it when a figure moved. Kent froze. The man bent over and pressed something on the floor. He picked up the phone and spoke.

"Kent Riley."

There was a pause.

"What do you think you're talking about then?"

Kent stood in mute shock. Callaghan was speaking in a low voice and putting on a suppressed Irish accent. "Why don't you stop your blathering and state your business," he said into the phone.

"Warn me about what?"

Kent could just hear the murmur of the voice on the line.

"Don't you be threatening me."

The boy sounded remarkably like him, Kent had to admit.

"Wait," Callaghan commanded anxiously. "Hello? Hello?"

Then he hung up the phone.

Kent spoke in a voice carrying pure menace. "What the bloody hell are you playing at, Callaghan? I knew I should never have given you that blasted key." He clicked on the light in the bedroom and it illuminated the other room slightly.

"Sir, I think I got a recording of your friend, Flynn Dolan, on the machine."

"He's not my friend, Callaghan, for God's sake! Play me the conversation," Kent commanded, dropping onto the couch.

Callaghan bent down and pulled the reel-to-reel out. He rewound and played. The conversation was mid-way through so he stopped the machine and rewound a little further. There was a silence, then, Callaghan's voice emerged, "Kent Riley."

Kent couldn't believe he had to endure Callaghan imitating his voice again. And then, Flynn's unmistakably elegant voice rose from the machine. "Kenny, you should really keep your eyes open."

"What do you think you're talking about then?"

"Haven't you learned yet that sleep is a dangerous place?"

"Why don't you stop your blathering and state your business."

"You know how I feel about you. I want to warn you."

"Warn me about what?"

"I hear you may be losing your head."

"Don't you be threatening me."

No response, just silence.

Then Callaghan's "Wait." His voice sounded anxious on the tape.

The line went dead and Callaghan turned off the machine.

"What do you think, Sir?" The boy sounded excited, even though Flynn was threatening Kent's life, and the sun hadn't even risen. What time was it? All Kent wanted was to go back to sleep and dream of wedding bells.

"I mean this is a threat," insisted Callaghan.

Christ Almighty. Thinking longingly of his revolver, Kent rubbed his eyes and asked. "What is it you're doing here, Callaghan, in the middle of the night?"

"It's the morning, Sir."

Kent looked daggers at him.

"I couldn't sleep," Callaghan explained. "So I wanted to get an earlier start on the day."

Kent's anger was mounting. The fact that Flynn Dolan was closing in made him want to break things. Lash out. He steeled himself. He reminded himself that Callaghan was just doing his job.

Callaghan had a little chuckle.

Kent considered throwing himself out the window to the cement below so as not to murder the boy in a moment of weakness. "Don't laugh like that Callaghan. You'll be driving me to drink."

"Sorry, Sir."

"What time is it, Callaghan?"

"Zero five hundred."

"I'm starving."

"That's another reason why swimming late at night—" Callaghan began in an officious tone until he caught sight of Kent's face and stopped.

"I'm going to have a shower and get dressed. Don't say another word to me until I speak to you," Kent advised him.

"Yes, Sir." Callaghan plunked noisily back down on the couch and stared out at the sun rising over the harbour.

The hotel lobby was like a polished marble and mahogany morgue, but a waiter put on a pot of coffee for them in the Bengal Lounge. The air was still and had a tinge of beer floating at the edges. All the surfaces were shining and the seats were in order expectantly waiting on the breakfast rush. The waiter served them coffee. "I'm pretty sure I can get you some toast or something, gentlemen. Just give me a moment."

Kent felt like dropping to his knees in gratitude. Moreover, Callaghan had remained quiet, which was another reason to praise God's bounty.

The waiter returned wearing a starched white chef's apron balancing a stack of thick cut toast, a bowl of raspberry jam and a small white plate with squares of butter. He went back to the bar and collected a pot of coffee. Hands on hips, he surveyed the table for a moment. "That's the best I can do, gentlemen. The kitchen doesn't officially open until seven-thirty."

"You're a saviour, honestly, thank you." Kent handed the man several coins.

Trying to make up for being so angry, Kent initiated discussion with the boy who had brightened considerably at the prospect of breakfast even if it was only toast. "The Deputy Commissioner is asking for a warrant to secure Chasseur at the Jubilee until after the Visit."

"Will we go and see him this morning?" Callaghan put a spoon full of sugar into his coffee.

"Yes, I'll be pushing him hard for information."

Callaghan was buttering, slathering on jam, and then folding pieces of toast into his mouth. Mesmerized, Kent lost his train of thought. He took a sip of the strong coffee.

"I need to know if Chasseur is connected to Dolan," Kent said.

"Do you mean working for Flynn Dolan here in Canada?" Callaghan asked, his mouth crammed full of toast and butter and jam.

Kent took another sip of coffee, letting it clear his mind. "Dolan is beyond our reach at the moment. The best we can do is figure out who here in Victoria might be connected to him. The fellow that called the other night knew specific details about our investigation, so there has to be a local connection." He worried for a moment about the boy's safety. "When the time is right, Dolan will find *us* unfortunately." He watched the child prodigy put another spoon full of sugar into his coffee. "I'm going to call the Staff Sergeant, so he can give us Chasseur's address. We need to search his place."

Kent forced himself to eat a piece of toast. Despite being so hungry, his stomach was acidic with the mounting threat of Flynn Dolan being in the same city as Queen Elizabeth. Hearing Flynn's voice had shaken him more than expected. He leaned back in his chair, waiting for Callaghan to finish. The boy was about to apply jam to his last square of toast when he seemed to realize that Kent was waiting. He hesitated and then put down the jam spoon with a sigh like a child who was being rushed to catch a school bus. Kent couldn't keep the impatience from his voice. "Can you go get your kit and that address? I'd like to get there sooner rather than later."

Callaghan got up quickly and exited. Kent went to the front desk and called the Staff Sergeant.

"Conrad Jones."

"It's Kent Riley. Sorry to call you at home so early."

"Not a problem, Investigator, I'm an early riser. I went and visited Gwen Heller at the hospital last evening and she's recovering nicely. Couldn't stop crying, mind you, but the doctor is talking about her being released in the next few days."

"I need access to Constable Chasseur's residence."

"Really? Is that necessary, Investigator Riley? I mean the man is out of commission. I'm not sure that looking through—"

"There's more going on than Chasseur's private life. I'm concerned he's involved in something more serious that relates to the Visit."

"Oh." For a moment, there was silence on the line and then Jones resumed. "Frankly, Investigator Riley, I think you're barking up the wrong tree."

Callaghan returned with his kit and perched on a chair in the lobby while Staff Sergeant Jones continued robustly. "Constable Chasseur is as fine an officer, as trustworthy a man as I could hope to have under my command."

"Surely, Staff Sergeant, you will agree that we cannot take enough precautions with the Visit and so a routine check to err on the side of caution is all I require."

"And I suppose Mick Callaghan will get you in?"

"Yes." Kent was starting to get frustrated.

"Alright, I'll need to go into the office in order to get Chasseur's file. I don't know where he lives. Can you give me an hour?"

"We'll meet you at the office in one hour." Kent hung up the phone and gestured to the boy to follow.

"Callaghan, let's go to the Staff Sergeant's office right away."

"Now? Why? What's the matter, Sir?"

"I don't feel fully confident about Staff Sergeant Jones." He set off with Callaghan positively skipping along at his side. "I want to get into the Detachment for the address," explained Kent, "and then I want to get over to Chasseur's place. We've only got about forty-five minutes."

"You want me to break into the Detachment?" Callaghan came to halt.

"Don't be stupid, Callaghan," Kent said still striding ahead. "It's manned around the clock. I want you to let *me* into the Staff Sergeant's office and specifically into his filing cabinet. I need to know where Constable Chasseur lives right now."

"Break into the—?" Callaghan had lumbered into an ungainly trot to catch up.

"Do you trust me, Callaghan?"

"Yes, Sir."

"Well then, let's go. Don't forget, you are working for me right now and I work for Deputy Commissioner Richard Tepoorten directly. He will approve *anything* I need getting done."

"Yes, Sir."

Kent gunned the Plymouth's V8. Tires racing, he screeched out of the Empress parking lot. Callaghan clung to his tool kit as though it might save him from a fiery death. Kent swerved around a slow garbage truck.

"What is it you're thinking, Callaghan?"

"I'm thinking that the lock on Sergeant Jones' office door will require a slim-jim."

Kent smiled. Much as Callaghan made him crazy, the fact that he was willing to break into the Staff Sergeant's office, a filing cabinet, and then Marcel Chasseur's residence, and all of it under an hour, was pleasing. He felt a fleeting moment of gratitude. As he went sharply around a corner, Callaghan gasped and slammed his foot to the floor as if to put on the brakes. Kent's jaw clenched.

There were only a few cars at the station. It was still early. Callaghan had set off briskly, but it was clear how nervous he was. Kent's eyes were dry from lack of sleep and he resisted the temptation to close them. He checked his watch, but only about seven minutes had passed. It would take the boy at least twenty to get through and find Chasseur's address, but then there he was. Kent watched Callaghan in the rear view mirror as he crossed the parking bay. He couldn't possibly have got the information that quickly. Something must have gone wrong. Callaghan collapsed into the passenger seat.

"He lives on lower Cook Street above a bicycle shop."

"How did you ever get in and out of the office so quickly?"

"Piece of cake, Sir, *piece of cake.*"

Callaghan might not like breaking the rules, but he was damn good at it.

Constable Chasseur's apartment was messy. The bed was unmade, dirty dishes were on the counter. Either he was not anticipating an extended absence or he had left his space purposely in this state to project his innocence. Was he friends with Paul O'Rourke? Did they spend time together in the Navy? They were both men who knew about ships. Were they targeting the Queen's yacht? Kent focused on slowing his pulse. O'Rourke was missing. Kent would feel better when Chasseur was contained in the secure ward at the Jubilee. Too bad Constable Cervide was so hazy on the details. His statement could even be used to protect Marcel Chasseur from further scrutiny.

"Sir, will you look at this!" Callaghan called out from another room.

Kent went rapidly into the bedroom, but Callaghan was not there. He was in the bathroom. "What is it, Callaghan?" Kent's heart was beating quickly with the hope that the boy had found something incriminating.

"Look, Constable Chasseur uses an electric razor as well!"

"Callaghan, if you ever so much as say the two words, 'electric razor' to me again, I am going to have to shoot you."

The boy's eyes widened and he pushed his glasses into position. "Yes of course. Sorry, Sir, it's just—" He trailed off.

The apartment was a waste of time. They found nothing, no papers, no notes, no clothing, no pictures, nothing. They returned to the Detachment.

"Good morning for the second time, Constable Callaghan," said the clerk at the front desk with a slight frown as he sent them to the Staff Sergeant's office.

"Good morning, Investigator Riley, Constable Callaghan." Jones said from behind his paper-strewn metal desk. "Here's the address for Constable Chasseur's residence. He lives on—"

"No need."

Jones stared up at Kent taking his measure. "But?"

"It doesn't matter. I'll be saying this once, Staff Sergeant, and only once."

The older man remained seated, his mouth tightened with anger.

"I need your full co-operation, is that clear?" Kent said. "I can tell you right now that something stinks in E-Division. Something that may well have implications for the Visit."

The Sergeant's face flushed an angry red. "How dare you suggest—"

Kent continued. "I know you're loyal to your men, but—"

"What are you talking about Investigator Riley? Where do you get off accusing members of my Detachment."

"Am I? I thought you might be in on it, especially when you failed to secure the dispatch tape," Kent admitted.

"I don't think it is—"

Kent put his hands on the Staff Sergeant's desk so that he loomed above the older man. "Don't make me change my mind about you," he warned.

"That's right," Callaghan added, deflating Kent's position. "I did a little research." He spoke with the tone of a kindergartener at show and tell as he flipped open his notepad.

"I've learned that Constable Dan Smythe was in Ottawa a week ago."

"Constable Symthe was where?" the Staff Sergeant asked.

Kent made sure to cover up his own surprise. He'd have to give Callaghan a piece of his mind later.

"According to Human Resources," the boy said primly, "Constable Smythe's trip was due to an urgent family matter. He was off work four days in total."

Constable Dan Smythe fit Chisholm's description, tall with light coloured hair.

"I'm wondering," Callaghan went on, "if he was the one who spoke to Fenwick Chisholm at NHQ about your wife. Sorry Sir, I know you don't like to talk about her."

"Constable Smythe was where?" repeated the Staff Sergeant.

165

Kent felt the time passing so quickly that even the Sergeant's repetition set his teeth on edge. The Queen arrived on the HMS Britannia tomorrow.

"Constable Dan Smythe," the Sergeant said, "is a seven-year veteran. He's a good man. I know him very well and—"

"Look," Kent interrupted, "the Deputy Commissioner is processing a detainment order to keep Chasseur in a secure ward at the Jubilee until the Visit's over. We can't afford to take any risks when it comes to the Queen's safety. Perhaps we need to make a similar move with Constable Smythe. Let's put him on ice for forty-eight hours."

"Dan Smythe has done nothing but very fine police work during his time here," insisted the Staff Sergeant. "I just can't see him suddenly getting involved in something like this. Locking him up for two days will tarnish his reputation and that kind of stain can't easily be removed, Investigator Riley."

Kent ignored the loyal Staff Sergeant. This must have been why he assigned Smythe to take Cervide's statement. He was more than trusted.

"Can I see Constable Cervide's statement that Smythe took?"

"I haven't had it done yet. The doctors were clear he needed time to recover. He's still heavily medicated."

"You had Constable Smythe take his statement, Staff Sergeant Jones," Kent fought to keep his voice down.

"I most certainly did not! What are you accusing me of now Investigator Riley?"

"Sorry, Staff Sergeant, when I interviewed Constable Cervide on Wednesday, he told me that Constable Smythe took his statement earlier that morning."

The Staff Sergeant grabbed the phone receiver, "I'll call him in right now and clear this up at once."

"No, no you won't Staff Sergeant," Kent said quietly.

Jones paused.

Kent looked over at Callaghan who was sitting on the couch, legs crossed, hands folded tidily on his lap. Still, he addressed his remarks to the boy as it helped him to concentrate. "We're not going to say or do anything right now about Constable Smythe. We're simply going to watch him."

The Staff Sergeant put down the receiver.

"I want a cop, a solid cop, assigned to keep an eye on Smythe," Kent said. "Tell him that you're worried that Smythe's shaken up by the shooting and you can't say more, but you want to make sure he's okay. Might be a harm to himself."

"Alright, consider it done," the Staff Sergeant said. "I just damn-well hope you're wrong."

"I may well be," Kent admitted. "I'll be trying to confirm with Constable Cervide exactly what he said to Smythe."

Callaghan got up and followed Kent out. At the door, Kent paused for a moment before he addressed the Staff Sergeant, who was gazing down at one of the framed photographs on his desk. "You have to have faith in me, Staff Sergeant, I serve no one but the Queen."

The Staff scrutinized Kent's face for a moment and then nodded.

CHAPTER TWENTY-THREE

Flynn watched Liam and Dan play croquet out the kitchen window. He had listened into the RCMP radio to see if there was mention of Feiring's body having been found. Henry's men had left it on the little beach below the Crawfords' property. A reminder in its own way about the danger of sleeping when one should always be awake.

His chair pushed against the wall, Marcel sat at the table staring into a cup of coffee. "Why can't I just sit in the yard? Who's going to see me?"

"We can't run the risk Marcel." Flynn said lighting a cigarette. "It's only a matter of time before Kent figures out that Dan's involved."

Flynn gazed back out the window to see Liam chasing Dan with a croquet mallet. Jesus, how Dan could go from single-handedly bringing Marcel out of a locked down psychiatric ward, to playing the fool with Liam in the backyard was beyond him. He turned his back to the window.

The screen door crashed open and Dan bounded in, grinning back at Liam. One look at Flynn, though, and the grin vanished.

"How did you get Marcel out of the hospital then, Dan?" Flynn asked quietly.

"The Head Nurse left early to attend a funeral. The young one was holding down the fort until the next shift came on. I only had a few minutes, but I told the girl she had something on the back of her uniform and I implied the mark was an ugly one."

Flynn could not get over his disgust for women, the oozing of tears and blood and vanity. How hopeless they made him feel.

"She was mortified and ran off to the washroom asking me to watch the desk for a moment. I grabbed Marcel and we simply walked out as if we owned the place!"

Flynn nodded, satisfied. He glanced at the Québécois still sitting glumly at the table. "You did a fine job, Marcel, but you've got to lay low now. I'll be needing you more than you know."

"Right Flynn," Marcel responded lifting his head a little.

Flynn unhooked the telephone receiver and spoke to the long distance operator. He waited, praying that William was home. If he could locate Sarah, he would once again own Kent Riley. The operator connected his line and Flynn heard the scratchy ringing start so very far away.

"Hello." It was a voice Flynn didn't recognize.

"William Gogarty there?" he asked.

"Who'll be calling then?"

"Not your business. Put William on the line."

"Just a minute."

"Gogarty, what is it?"

"Keeping well I trust, William?"

There was a distinct pause on the other end of the line.

"Flynn Dolan, what is it you're needing?"

"I'll be needing a favour."

"As always, Flynn. What is it you're needing on this occasion?"

"I'll be wanting you to track down a young lady for me."

"To marry?" William laughed.

"No, it's a woman who has gone missing."

"Is she a runaway, then?"

"I'm telling you," Flynn tried to keep the fury out of his voice. William Gogarty always asked too many questions.

"I'm listening Flynn, that's what I'm doing. No more questions."

"Her name is Sarah Flint-Rochester. Her married name is Riley."

"Riley?" Gogarty interjected.

"She could be living with her parents," Flynn pushed on. "They have a place in Kensington or maybe she's at a girlfriend's house. She used to be close to two girls, Catherine Hatfield and Julia Baxton-Miller. Catherine's family are in Kensington just down from the Flint-Rochester's and Julia's are in Chelsea."

"Isn't that Sarah, the one who died a couple of years ago in the car crash? Kent Riley's wife wasn't she?" Gogarty asked.

"She's not dead," Flynn closed his eyes willing the call to be over and Sarah to be found.

"How is it you know that Flynn?"

"I know things William. I know a lot of things."

"How will I know it's her?"

"She's rich, well-dressed, long dark hair and blue eyes, pale skin."

"There are a number of rich women in London who fit that description – can you be a little more specific, Flynn?"

169

"She has a scar across her neck."

"Across her neck?! Across her throat then?"

"Yes," Flynn replied with a weary tone, but Gogarty wouldn't let it go.

"A jagged one then Flynn?"

Flynn almost whispered. "No, it'll be a nice clean scar."

"Must have been a hell of a crash."

"There was no accident, William."

There was a silence on the line.

"Right then, give me a day and call me back at this number," Gogarty said.

"Thanks, William. I'll be calling you." Flynn hung up the phone. Pulling at the ends of his fingers, he snapped the tension from his hands.

CHAPTER TWENTY-FOUR

Kent expected a significant police presence at the Crawfords, but the property was deserted except for Staff Sergeant Jones. He was standing at the edge of the driveway smoking a cigarette next to his cruiser. The leaves were dripping and fragrant from the mid-morning drizzle. The sky was darkening with more rain over the sea beyond the low house. Behind them another patrol car pulled up. The driver shut off the motor, but the two officers remained sitting inside.

"Come on. Let's go," Kent said.

Kent waited for the Staff Sergeant to approach. Suddenly the Plymouth's siren went off making Kent nearly jump out of his skin. He whipped around to see Callaghan fumbling with the controls. Mother of Mary and all the Saints—"

Callaghan bumbled out of the vehicle. "Sorry, Sir, was trying to reach my—"

Staff Sergeant Jones glared him into silence as he walked over to meet them. Kent felt a little surge of smugness that Jones witnessed what he had suffered, without complaint, since the beginning of this assignment.

"I received a call from Charlie Crawford, said he couldn't reach you. That's why I called you. He specifically asked for you."

"About an unidentified body? Left on his beach?"

"Washed up on his beach. That's what he told me."

The men arranged themselves at the Crawfords' front door. Kent was about to knock when the door opened a crack and Susan Crawford peered out anxiously at them. She unlatched the chain and opened it wide for the three officers.

"Thank you for coming Investigator Riley. It's rather dreadful I'm afraid, but please come this way." Her eyes were bloodshot.

171

When they reached the studio with its doors out onto the patio, she stopped. "I'll make us all some coffee." She backed up and went into the hallway.

Charlie Crawford was gazing out at the ocean. His studio was tidy and the vast canvas of the horse about to take off was no longer on the easel. Instead, another canvas was in its place. This one had a large horse painted with a thin white outline in the foreground. The horse was positioned behind a gate and it was gazing into an open pasture. At the far end of a swirling field of sun-browned grass stood a little horse with willowy, awkward legs.

Crawford spoke without turning around. "Investigator Riley?"

"Hello Mr. Crawford," Kent said to the painter's back. "This is Staff Sergeant Jones and you remember Constable Callaghan."

"Good morning!" gushed the child prodigy.

Crawford scowled at the men. "No one else came with you? I said in no uncertain terms—"

"No one but us three," the Staff Sergeant assured him. "However, I need an officer to secure the beach. The corpse will have to go to the Coroner, and the sooner we do it, the better." There was a hint of frustration in his tone.

"Since my Brancusi is still missing, I'm afraid I don't have much faith in your people's ability. Now there's a dead man on my beach."

Stiffening, the Staff Sergeant informed him. "I've told them to give us twenty minutes. They'll arrive shortly."

"Maybe you'll take me seriously now," Crawford said. "I'm telling you, back home in Texas, criminals couldn't run the show like they do here."

Kent glanced over at the Staff Sergeant to see if he was going take the bait, but Jones looked steadily at Crawford and did not speak.

"Follow me," muttered the painter. He set off toward the steps down to the beach. "I told the officer I spoke with on the phone that we still needed a guard," Crawford said. "I'm not afraid, but my wife—"

Kent assumed that it was Staff Sergeant he was talking to, and while Jones' face had taken on a ruddy hue, he was still not responding to Crawford's jibes. The three men made their way single file down the damp steps to the small beach. The air was colder by the sea and the wind had set the trees above swaying. Kent heard the Staff Sergeant behind him speak quietly.

"I *had* assigned Constable Davies. The past two days, he was alternating shifts with a second officer to ensure there were no more attempts to steal the Crawfords' art collection." He lowered his voice so that only Kent could hear. "I pulled them off late last night because of tomorrow's Visit."

"You can't be blaming yourself, Jones," Riley felt sorry for the Staff Sergeant. So much pressure.

Crawford stood rigidly, even though the other men had now joined him on the rocky platform. Keeping his eyes fixed on the stairs, away from the body that was lolling lightly in the water's edge a few feet away, Crawford motioned them forward. Callaghan marched across the narrow stretch of sand to get a closer look at the body, but he backed up abruptly. Hand over his mouth, he stumbled up the beach a ways and promptly vomited on the wet hard packed sand. Kent approached the body more cautiously.

A slow reel of the dead bodies he'd seen crossed the screen of Kent's mind, and they layered themselves softly upon the man lying partially in the water. Callaghan was heaving over on the far side of the beach. He never should have gone up to the corpse without first planning on how to look at it. The way to look at a dead body was carefully. You never looked at the whole thing at once. It was safest to just concentrate on parts slowly like you might study a vicious animal that was approaching.

Kent started with the man's feet. They were an average size in his boots. Then, he looked at his legs which were slim and clothed in dark trousers. He examined the hands that were fluttering slightly in the waves. He examined the man's bare chest and shoulders. They looked cold. He looked at the neck, but couldn't see it. His eyes blurred in a protective way.

Risking a glance at the face, Kent thought he might have seen this young man before. Almost black hair, muddy blue eyes, something familiar about him – *Constable John Feiring*.

"Do you think he was dumped in the ocean and washed up here?" Crawford asked.

"No, he hasn't been in the ocean that long from what I can tell. He was placed here." Kent replied.

"How the hell?!" Crawford muttered. "Why would someone do that? Is it meant to be a threat?"

"Yes, I believe it is, Mr. Crawford," Kent shook his head, "but it's not directed at you. It's meant for me."

Crawford studied Kent's face. "Meant for you. Do you know who left this fellow here?"

"Yes, Mr. Crawford and I am quite sure you won't be bothered again. I'm sorry you've been put through so much trouble."

Charlie Crawford put his hand briefly on Kent's arm. "I trust you Investigator Riley. I trust you'll return my Brancusi. Now, I'm going to see to Susan. She's incredibly upset about this."

Kent watched him go up the stairs and prayed that Flynn and his men would leave the Crawfords alone. A wave curled over the body and as the water pushed against the corpse, Kent could see the man's head had nearly been sliced off and was barely attached to his body. *Jesus Bloody Christ.*

The Coroner came down the stairs carrying a large bag of equipment. He was followed by the two officers Kent had seen sitting in the squad car at the top of the drive. One of them carried a body bag. Retreating, Kent moved to the side of the beach so that he was standing beside Staff Sergeant Jones. He felt anxious like he was floating on water that had a nasty undertow. The Staff Sergeant didn't say anything. Kent took a glance at his face. Jones had tears on his cheeks. Pulling a handkerchief from his pocket, he watched the men slide the body into the bag.

Jones mopped his face and cleared his throat. "That's one of ours," he said. "Constable John Feiring."

Kent's skin prickled. Again, he saw Feiring approaching him in the Bengal Lounge and giving him the photographs of Gwen Heller. If it hadn't been for Feiring, he might never have found Paul O'Rourke. Feiring knew the danger he would be in if he gave the photographs to Kent. He worked for an illegal club, but wouldn't stand by when a woman was raped. What a way to die.

Hopefully, Charlie Crawford didn't put two and two together. Feiring's severed head a violent version of the disembodied head of his Brancusi *Muse*. Kent's mind flashed to the knife wound across Sarah's neck before he could stop it and bile was flung up his throat.

He looked for Callaghan who must have left the beach unnoticed. They had to secure Constable Chasseur. God willing the paperwork had gone through and the ward was on lockdown. His gut clenched. What if the corpse had been placed as a diversion to secure Flynn's men time at the hospital to get Chasseur out? Dammit. There was no time to waste. Callaghan insisted on driving. He said it was so that Kent could think, but they both knew it was because the boy feared for his life when Kent was behind the wheel.

"We need to make up some codes, ones that only we understand, Callaghan," Kent said.

"Codes, Sir?"

"Well, think about it. Marcel Chasseur is a suspect. You've discovered that Constable Smythe may well be involved. I even have my doubts about the Staff Sergeant. We can't afford to say anything material to this case in front of anybody. We need to be mindful of the words we use."

"Can you give me an example, Sir?"

Kent thought. "Do you know anything about polygraph, Callaghan?"

"You mean the lie detector machine?"

"No, not exactly. A lie detector machine shows physiological changes when someone's lying but a trained polygrapher studies the confessions."

"Confessions, Sir?"

"I mean statements."

"Studies them?"

"The polygrapher analyzes the statement, then uses it to their advantage in the interrogation room," Kent explained. "When a person is giving their statement and they're lying, they get mixed up in their verb tenses or their pronouns. When you are not telling a sequence of events as they happened, it's extremely difficult to get the subjects, verbs and the timing right."

"That's very interesting Sir. One thing I've noticed is that when you talk about your wife, you use the present tense."

Kent looked out the car window so that the boy could not see the fear in his eyes. "That's an excellent observation, Callaghan. That's exactly the sort of detail that can tell you things." He said in a softer, hopefully convincing, tone. "I guess that shows how much I loved her, because I don't think of her as really being gone, even after she died."

Callaghan pulled into the Jubilee hospital parking lot. "I think I'd feel exactly the same about Courtney, Sir. I just can't imagine the world without her in it. If she died, I'd probably just pretend that all was well and she was still around. Like on vacation or something."

As they got out of the Plymouth, Callaghan polished his glasses with the cloth he always seemed to have at the ready. Kent took off for the psych ward. He searched for another example to try and get his point across. "When someone has colluded in a crime or is an accessory to a crime, they make mistakes."

Callaghan was breathing hard alongside him as he trotted to keep up the pace.

"They will use 'we' accidently at times and then correct themselves," Kent explained. "Again, this is the gap or the error that allows the interrogator to push hard and extract the truth."

"So when you say code, you want me to change details so that only you understand what I'm saying?" Callaghan puffed out.

"Yes, exactly. We can take this same idea and say things to one another that will be having meaning to us, but that no one else can pick up on."

Callaghan pulled open the hospital's glass door and addressed Kent formally. "I want a smooth shave locked down."

Kent thought for a moment. "You want to secure Marcel Chasseur who uses an electric razor as we discovered," he said slowly. "Not bad. You've got the idea already, well done."

They hurried into the hospital lobby. Despite how irritating he could be at times, Kent had to admit that Callaghan was the fastest learner he'd ever worked with. They waited at the lift.

"Courtney wants to have five children. Can you imagine?"

What Kent couldn't imagine was that he had to endure a conversation like this. Or was Callaghan speaking in code? He decided to remain silent in the hope it was code speak.

"She works as a librarian."

Kent pressed the lift button again more forcefully.

Callaghan asked with a few low clucks. "Did Sarah want to have children?"

"Callaghan, we don't talk about Sarah, remember?" Kent willed the lift's doors to open and save him.

"I know it's a very difficult topic for you, Sir, but sometimes it helps to talk about people we love who've passed away. I remember when my grandmother died—"

At that blessed moment, the lift doors opened, people exited and Kent busied himself with pushing the button for the correct floor. Callaghan seemed to get the message and the ride to the fourth floor was silent. There were three nurses huddled talking in low tones behind the desk. One of them was crying and Kent realized that Dr. Mason was also there. Kent's heart sank. They were too late. He quickened his pace. Dr. Mason looked up. "I'm so sorry, Investigator Riley, Marcel Chasseur is *gone*."

The crying nurse started to sob. One comforted her, while the grey-haired nurse had her arms crossed over her chest, a scowl on her face.

"You mean he escaped? How is that possible?" Kent wanted to grab Mason by the shoulders and shake him. He looked over at the sobbing nurse and snapped at her. "Stop crying. Tell me exactly how this happened."

The nurse, who was comforting the crying woman, shot an appealing look the psychiatrist's way. "Dr. Mason, can't Cynthia have a moment. She's very upset."

"I don't have a moment," Kent interjected trying to keep his voice calm. "Marcel Chasseur is dangerous. I need to know exactly what happened."

The sobbing woman choked out. "I only left the desk for thirty seconds. Marie had to leave ten minutes early for a funeral and, and, and, I needed to go to the – I never thought." Her voice trailed off.

"Did you see anybody? A hospital staff worker or a doctor you don't know?"

"No one came by at all. It was quiet all day."

The older nurse spoke severely. "She's told you what you need to know."

"I know you're lying," Kent directed his words at the older woman, but the young nurse began to cry harder. "Luckily for you, I don't have time for this right now. "Mason, call me if your nursing staff decide to fess up about who and what they saw." Ignoring the nurses' protests, he walked rapidly away. Callaghan skipped along to keep up.

"What did she need to do, Sir?"

"Jesus and Mary," muttered Kent. "Who knows, but this is serious, Callaghan."

Kent phoned the Deputy Commissioner from the hospital lobby.

"Richard Tepoorten."

"Deputy, it's Kent Riley. Marcel Chasseur has escaped."

"What do you mean escaped? I've got the paperwork right here. Miss Lennox has been in touch with Dr. Mason. I was assured—"

"He left the hospital unauthorized. Some nurse missed his exit. She's not talking."

"He's gone?"

"Yes. I think we should cancel the Visit. I don't—"

The Deputy Commissioner cut him off. "I already spoke to London, to Neville Heath and to the Prime Minister. I briefed Chisholm and he has spoken with Prince Philip as well as the Queen herself. I have spoken to the President's Chief of Staff who is presently with her Majesty in Seattle. They will not cancel. They will not alter the route. The Queen will arrive tomorrow morning in the Inner Harbour on the HMS Britannia as planned."

Kent now had a death grip on the telephone receiver. "Paul O'Rourke and Marcel Chasseur are both Navy men."

"Lieutenant Commander Coles has briefed the Admiral. There's a warrant out for O'Rourke's arrest and now there will be one for Chasseur."

"Any more information on Constable Smythe?"

"As it turns out, he *has* family in Ottawa, but whether or not there was a crisis last week, we still don't know. The Staff Sergeant has him being followed at all times."

"Just maybe he'll lead us to the others."

"I have to go to a meeting, Riley, keep me posted."

"Yes, Deputy." Kent stood staring at the phone receiver in his hand until Callaghan gently extracted it from his grip and set it back down on the cradle.

"What about swamp candle, Sir?" Callaghan asked, his eyes sparkling.

Kent looked at him quizzically. "I get the candle, the 'wick' part of Fenwick's name, Callaghan, but swamp?"

"Swamp is another word for fen, Sir. I figured that was something *you* knew."

Kent felt ignorant and angry at the same time. "Fen, alright, so Fenwick, candle swamp." He nodded. "Good, Callaghan, good job, you're a smart kid." Kent paused. "Fenwick's okay, we can trust him."

"How do you know?"

"He owes his life to King George."

"Oh, well then, the other concern of mine would be 'the medical jar'."

"Dr. Mason? How so?"

"I just don't see how Chasseur could have walked out the door without Dr. Mason knowing about it."

"He's in meetings all day, consultations," said Kent. "It's the nurses that are to blame. They saw him leave or saw someone else and they're afraid to talk. They'll lose their jobs, Callaghan."

"They *should* lose their jobs."

Kent looked over at Callaghan and saw something in him that he hadn't noticed before. The boy didn't suffer fools gladly.

Outside the hospital, the sun was bright and warm. It must be close to noon. They hadn't eaten since the early morning visit to the Bengal Lounge. Kent walked over to the Plymouth and took the keys from the boy. "How do we get to the ladies' restaurant where we went the other day for lunch."

"What a dandy idea, Sir. I'm *so* hungry and the food—"

"Where is it, Callaghan?"

"Turn left down Richmond, then we'll go left again on Oak Bay Avenue."

Kent drove in silence. He must have been hungry because he could not put two coherent thoughts together. He worried that he was becoming more like Callaghan, because instead of being able to sort out exactly what he had to do, all he could think about were the fish and chips at the diner.

"Corruption so often happens at the top, Sir, and trickles down," said Callaghan with a grin. "Are you completely confident in steeped drink pouring?"

Kent tried to decipher the code. "Tea Pouring. Tepoorten? He's fine. That's *enough*, Callaghan. This isn't some kind of game. The Deputy Commissioner is rock solid. Trust me."

CHAPTER TWENTY-FIVE

As the lift rose, Flynn stood close behind the Scottish chambermaid and she giggled a little. She pressed the button for the fifth floor.

"You look very snappy in your uniform Jamie," she teased.

Flynn looked down at the slightly worn black tie uniform that matched the girl's French servant's outfit. "Thank you kindly, Emily. You look quite lovely, yourself."

When they reached the fifth floor, she peered around both sides to see if anyone was about. It appeared most guests staying at the hotel were out enjoying the bright mid-afternoon summer's day. She gestured for him to come over to the stairwell.

"Shhhh, there could still be guests lingering or housekeeping about, there are still rooms to be done on the third. Not to mention the police are all over the Vice-Regal suite up on six."

They slipped up the two flights of stairs to the seventh floor. Ignoring the sign about 'Restricted Access, Danger, Severe Penalties,' Emily pulled the heavy door open and peered into the long carpeted hallway. She eased open the door and whispered for him to wait. Flynn could feel his heart beating rapidly in the quiet space that in a little more than twenty-four hours he would be racing down after the bomb blast.

Emily came and signalled to him the corridor was clear. He slipped out, trying not to rustle the paper package he carried. She pulled out a ring of keys and opened the door to the corner room at the far end of the hall. Flynn followed Emily into an odd little room that looked like a military camp, but still had a pink marble tub in one corner.

"This is Mr. Chisholm's room," she whispered, evidently surprised by what it looked like. "I thought he would have something much more fine than this."

She pulled Flynn over to show him the hundred and eighty degree view. "This is one of the turret rooms, that's why it's circular in shape. I don't know what he's done with the guest furniture and the proper bed. They'll have his head when they see he's taken down all the pictures."

"Is this the only room you've seen him go into, Emily?"

"No, there's another one, but—"

He clasped her hand. "Show me!"

She carefully closed the door behind them and took his hand to lead him down the hall. They didn't make a sound on the carpeted floor, but she stopped and cocked her head for a moment, squeezing his hand. The murmur of male voices dwindled away. It must have come from the stairwell. She opened a door mid-way down the hall from the turret room. There was an elegant, but discreet golden 702 to one side. "This is one of two harbour view suites on this floor. It's like an apartment and costs a fortune."

The door opened into a sitting room with paintings of ships and handsome couches and chairs. The dining room table gleamed beyond. The harbour was right outside, glinting in the summer sun. The sea stretched out beyond the two headlands marking the entrance into Victoria's Inner Harbour. The seascape looked strangely like home Flynn thought, but was blue rather than grey. He could see into a large bedroom through a door that was ajar.

"This is the room that I saw Mr. Chisholm go into," she whispered. "We've been told the maintenance boys were doing a few updates and fixes so that's why there were no guests, but I think it's because the Queen's Ladies-in-Waiting will be staying in the Suite down below. No one's been allowed up here for weeks except for Mr. Chisholm."

"What do you mean no one's booked onto this floor, but Fenwick can come and go as he pleases?" Flynn asked shifting the package in his hands, the paper crinkling too loudly.

"That's just what I want to know," Emily said bitterly. "How'd he get a turret room when he's on hotel staff? I'm going to ask my super—"

"I asked around, Emily, and I've heard that he might actually be doing military work," Flynn said. "Secret work. I think he's part of the team in place to protect the Queen's Ladies-in-Waiting."

Emily's eyes widened.

"You can't tell a soul," he whispered down the girl's neck.

She straightened up, turning her face to him. He pushed down a stab of irritation and pressed his lips hard on hers. She recoiled a little and her eyes flashed up at him.

Just then, Flynn saw Kent's jacket flung onto a side chair and he went straight to it. Emily went nervously to the door and opened it a crack. She kept looking down the corridor.

Flynn fingered the fabric of Kent's jacket and then lifted it trying to catch the scent. There it was. Kenny always smelled like a match just as you strike it, a smoldering warm smell. Even when he was a boy, he had this scent on his clothes.

After his own dad died, he'd have dinners at Kent's house five or six times a week. Kenny's father used to light candles at dinner. Flynn could see him, a little stooped, serving food into bowls for the two boys. Flynn's eyes swam with the memory.

The stupid girl cleared her throat and asked as if amused. "What're you doing there with that jacket, Jamie?"

Flynn steadied himself. "I'm trying to be sure it belongs to Fenwick and I think it really is his. He must be using this room for work as well. This will be such a grand surprise. I can't thank you enough for your help."

The girl blushed and smiled shyly. Flynn thought with regret that she was a person not often praised. He resisted the temptation to tell her the truth about what he was doing. The truth that he needed to find Kent and that without him, his beautiful plan might not work. He wanted her to know that they were closer than brothers and that they had been at war together ever since they were kids and it had been a losing battle up until now. The girl must read all of these truths in his face for she asked him.

"What, what is it Jamie? What are you thinking?"

"Nothing, Emily, nothing at all. I'm just relieved we've found the right man." Flynn put the jacket down and picked the package back up from the chair. He walked over and placed it carefully on the table.

"What's that you're leaving for him?" Emily asked.

"Oh it's a surprise that'll give him a hint that I've finally found him. Bit of a lark really, a mystery of sorts that will tell him where to meet me after all this time."

"Can I see what it is?"

Flynn studied her. He opened the brown paper bag and pulled out a mannequin's head. It looked gruesome with smeared moon painted eyes that forced the face to seem sleeping while awake. The girl took in a sharp breath.

"That's a very strange gift."

"He'll know what it means."

"What does it mean?"

"It'll be reminding him about the war and how you can't just sleep when injustice rules the day."

"Oh, well then," the girl laughed anxiously. "Come on, we shouldn't be here. I'd lose my job if I was seen anywhere near this room."

• • •

Flynn changed out of the waiter's uniform and divested himself of Emily. He cut through the Empress Hotel's rose gardens, skirted the Union Club, and ensuring no one was around, slipped into the laneway. He prayed the men had secured Michael Callaghan as planned. He expected the usual gloom in the warehouse, but found that the vast room was brightly lit. He looked at Scotty in surprise and the older man gestured with his chin past the wall of dusty boxes to the centre of the room. The man on the catwalk had even slipped away and was standing above a table covered in wires, tools and circuits. Rooke and Henry's other thug hovered far away from the table where Callaghan hunched intently over the square black receiver. The bright lights in the dusty warehouse made it seem like a dissecting room.

Henry had actually left his office to watch the boy at his work. Flynn had never seen him leave the shadows of the green-lit office. He looked like a different man without his desk and banker's lamp. His skin had the pallor of lichen and his hair was thin and wispy.

While the boy worked on hooking up the remote to the bomb, Flynn let his mind wander back over the details of the wound he was about to inflict. It had begun so long ago, the meetings where he preached justice to men who would never have imagined crossing the line. Flynn had taught them the virtue of claiming their rights rather than waiting for suspect authorities who promised, but always failed, to deliver on their commitments. Convincing Dan Smythe and Marcel Chasseur to join his cause and topple the old British order had been his first coup, then the Brancusi robbery, a simple theft worth hundreds of thousands of dollars had been his second. He lured Michael Callaghan away from Kenny and they would use his remote to take the Queen alive. This meant they could make demands, rather than just a single deadly point about the injustice that had torn Ireland apart.

Finally, they were gifted with the hubris of Fenwick Chisholm. He was so sure that he was in control of the Empress Hotel staff that he had led them straight to suite 704. The suite thought to be safely positioned between Chisholm's corner room and Kent's room. The final move hinged solely upon Flynn. His fingers tingled with nervous energy. How to get Kent? Sarah was the key. He had William Gogarty looking. It was only a matter of time before Gogarty found her. Flynn imagined the things he needed to say to bring Kent back on side. 'Come back home. It is time. It is time for everyone. It is time for change.' The Empire was dying and now Ireland could be one and the British forever driven away.

Going over the details, Flynn's mind hummed: Rooke would take out the Queen's man. Flynn would approach Kent who would join them, especially when he saw that even Callaghan was onside. Dan would do a final check on boat, cars and drivers before returning to the Detachment to be on alert for anything going awry. The bomb would be activated. Liam would take the Prince down the east stairwell and across Government Street to the dock. Flynn would help Marcel create conditions so that Kent could bring the Queen, so that she disappeared in the explosion and so she wouldn't be hurt. Not yet. Not hurt yet. Henry would be in his warehouse office waiting for the Queen to be delivered and imprisoned.

Kent wouldn't have a chance on his own and even with all his pride, he would realize in this moment that he too needed Flynn. Maybe he had even missed him. Assuming the bomb went off as planned, there would be very few deaths, which would surely win the press over to Flynn's side. When he talked to the reporters on Sunday, he would explain that he wouldn't harm the Queen, but changes needed to be made and that the Irish deserved justice after centuries of English tyranny.

Flynn wondered, had his father been alive, what he would say on this day when Flynn, brought the world's attention to Ireland's suffering. All the people wanted was a chance, an opportunity for justice and equality, and the Queen held the reins. And now Flynn would have the Queen.

CHAPTER TWENTY-SIX

Kent and Callaghan walked along Government Street. Kent didn't want to go into the Empress just yet. He felt cooped up. He wanted to talk, and couldn't tell the story without walking. Callaghan did a good job of keeping pace with him as they dodged the tourists strolling up and down looking in shops, buying ice cream, watching the street musicians and whiling away the late summer afternoon.

Kent had tried everything from swimming lengths to pummelling the punching bag in the hotel gym while Callaghan had taken the afternoon off.

"You need to know more about Flynn Dolan," Kent explained.

The kid remained strangely quiet, like he didn't trust himself to speak. The last couple of days were clearly taking their toll on Callaghan. Kent had told him he had to rest.

"I told you how Flynn and I were close at school when we were teenagers."

Kent glanced at Callaghan willing him to interrupt, but the boy remained silent.

"But the truth is I actually grew up with Flynn Dolan. Our fathers were good friends. After his dad was beaten to death, my father made sure Flynn and his mother never went hungry. It made Flynn hate me more. The more he loved my father, the more he wanted me to pay. He had this kid that followed him everywhere, Liam O'Rourke. They were inseparable."

O'Rourke. No possible way. There was certainly no physical resemblance between Master Seaman Paul O'Rourke and whiny Liam, but the shared name was too coincidental for Kent's liking.

"So what trouble did you, Flynn Dolan and Liam O'Rourke get into?" Callaghan asked pushing his glasses up so that they were once again at the bridge of his nose.

"We started to do some small jobs for the Army. We were just kids really."

"The Army?"

"The IRA, I was telling you before."

"Oh, I see," Callaghan said.

"I didn't kill anyone, Callaghan. I just beat people up, carried stuff from one place to another and was one of their lookouts. I was only fourteen, maybe fifteen at the time."

Kent wanted to get close to the sea. He started down the causeway steps towards the dock at the foot of the Empress. Callaghan fell in behind him.

"For Flynn it always had to be more. It took me a long time to realize that he took pleasure in hurting others. That it wasn't just trying to stop the division that is the terrible legacy the British left in Ireland. It was something that Flynn yearned for like some men yearn for a woman. I started to drift away from him. He and Liam became closer than ever."

Kent walked up and down the creaking boards of the dock. Above on the street, cars were meandering by. Callaghan followed close behind without saying anything.

"Finally, I was old enough to do my part for the war effort. I worked for a year—"

Still the kid remained silent.

"Irish neutrality meant the U-Boats left our fishing ships alone, so I spent my days on a fishing vessel giving ship and U-boat movements to the British and hauling sailors – men from all over the world – out of the Atlantic. Flynn said I was a traitor, but it changed the way I felt about England and everything I believed to that point."

Suddenly, Kent got a flashing memory of Paul O'Rourke.

"Jesus and Mary! That's where I know him from!"

"Who, Sir?"

"Paul O'Rourke. I knew I recognized him from somewhere. It was maybe thirteen, fourteen or so years ago. He was rescuing torpedoed Allied sailors. I only saw him briefly, didn't even speak to him. But I remember his face. He must have transferred to the Canadian Navy after the war."

Callaghan's shorter legs caused him to hustle alongside Kent's longer strides and he missed a step and almost pitched into the water. He grabbed Kent's arm and almost wrenched it out of the socket. "What the hell Callaghan!" Kent nearly decked him. Callaghan carefully put down Kent's raised fist and patted his arm.

"Oh sorry, Sir, you're going so fast." He was out of breath, maybe that's why he was so quiet. Kent concentrated on walking slower, for both their sakes. Despite his sudden frustration, it was a relief to tell Callaghan this story. He needed to tell Chisholm this tale too, but that would be painful.

"When I started UC Dublin, that was the fall I stopped being one of Flynn's boys."

Callaghan shuffled along in silence.

"Like I told you, I worked for the Garda Síochána nights and weekends. When I married Sarah that fully severed my ties to Flynn and the IRA."

Kent could see Sarah's face. She seemed like a marble bust she was so white with fear. Flynn was standing next to her with his knife and tracing it across her throat like a pen, but the ink that flowed was brick red in colour. Kent physically shuddered at the memory.

"Did a ghost walk over your grave, Sir?"

Kent pretended not to hear.

"Flynn was rising up the anti-Treaty, IRA ranks, becoming more powerful with every passing day. He became their bomber." For once the boy didn't have a hundred questions. He must have been too afraid to even ask about Flynn's skill with explosives. The quiet allowed Kent to think. They had reached the end of the dock. Kent bowed his head to the sea. Clinging to the wooden frame were mussels and barnacles. Kelp fanned in the currents beneath that.

"Flynn claimed that he hated Sarah because she's British, but really it's because, as he saw it, she took me away from him. And you're going to think this sounds strange, Callaghan, but Flynn loves me like a brother."

"I know exactly what you're saying, Sir, exactly what you're saying."

Kent realized that the boy was listening to the story like it was one of the chapters out of the *Jungle Book* and he felt sorry that he was getting the sense of adventure, without realizing the danger.

"But Flynn couldn't let go. He kept after me. Anytime he thought I might want to make some money or do something for Ireland, he came after me."

Kent tried to read Callaghan's expression, but couldn't see his eyes for the spectacles.

"He even tried to set me up with other girls. He hates Sarah because I love her."

"You still love her, don't you, Sir?"

"Yes." Kent let out a sigh and shook his head in disbelief. "There's one more thing you need to know, Callaghan. Neither Tepoorten nor Chisholm can do a thing about it and so you will have to bear this burden with me. The Queen and Prince Phillip are in danger – just how much I don't know. I suspect that Flynn Dolan, or his men, are going to make a move on them at some point during their stay here in Victoria."

The boy looked like he wanted to say something, but Kent cut him off. "Just listen, Callaghan. You need to listen."

Kent took a deep breath.

"Flynn couldn't really get at me because I was in Canada, but two years ago, my father, Sarah and I went home to Dublin to bury my mother. Flynn abducted Sarah when she was out alone for a walk. I never should have let her out of my sight. He had a knife. So she did what she was told. He called me to come to Liam O'Rourke's flat where he was holding her. She was sitting perfectly still on a chair in the kitchen. From the doorway, I could see the knife."

Callaghan gasped. Kent ignored him.

"Flynn asked me to place his latest bomb in Paddington Station in the heart of London's underground. At the time, I was pretty much the only one who could place it and get out before it blew. He held the knife to Sarah's throat. I told Flynn I wouldn't do it. I was a cop for God's sake, and the days of Flynn ordering me around were long over. But he knew me better than that. He trailed the knife across Sarah's neck deep enough that it started to bleed."

Reaching out to pat his arm, Callaghan let out a few clucks.

"Tears were rolling down her cheeks, but there was defiance in her eyes. I cracked. I would not let him torture her. Sarah begged me not to do Flynn's bidding, but I agreed to his plan. He put down the knife and came over and shook my hand warmly as if nothing had happened."

Kent paced up and down the dock. Callaghan hovered trying to stay out of his way and keep up at the same time.

"A week later, Liam O'Rourke held Sarah captive while Flynn and I travelled by train to London. Sarah was Flynn's insurance policy. I took Flynn's bomb into Paddington Station as if I was keeping up my end of the deal, but my father met me in the station toilet as we had planned – unbeknownst to Flynn – and he used an old watchmaker's trick on the clock timer so the bomb never activated. I placed the bomb in a garbage can on the platform and made my grand escape, witnessed by Flynn's men. The bomb didn't blow. The next day Flynn's men retrieved the bomb, and by all appearances it simply seemed to have malfunctioned."

"Was your father afraid?"

Kent paused. He'd never really thought about it. "No, not really. He's used to dealing with mechanical devices – much like you. He just treated the bomb like it was another clock that he had to fix."

Callaghan nodded and Kent resumed.

"Flynn figured that something had gone wrong with the clock mechanism, but never suspected it had been tampered with. I was off the hook."

"Sir, I really need to—"

Kent cut Callaghan off. "Three days later, Sarah died in the car accident. Flynn has left me alone until now."

"Why didn't Flynn go after your father to get you back?"

"He would never touch my father. Some bonds are sacred, even to Flynn."

They returned to the Empress in silence. Kent steered Callaghan into the Bengal Lounge. They sat down in the heavy leather chairs and Callaghan took a handful of peanuts and pushed them into his mouth.

Kent thought he had finally told Callaghan a story that might actually succeeded in quelling the boy's appetite. Today's story was clearly not it. A waiter materialized at their tableside. "Two pints of beer," Kent said and he hurried away. "Callaghan, I'm just going to go to the room and get my jacket. I'm cold after walking along the docks."

"Okay, Sir."

"Are you cold?"

"No, not at all." The boy threw another handful of peanuts in his mouth and chomped away.

Kent's coat was not in his sixth floor room. He must have left it in 702. He sprinted up the stairs and let himself into the suite. Something was wrong with the room. Kent put his hand on his gun. Doing a slow survey, he noted his coat lying on the blue chair off to the side and a round package in a brown paper bag on the table. He reached over and whisked the paper off.

Inside was a mannequin's head lying on its side. A grotesque version of Crawford's stolen Muse stared back at him with crudely painted eyes.

"*Christ Almighty.*"

The phone rang jarring Kent even more.

It had to be Chisholm or Callaghan. Kent's hand paused over the receiver. His heart was beating rapidly. Maybe it was the Deputy Commissioner. No one else knew about this room. How did the package get into this room?

"Kent Riley."

"Kenny, it's good to hear your voice. I'll be knowing where Sarah is."

The floor slipped away beneath Kent's feet. "She's dead, Flynn," he said gripping the receiver. "I would think that even you could be respecting that."

"She's not dead, Kenny."

"Where are you?"

"I know where she is."

Kent's head was pounding. He levelled his voice. "Don't waste my time, Flynn. What is it you'll be wanting? Where are you?"

"I have a job for you."

"I already have a job."

"Does it make you sleep well at night to be working for the enemy?"

"Canada's not my enemy, Flynn. It's my home."

"It's ruled by the Monarchy, Kenny."

"Leave me alone."

"You'll never be alone, Kenny, for as long as I'll be living."

"Flynn, we need to—"

Flynn had already hung up.

Kent slammed down the phone. His eyes travelled to the mannequin's head lying on its side on the table. He stared at the black pen markings that made the eyes look as if they were closed. The mouth too had been painted over in black so as to resemble the moon shape of the Brancusi Muse. The eyes and mouth looked stitched shut. Kent wanted to hurl it through the window.

"How did he get in?" Kent demanded of the empty room. How did he know about this room? *Dammit all to hell.*

He needed to inform Fenwick Chisholm that the hotel staff had a collaborator in their midst. Now they might cancel the bloody Visit. Kent grabbed his coat and locked the room behind him. As the lift descended, he thought maybe he should tell Tepoorten he was done with this case. It was too close to home. He was jeopardizing the Visit. But the only reason this was all happening was because Flynn wanted him here, needed him here. Kent just had to figure out exactly why. This was just like Paddington Station all over again. There would be a deal laid out, he'd simply have to wait and find out what it was. What about Callaghan? How much real danger was the boy in? Kent never really understood Callaghan's thought process at the best of times and that made him a bit of a live wire. Damn the whole bloody thing! He slumped back into his seat in the lounge. The beers had arrived and Kent drank deeply. Callaghan had already taken what looked to be a few sips.

"A terrible thing just happened."

"What's that, Sir?" Callaghan asked leaning forward in his seat.

"Flynn Dolan knows about 702."

"That's impossible. Are you sure?"

"Yes, he left me a gift."

"What gift?"

"It's a mannequin's head. A crudely painted one made to resemble Crawford's stolen Brancusi."

"No, that's just not possible. How could anyone know you were going to be staying in that room? Does that mean they know about the Visit and where—"

"I don't know," Kent interjected. "I don't know anything anymore."

"You have to tell Mr. Chisholm."

"I know, I will, but the Deputy Commissioner says they won't cancel. No matter what."

Kent ordered two more beers. His glass was empty and he had a serious thirst. Callaghan drained his and then wiped his mouth with the back of his hand. That must have been a first.

"Sir, even if 'Swamp Candle' can't address your concerns, your friend in fact is interested in you and the Visit. He has shown today that he's involved in the Crawford theft and somehow everything that is happening is being used to make you work with him once again." He smiled shyly. "For old times' sake."

Kent felt a great surge of appreciation for Callaghan. Two more beers arrived. Callaghan only acted like a complete fool, but really, he was not so foolish.

"You are smart, Callaghan." They both drank and Kent considered the situation.

"Why didn't you tell Mr. Chisholm about knowing Flynn Dolan since you were a boy?" Callaghan asked.

"He didn't give me a chance."

Both Callaghan and Kent knew that was a lie.

Kent was embarrassed to know Dolan, confessing that part of his past to Chisholm was simply unbearable. "We'll tell him, Callaghan. We'll tell him tonight. We have to meet him at nineteen hundred hours, but I'm already dead tired."

"I'm exhausted too, Sir."

"I mean the flaw may well lie with Chisholm's assessment of the hotel staff. Flynn's got someone on the inside. That's the only way someone could get into the seventh floor suite."

Callaghan shifted in his seat and then called for two more beers. Kent could feel the alcohol warming him from the inside out. Every bone in his body ached. The waiter came by with two more glasses. Callaghan reached into his pocket and drew out a beaten up leather wallet.

"Sir, I want you to do something for me."

"Sure, Callaghan." The boy reached over and gave him a photograph. A young woman with a pointy chin and upswept blond hair stared out at him. Her eyes were dark brown. Kent could not imagine for the life of him what she saw in Callaghan.

"That's Court."

Kent looked at him blankly. Callaghan beamed at him.

"Court, short for Courtney. That's her nickname. I call her that because she's a law librarian at the Courthouse."

"Ah, Court, of course."

"Did you have a nickname for Sarah, Sir?"

Here we go again, thought Kent. He resisted the temptation to grind his teeth. "No, Callaghan, I don't."

"Do you know what Court says about me?"

"No, Callaghan, I can't say that I do."

"Well, she says she loves me because I'm so curious, because I ask so many questions."

Well, that's one of us. Kent drained his beer.

"I'm going to get the waiter to bring us more beers if that's okay," the boy said. He hadn't even started the one he still had on the table.

"It's not okay, Callaghan, it's a great idea."

"Sir, could you do me a favour and write down this number for Court here. If anything, I mean, if anything happens to me."

When the waiter came and put the beer down. Kent ordered roast beef sandwiches for them both. He didn't feel much like eating, but had to off-set the beer.

"Callaghan, give me the number. Nothing's going to happen to you. I wouldn't ever let anything happen to you. I know I'm hard on you, but you've got to know that I've got your back. I've always got your back."

"About that, Sir, I need you to know—"

"Enough serious talk, Callaghan. Let's relax. Old 'Swamp Candle' doesn't think we have a thing to worry about so we're going to relax."

"What about the mannequin head, Sir?"

"Yes, you're right. We should tell him about that, but then he'll act like it's tomfoolery on our part and make us look like a couple of stupid colonials."

"No, Sir. We need to tell him. It's important."

"Of course, Callaghan, of course we'll be telling him."

Kent felt angry and a little dizzy as they ascended in the lift. He'd need to sleep off the drinks. He knew there was someone in the hotel that had access to 702, so he and Callaghan would have to take shifts when sleeping there tonight. They couldn't fully trust the police guarding the stairwells. No one could be trusted anymore. He would brief Chisholm as best he could.

They didn't have to wait outside the turret room for long before Fenwick Chisholm came down the hallway. Kent hoped they didn't smell too much like a distillery. Chisholm let them into the small circular room.

Kent cleared his throat. "Chisholm, somebody left a mannequin's head in my room, an obvious homage to Crawford's missing Brancusi," he paused, "not room 602, Chisholm. The head was left in the suite, in 702."

Chisholm remained very still.

"It gets worse," Kent continued, "Flynn Dolan called me in 702 less than an hour ago."

"You never mentioned that, Sir!" Callaghan blurted.

Chisholm's mouth tightened. "Dammit Riley, you or Callaghan must have let your guard down along the way, how else could this have happened?" Chisholm's eyes flashed. "And how the bloody hell does the Irish Republican Army's most prolific bomber know who you are?"

"I've known Dolan all my life. We grew up together back in Ireland, but I severed all ties with him years ago."

Chisholm's damaged hands tensed.

"Look Chisholm, I know you don't want to cancel the Visit."

Callaghan was nodding his head vigorously, but mercifully remained silent.

"You know Flynn Dolan personally." Chisholm's tone was flat.

"Yes."

"Let me see if I understand, Investigator. You grew up together? In Ireland?"

"They went to school together!" Callaghan broke the silence despite Kent's warning glare.

"Yes." Kent could feel the impending explosion.

"And on the eve of Her Majesty and Prince Phillip's Visit, you find a mannequin head, clearly linked to an ongoing RCMP investigation and moments later take a phone call from a known terrorist – in the top secret room assigned to you, so that you can protect the Queen and the Prince who will be stationed beside you tomorrow night?"

"Yes, but at least we know—"

"Jesus H. Christ, Investigator Riley, this is a bloody mess!" Chisholm's shout reverberated around the turret room.

Kent kept his face neutral, but Callaghan's eyes went wide. He pulled out the inevitable cloth and began polishing his glasses.

"You're not holding any soft feelings for Ireland, are you, Investigator?" Chisolm asked bluntly.

Kent put his shoulders back automatically. "I'm a member of the Royal Canadian Mounted Police, Chisholm, if you cut me, I bleed red serge."

Chisholm took his measure.

Kent continued. "What you need to be worrying about is who on your hotel staff got Flynn Dolan into 702 and whether or not Flynn knows that Her Majesty will be sleeping in the suite next door to mine tomorrow night. You told us the staff were clear."

A slightly calmer Fenwick Chisholm scrutinized Kent. "We can discuss moving the Queen tomorrow morning before the briefing." He looked at his watch. "In the meantime, my shift just started. I can't be late especially now. I'll see what I can find out about the hotel staff and meet you back here in two hours." He opened the door a crack and exited quickly.

Kent and Callaghan went down the stairs to 602. The hotel was quiet as people must have descended for dinner. He gave a nod to the officers guarding the Vice-Regal suite. With a great sigh, Kent opened the door, half expecting to see Flynn on the couch having a cup of tea.

The room was empty.

CHAPTER TWENTY-SEVEN

Dan's house was too dangerous, especially for Marcel. They had moved into Henry's warehouse and sat around a dark table picking at the remnants of dinner. The men looked strained and tired.

The solemn mood didn't touch Flynn, though, as the path to victory unfolded so clearly before him – as long as he didn't think about Kent.

So far Gogarty had failed to find Sarah, but Flynn wouldn't stop until he found her. It could happen at any point. On this night especially, he would not give up hope. He tamped his cigarette down before lighting it. Tonight was for celebration and anticipation. So much suffering, so much work. Now they had reached the turning point where the world would see things based on Irish beliefs and Irish values. The soul-destroying colonialism would end tomorrow night and a new era would dawn where an undivided Ireland would take its rightful place at the table. Flynn would sit at that table and speak for all those who had suffered at the hands of the British. Flynn leaned back in his chair and released the blue smoke from his lungs. It wafted up into the warehouse rafters before dissipating into nothingness. Paul O'Rourke had brought them a well-aged bottle of *Bushmills* to mark the occasion. He raised his glass and the other men fell silent.

"Tomorrow, we change the course of history. Tomorrow, we stop being men who take orders; instead, we give them. Tomorrow, we establish the rules for equality, for justice, and for a better future. To a united Ireland!"

"To the future," Dan cried over Marcel's approving roar. Liam's eyes gleamed as he took a draught of the whiskey. Paul bowed his head to Flynn and drained his glass, growling with the liquid heat. Flynn closed his eyes letting the warm marzipan flavour slide down his throat and warm his heart.

SATURDAY

CHAPTER TWENTY-EIGHT

Kent was up at zero six hundred, not that he had slept much. He had sent the boy home noticing his exhaustion and something more. He was jumpy. Besides, Kent thought it best to be on his own if Flynn's men paid him a visit. Gratefully his night in the seventh floor suite was entirely uneventful. His check-in with Chisholm had not produced any insight into who on the staff might be working for Flynn. The refusal to cancel the Visit was once again issued from on high. Maybe Kent gave Flynn Dolan too much credit when he couldn't actually get close to the Queen.

Kent showered and shaved, mentally rehearsing each minute of the day. Staring at the harbour where the Queen's yacht would arrive in mere hours, he wished Callaghan would arrive so they could have coffee and go over the day's details once more. The child prodigy was very put out about not being allowed to accompany Kent through the tunnel, but access between the Legislative Building and the Empress was highly restricted. To Kent the day looked as if it would be hazy for a time, but then the summer sun ought to burn off the cloud cover in time for Her Majesty's arrival.

Callaghan arrived promptly at seven, but didn't look particularly refreshed. Kent was suggesting coffee in the Bengal Lounge when he noticed the boy's right hand. "What happened, Callaghan? You'll be having a nasty burn!"

His thumb and forefinger were badly scorched.

"It's nothing, Sir. I just need to keep the air on it since it was covered up through the night. My father and I often get little burns while repairing appliances."

"What happened?"

"What happened? Um, it was a toaster that didn't really—"

"I get the picture. Funny, I always think police work is the most dangerous thing, but maybe being an electrician is more hazardous."

"Yes, maybe it is."

By mid-morning, Kent and Callaghan were stationed in the Legislature sizing up HMS Britannia now looming over an adoring crowd of thousands at a secured berth to their left. Standing ramrod straight, immaculate in their uniforms, the Royal Canadian Navy's band greeted the Royals first with *O Canada*, followed by *God Save the Queen*, and finally a rousing rendition of *Rule Britannia*, which had set Kent's teeth on edge. Queen Elizabeth II and Prince Philip strolled along a barricaded path, shaking hands with their fans, accepting bouquets of flowers. They crossed Belleview Street and on to the Legislature. Soon Kent and Chisholm would brief the Queen and Prince.

"Good luck, Sir," said Callaghan, clearly excited. "This will be an experience to remember. I'll just be right here in the hallway if you need me for anything."

Kent didn't reply, his nerves so taut he didn't trust himself to speak. He left Callaghan without a glance backward and followed the Royal Navy officer who had arrived to escort him to the Premier's office.

Premier Bennett's office was large, but with the crush of dignitaries, security and aides, Kent felt stifled. The Premier gave a formal address in the Queen and Prince's honour, and much to Kent's irritation many pleasant words were subsequently exchanged by all parties. Kent remained silent, trying to disappear at the back of the elite crowd.

After the formalities, Deputy Tepoorten motioned Kent forward to meet the Queen. Fenwick Chisholm suddenly appeared at his side and the Queen's regal expression shifted to a beam of pleasure.

"We are quite pleased to see you again, Mr. Chisholm."

Chisholm bowed slightly from the waist. "It is my pleasure to continue to serve Your Majesty."

Kent felt utterly out of place, and was suddenly glad that Queen Elizabeth's gaze was not upon him. He kept reminding himself that all he was responsible for was this evening through until when the Queen and Prince joined the motorcade that would deliver them to the airport on Sunday. All Kent had to do was keep them safe for one night, with the assistance of dozens of RCMP and British security officers.

Queen Elizabeth sat across from Kent and Chisholm, her hands folded in her lap. Dark curls framed her face and her bright blue eyes were alert. She was dressed in a flared yellow skirt with a matching short-jacket and hat. She wore a red and gold maple leaf on the left above her heart.

Deputy Commissioner Tepoorten introduced Kent as the RCMP's Chief of Security at the Empress.

"Good-morning, Investigator Riley. It's nice to finally meet you."

"Thank you, Your Majesty. It is a great honour to meet you and the Prince. I look forward to ensuring your safety and comfort while you are with us in Victoria."

"You have quite a reputation, Investigator Riley."

Kent flushed unsure as to what she meant.

"We carefully selected Investigator Riley and feel completely confident in his commitment to your security, Your Majesty," the Deputy said giving Kent time to gather himself.

Kent briefed the Queen on her itinerary after leaving the Legislature, including the escort up to their seventh floor suite at the Empress. Checking off each detail on his list, Chisholm's presence eased the pressure slightly. He couldn't imagine how the Queen and Prince lived on such a schedule. Every moment had to be accounted for, every minute had to be devoted to so many clamouring individuals, groups, communities, and counties that required her attention and focus. How did the Royals choose what was important and who merited their valuable time? He could hear the crowd outside hoping for another appearance and the dull roar was giving him a headache.

Prince Philip was at the far end of the great room. He was surrounded by a series of gentlemen who were gesticulating and speaking in raised voices. The Prince extricated himself from the impassioned discussion and came over to where his wife was sitting. Chisholm and Kent stood, but Queen Elizabeth remained seated and patted the place beside her. The Prince appeared energized and warm. He gave Kent's proffered hand a firm shake and followed suit with the Deputy Commissioner.

"So sorry to keep you waiting. It's good to see you Chisholm." The Prince clapped him on the shoulder. He took his seat next to the Queen while Chisholm made formal introductions to the Deputy Commissioner and to Kent. The Prince set Kent at ease with his evident faith in their abilities and his delight in Victoria's handsome harbour. He was remarkably handsome, dressed in a light grey suit, white shirt, and blue striped tie. Kent had never seen such elegance.

Queen Elizabeth smiled at her husband. "These gentlemen are now going to tell us about the route which will take us to the Empress Hotel – via a secret passageway no less."

"It's all quite marvellous I'm sure," said the Prince.

"The underground passage was originally constructed between the Legislature, the Union Club and the Empress Hotel at the turn of the century," explained the Deputy Commissioner. "To let the politicians take their – rest and relaxation out of the public eye."

"Chisholm, I thought you were pulling our leg when you first told us about this tunnel," Prince Philip exclaimed.

"The covert passage is really the lasting legacy of marital difficulties and an architect's fanciful imagination," the Deputy explained.

"I think a decent tunnel is *de rigueur* for any serious building," the Queen announced.

"It must have been an Englishman who designed this labyrinth," said Prince Philip.

"As a matter of fact it was," Chisholm said and Kent thought for a moment he may have even smiled.

"Francis Rattenbury," said the Deputy, "designed both the Legislative Buildings where we are now and the Empress Hotel which is facing the harbour. He was born and raised in Leeds."

Prince Philip nodded with interest. The Queen took a sip of water from a crystal cut glass and listened politely. Kent could not think of a single thing to say and felt completely foolish sitting beside Chisholm. He looked over to the far end of the room where three RCMP officers were smiling and chatting with an extremely well-dressed personal assistant or Lady-in-Waiting or whatever those ladies who assisted the Queen were called.

Kent tried to think how he might add in a comment, but his mind was completely blank. The more he thought, the more tongue-tied he felt. Chisholm laid out a line diagram of Victoria's Inner Harbour, which clearly showed the Legislature, the Empress Hotel and the Union Club, the latter nestled amongst the other downtown buildings. "The Legislature has been completely secured so there is no possibility we will be seen as we enter the tunnel. Even the Members of the Legislative Assembly will have to remain in their seats until after we have departed. Your Majesty, we will be very discreet and it will only be myself and Investigator Riley," he nodded briefly at Kent, "who will be accompanying you both through the tunnel."

"I must say," said Prince Phillip, "from my glimpse of the Empress Hotel and our arrival at the Parliament Buildings, this Rattenbury was a damned talented architect. Don't you agree, Investigator Riley?"

"In all honesty, Your Royal Highness," Kent replied, painfully aware of his Irish accent, "until tomorrow, my mind is focussed solely on your safety and that of Her Majesty. All that I can see in this," he gestured at the line diagram, "is a blueprint of potential threats."

Queen Elizabeth's face lost its look of delight for the briefest second, and in that moment, Kent realized it was nothing but a polished and useful façade.

"Well said, Investigator Riley. While my husband and I both appreciate Officer Chisholm's presence, we are also fortunate to have you with us, considering the safety of our every move. I know there have been some serious concerns given recent developments."

"Not that we have any worries," Prince Philip assured them. "We live in a perpetual state of so-called 'threats' as you are well-aware Riley and we must continue to conduct ourselves with our trust well-placed in highly skilled individuals such as Chisholm and yourself."

The Queen stood, and the assembled men scrambled to rise. "May we see the entrance to the tunnel prior to our luncheon event?" she asked.

Kent noticed several attendants glance at their watches, but no one dared object as Chisholm led the way. They walked through the deserted, wood panelled corridors of the Legislature, the floors had elaborate tiled patterns. They went down a wide set of stairs in silence to a wooden door labeled Furnace Room. Chisholm opened it and ushered them in. Kent thought he might have made an error as indeed they were in an oily, dingy furnace room. Chisholm proceeded to the back wall where there was a heavy metal sliding door that he unlocked and slid to the right. The old door opened with surprisingly little effort. There was second door beyond the wooden one that he also unlocked and pulled open. A smooth and dry stone tunnel extended beyond.

Chisholm peered in then took a few steps into the dark. Queen Elizabeth came boldly up beside Kent at the doorway entrance, despite how forbidding it looked.

"Does it look safe to you, Investigator Riley?"

"Yes, Your Majesty, it does," he assured her.

"There is a certain comfort in people being unaware of how one moves from one location to another," she mused.

CHAPTER TWENTY-NINE

Flynn grabbed Dan Smythe by the collar and pulled him in close to his face.

"Where is she?" Flynn demanded. "The decoy went in the cavalcade, but the Queen never left the Legislature."

"I don't know, Flynn, I don't know," spluttered Dan.

Flynn shoved him away and turned on Liam with narrowed eyes. "What did you see?"

"I couldn't see anything of the luncheon," Liam said. "It was crawling with police, but from the hotel lobby I would say they were at it until about one. Then there was a children's choir or some such. They left the Empress through the main entrance at one-thirty."

"Through the front," Flynn repeated. He slumped down in a chair and lit a cigarette.

"They arrived at Butchart Gardens a little after two and were there until three-thirty." Chasseur confirmed. "Then they returned to the Legislature and entered through a side entrance on the left."

"I was told she had a meeting with the Premier," Dan spoke softly as if it would save him from Flynn's anger.

"Yes, yes I know that," Flynn slammed his hands down on the kitchen table. The ashtray clattered. He closed his eyes. "Is there another way to get from the Premier's Office to the Empress Hotel without being seen?"

"They may have left through a side passage we don't know about," Dan suggested.

"Maybe they dressed down and blended in with the crowd," Liam offered.

"Too risky," Flynn's temper was easing. "Too many people watching and waiting," he added. Liam picked up a fork that had fallen to the floor.

"There were newspaper men that followed the cavalcade to Government House and another that followed the Ladies-in-Waiting who went through the front entrance of the Empress Hotel," said Dan.

Flynn's face changed. "That's it. They weren't going through the front or the side to the Hotel. They were going beneath it—"

"Like an abandoned line of the métro," said Chasseur.

"That will have been Kenny's assignment then." Flynn's calm had fully returned. The summer light was beginning to wane. "Given what we already know, the Queen and Prince are now on the seventh floor of the Empress."

Flynn looked each man in the eyes. "Alright you all know what to do."

● ● ●

Marcel spotted Henry's thug Rooke in the lobby, but walked past him as planned. He took the east stairs, carefully bypassing the police presence on the sixth floor and reaching the seventh to wait for Rooke to trudge up the stairwell landing. He eased out through the door and onto the seventh floor. Marcel checked his watch. It was nine. He signalled to Rooke. They were right on schedule. And, sure enough, there was the Queen's guard backing out of the corner room Flynn had told them to watch. He was pulling behind him a rolling cart of sheets and towels. Marcel leapt ahead and put a gun to his back. Rooke loomed alongside him.

Abruptly, the Queen's guard tensed like he was going to make a break for it. Marcel held the gun hard against his back. He glanced over at Rooke who closed the door. Marcel marched the Queen's guard down the hallway toward 704, pushing the gun into his spine with each step. Rooke's foot fall was heavy as he treaded behind Marcel. The man didn't speak. Marcel's hand was sweating on the gun. He shifted his fingers to get a tighter grip. Outside 704, Marcel said into the guard's ear, "Open the door." He didn't want to be too loud and alert Kent if he was in the room next door.

The Queen's guard started to unlock the door, but Marcel could tell he was about to try something. Chisholm hurtled backward, crashing into him, but Marcel was ready for it. He braced, absorbed the hit and smashed the gun hard across Chisholm's head. The man moaned and slumped against the door.

Marcel said in a low voice. "Open the door or I'll do it myself and leave you dead in your room." Chisholm seemed get some life back after a moment. Blood was oozing through the hair on the back of his head. He was staring at the length of rope that Rooke held in one hand. Really, they should just tie him up and leave him in his room where he would be out of the way, but Marcel worried a man like this would get loose. It was better to have him within arm's reach.

"Who's there? Chisholm?" A man's voice called through the door. It must be the Prince.

Marcel pushed the gun hard into the back of the Queen's guard.

"Answer him," he ordered.

But the Queen's guard didn't say anything. Marcel had to resist the temptation to kill him right there. If he pulled the trigger, the cops stationed on the sixth floor below would come running. Flynn said this whole job had to be quiet, very, very quiet, until he set the bomb off.

"Okay, take the fool and tie him up, we'll leave him in the closet and go in ourselves."

"No," the Queen's guard spoke. "Mountbatten, we have a problem. We have intruders. Open the door and—"

Marcel slammed his gun into the guard's cheek and leaned in so his mouth was right by his ear. "No instructions," he said to him softly, "no instructions."

There was a pause and then the door opened a crack. Rooke pushed it open and the three of them stumbled in. Marcel felt elated and then quickly embarrassed at the sight of the Queen. He felt like a small child who had snuck into a classroom only to find the teacher standing right there. He wanted to apologize for the rude intrusion, but he stopped himself. She was in a silk dressing gown that made it all worse. He had rarely seen a woman so beautiful. The Prince was in pyjamas and still managed to look imperious and enraged at the same time. They both looked tired. There was a cheese and fruit platter sitting on a table next to a pile of embossed paper and envelopes. Marcel's gun hand started shaking slightly and he had to will it to stop.

"I am sorry about this," the guard said to the Queen.

She reached out a hand. "Fenwick, you're hurt!"

"I'm fine," he assured her.

"You're bleeding." She wheeled on Marcel. "How dare you—"

"Elizabeth, stand down," snapped her husband.

Marcel raised his gun so that it pointed right at her face and she took a step back. The Prince moved toward her and Marcel put him in his gun sights. He stopped and raised his hands.

"No one's going to get hurt if everyone stays calm." Marcel pushed Chisholm over to Henry's silent thug. "Take him into the bathroom and fix him up. Bind his hands and feet so he won't be any trouble."

Gun in hand, Rooke manoeuvred the Queen's guard into the bathroom. Marcel could hear a chair scraping across the floor. There was a struggle, grunting. Marcel stopped breathing. What the hell? That Englishman was clearly impossible to contain. He trained his gun on the door, away from the Queen, and as he did the Prince grabbed a knife off the cheese platter, knocking envelopes to the floor, and came at him.

Marcel felt a searing pain across his gun arm. He dropped his revolver. He shoved Prince hard and he fell backward, crashing heavily to the floor. There was a push against the bathroom door and the thud of a fist hitting a body. The Queen was moving towards the door. Marcel whipped his backup gun from its holster and pointed it at the Queen. She stopped moving. He expected to see fear, but her eyes were closed off and if anything, angry. The Prince was struggling to get up, knife still in hand.

"Philip, please put down the knife. I want you safe," the Queen stated flatly.

The Prince placed the knife carefully on the table with exaggerated gesture. Marcel walked backward so that he had them both in his sights. He was breathing hard and his arm was screaming at him. This wasn't going well. Not well at all. Flynn would be angry. The window was dark. He didn't know if the battle raging in the bathroom was Queen's man giving Rooke a good beating or if it was the other way around. Marcel was having trouble focusing.

"Pick up the knife and put it away in that cupboard over there. Do it slowly. So much as one step towards me and I'll kill your wife." His voice sounded strained, but hearing himself issue a command made his racing heart slow down slightly.

The Prince picked up the knife and went slowly over to a tall ornately carved wooden cupboard Marcel had waved at. He opened the door and placed the knife in it on top of a stack of blankets and pillows. Closing the cupboard, he faced Marcel.

"What do you want?" he asked.

Marcel felt like laughing out loud at the man's ease, at his entitlement. Hate rose in Marcel's throat. "We want the Queen." He felt of rush of power just saying such a thing.

There was a presence at the bathroom door. It was Rooke, Thank God. Behind him, Marcel could see the Queen's man beaten senseless. His head hung down and blood dripped on the floor. Relief coursed through Marcel's veins.

The Prince continued to speak evenly, although he too had seen his guard ruined by Rooke. "You'll never leave this hotel with the Queen. There are police everywhere. Why don't you set your sights on something more achievable?"

Holding his gun in both hands, Rooke positioned himself on the other side of the Prince.

Where was Flynn? He should have been here by now. Marcel's arm was aching. His fingers felt stiff. Warm blood was soaking into his shirt and jacket. He flexed his fingers and forearm. The cut to his arm wasn't serious, but it felt disgusting. The Queen was looking right at him, so he cast his gaze out the dark window.

"What do you want from me?" the Queen asked simply.

Her voice sounded caring, not proud like her husband's. Marcel wished that they could sit down and discuss a plan together.

"What can I do?" she asked again.

He shook off the daydream. There was no changing the plan. "It's too late, there's nothing you can do to help me, or yourself."

The sacrifices he had made for this moment, for this moment of justice. He would not let this woman deter him with her persuasive calm. The degradation of his parents, of all French people in this British colony, treated as second-class citizens in their own country, and she was the one with her castles and crown that kept Québec humiliated. One wave of her sceptre and she could return to them their language, their culture, their heritage. He couldn't wait for Flynn to arrive and put her in her place.

"Do you know where I'm from?" he asked, and then before she could speak, he answered his own question. "*Je suis Québécois-*" his voice began to shake with rage so that he couldn't finish the sentence.

• • •

Standing in the dark in Kent's suite, Flynn found the repeated blows emanating through the wall reassuring – almost pleasurable. Rooke or Marcel was evidently giving Fenwick Chisholm the thrashing he so rightly deserved. He longed to join them next door. Kent and Callaghan were late. He was about to light a cigarette when a key rattled in the lock. Then Flynn saw the shadowy forms of Kent and Callaghan enter the suite. As they came closer, completely unaware, Flynn gripped his gun a little tighter. The lights came on and Kent's eyes immediately flicked over to Liam sitting on the couch, then he stared straight at Flynn. There was no surprise, no change in expression. Kent moved rapidly so that he was standing directly between Flynn and the boy.

Kent's face was completely blank. Where was the boyish smile or the flashing scent of a lit match that Flynn remembered so well? Even five feet away, he could see Kent had aged. His face was harder and more drawn. Keeping perfectly still, Kent shifted his eyes from Flynn to Liam. Flynn knew him well enough to see that he was scoping out the space, recording every detail, formulating a plan. He was about to attack and Flynn needed to take charge before that happened.

"It's been a long time Kenny."

"Let the boy go, Flynn," he said, trying to remain in front of Callaghan, who was trying to move out from behind him. "He has nothing to do with this."

"Let him go?" Flynn smiled at Kent's double-crossing partner. That was Kent's problem right there. He trusted people. Kent was still talking.

"Lock him in the bathroom and then we'll deal with what we have to. He has nothing to do with us. He's just a kid."

"He's a genius, Kenny. It's the boy we wanted all along. Don't you understand?"

Kent wasn't quick enough to cover up his confusion.

Hang-dog face, the kid walked over and sat down beside Liam who let out a high-pitched guffaw.

"Callaghan?" Kent exclaimed.

Now Kent didn't look so sure of himself. The boy kept his eyes cast downward.

"Good evening, Michael," Flynn said.

"Hello, Mr. Dolan," he replied, like a schoolboy.

Liam laughed quietly, shaking his head.

"We weren't after you, Kenny," Flynn explained, "We were wanting your partner.

"Callaghan—" Kent said again, his voice now menacing.

"Put your gun on the floor at your feet, Kenny. Kick it my way." Flynn gestured at Callaghan. "You, give yours to Liam. Easy my boy, nice and easy."

Liam took Callaghan's gun. Kent pulled his gun from the holster beneath his shoulder and laid it on the carpet, giving it a push toward Flynn.

"As soon as they're done with you, they'll kill you, Callaghan," Kent said. "And then you'll go to hell."

The boy pushed up his glasses. "Hell's not the Court I care about, Sir."

Kent's eyes widened at the feisty answer from his backstabbing partner. Callaghan's insulting 'Sir' added the ideal finish. Flynn wished he could put the gun down and release the tension in his fingers.

"The Brancusi head – the easiest robbery I've ever done, just let me add – was worth a pretty penny," he said, finally laying out his plan to bring Kent into the fold. "There's a man in New York who's waiting for it. Michael Callaghan is now set for life. No more policing. He can do anything he wants. Go anywhere he wants. And best of all, his parents stay alive. We're not going to be killing him. He's one of us, Kent. You wouldn't understand because you like to work alone."

"Flynn, you're in Canada now," Kent took a step toward him. "So escape from all this. You can make a real life for yourself. You won't be changing Britain and Ireland with a bomb. It doesn't work that way."

Callaghan kept his eyes cast down. He seemed to be muttering under his breath. He must be afraid.

Flynn was back in control and could afford to be generous. "But Kenny, I need you too," he said looking directly into Kent's hardened eyes. He could barely see a trace of the boy he once knew so well.

"I'm here protecting the Queen, Flynn!" Kent hands flew up. "I won't let anything happen to her."

"Oh really? How noble." Sarcasm infected Flynn's tone even though he promised himself he would only be direct and kind, but Kent was so provoking. "You're protecting the figurehead for an Empire that has sucked the lifeblood out of your people and your land for centuries," he countered. "How very, very noble." He dropped the sarcasm and spoke from the heart. "This is why you need me to jolt you awake, Kenny."

"If you hurt her, Flynn," Kent warned, "it will simply confirm the British view – that the Irish are beyond control. Think about it for once."

"Think about it?" Flynn's voice rose in despair. "Think about it?" He could feel his eyes burning with tears. *"That's all I think about,* Kenny. I think about making a change and I think about you and bringing you back."

Kent spoke through clenched teeth. "The day you hurt Sarah was our last day, Flynn, and you damn well know it."

Flynn took a step toward him, anger pulsing through him. "What I know is that Sarah's alive and I'm having her tracked down right now," Kent's eyes narrowed slightly, but he recovered quickly. "I have men watching her family's home in London around the clock. I have a man at each of her girlfriends' houses. She'll be found Kenny. It's only a matter of time."

Kent let out a low growl and lunged at Flynn, who took several brisk steps back. Liam leapt to his feet, revolver trained at Kent's head. Pulling back from the lunge, Kent dropped his hands to his sides.

Flynn should never have mentioned Sarah. What possessed him? It was a stupid move guaranteed to cause more trouble than it was worth. He felt like a boy who pushed a stick in a dog's face, poking and teasing until the creature came at him all teeth.

"Think how much work we'll be able to do with the Queen of England under our control. And to think she's right next door."

"The hotel is full of police. You don't have a chance."

Flynn laughed slightly, feeling suddenly uneven and strange. He cocked his head at the rhythmic, angry thumping through the wall that had started up again. "Ah, how I do love that sound. Do you know what that is, Kenny?"

Kent remained silent.

"That's the sound of Fenwick Chisholm being beaten to death next door."

Kent's face was so tense. Flynn suddenly wanted to comfort him. There was a shattering sound. The boy started talking to himself again, muttering as if he'd finally lost his mind. Flynn approached with the gun, but Kent didn't take a step back.

"One of ours is taking care of Mr. Chisholm," Flynn explained. "He's come to Canada too, Kenny, but he hasn't forgotten where he comes from. He hasn't abandoned his people, just because he's come to a rich, fat land."

Liam began to approach and Flynn held a hand up to stop him.

He was close enough to smell the ocean on Kent's coat. "Look Kenny, one more job," he said softly. "It would set you up for life, just one more job. We're not going to be hurting the Queen, just hiding her away for a time."

Kent spat bitterly.

"We're doing a grab and run like in the old days." He wanted Kenny to understand. "I've got a spot set up for her. She'll be safe and comfortable and when we get what we want, the change that we want, Kenny, then we'll let her go."

Flynn could feel Kent starting to consider the plan. As long as he thought the Queen was safe, he might go for it.

"Why do you need the boy?" Kent asked. "He's slow and doesn't see well."

"He's setting up a remote for us."

"A remote? What does—"

"He's the key to our 'distraction' that's how we're going to get her Majesty out. You'll be in charge of the Queen. You'll have to carry her and move like lightning. Few men could do it, Kenny. It's why we need you."

"Where's the bomb being planted and how much damage can we expect?" Kent asked.

The boy leapt up. "Uh, the bomb has the capacity to blow up the elevator and create a great deal of smoke. Please God, there'll be no casualties! I'll set the remote from the end of the hallway. We remain behind the fire exit door to the stairwell and after the men have come up the stairs and run into the smoke towards Her Majesty's room, we'll exit down the stairs at the opposite end of the corridor."

Kent was looking at the kid like he was contemplating his murder. Michael Callaghan suddenly looked sheepish. He plunked back down on the couch.

"There'll be two cars waiting for us out back," Flynn continued, "out where the garbage is stored. Beneath the main floor, the stairs lead straight out."

Kent was clearly thinking over the job, the logistics. He looked at Flynn like old times. His voice was all business now. "What about Prince Philip?"

"There's a man stationed on the Prince. He'll be the last to leave, but he'll take the Prince. They'll go straight from the harbour by boat. He's the distraction. Everyone will assume the Queen is with him. Our inside man will make sure the police keep focused on the boat."

"Who's our inside man?"

"Someone I trust."

The pounding next door had ceased, and silence fell in the room.

Then, Kent started to speak and it was so quiet. It was just for Flynn to hear and his heart began to beat rapidly. This was exactly the moment that he had worked toward, this turning point in history, this great claim for the country and the people that he loved. Suddenly, all the work, all the hours and the thinking and the dealing with lesser men, cruel, blundering men, was worth it. He could tell in Kent's first few words that he was coming back. He was coming back home. He was forgiving Flynn for the mistake with Sarah. He was remembering their brotherhood, the promises they made one another. He heard in Kent's voice the echoing sounds of his sweet father, the clockmaker, the sweetest man who ever lived. 'Ah, Flynn my boy, my second son, few boys have your charisma. I know by the very stars, you will make a great man, Flynn, a very great man.' He focused on Kent's words that were spoken so low.

"Flynn, oh Flynn," Kent swallowed hard. "You are not your father's son."

What's this? What could Kent mean?

Flynn felt pulled apart. He felt sick in his gut.

Kent spoke in a strained voice, a little softer until his voice became almost a whisper. "Flynn, you've become the British jailers who beat your father to death."

Flynn recoiled. His head snapped up. His eyes dried out in his head so that they felt small and hard. His lip curled and his blood pumped hatred through every vein and artery in his body. Flynn gestured at Kent with his chin, as if saying his name was too good for such filth, "Liam, get rid of him. Make sure his body is never found."

CHAPTER THIRTY

Kent knew Flynn couldn't kill him. That was where he had a chance, a very small chance. Callaghan looked portly and weak and slightly crazy as he sat muttering on the couch. Kent strained to hear what he was saying and it sounded like some sort of formula. It sounded like letters and numbers, an equation of sorts. He kept saying it over and over.

Liam O'Rourke got up and started walking around the table, closing in on Kent. Flynn had a sick, strange smile playing across his features that Kent had never seen before.

Suddenly, Callaghan stood up. "Remember, you can't shoot him, Mr. Dolan. The hotel is crawling with police. Any noise is too much of a risk."

Flynn didn't seem to hear what he had said.

"It's going to take me time to prepare the bomb and the timing device," Callaghan insisted. "I can't have the police up here now."

Liam O'Rourke rocked back and forth on his feet, waiting for an order.

"I think the smartest thing is to drown him," Callaghan suggested, ignoring the startled look on Kent's face.

"I'll fill the tub," he explained. "And then I can make the Staff Sergeant think he killed himself, that he was so upset about the—"

"Drown him?"

"Yes, don't you see? A suicide, the despair over the death of his wife simply became too much. Losing the Queen was the final straw. You know?"

"His wife's not dead," Flynn said.

Getting ready, Kent rubbed his palms on his jacket. Flynn took an agitated step forward. Kent put one leg slightly forward where he had his second gun strapped in its ankle holster.

"Okay," said Flynn, "I like drowning." He spoke as if he had thought up the idea himself. "Michael, go and fill the tub."

Callaghan walked quickly into the bathroom and shut the door. Moments later, the room was full of the sound of rushing water.

"You know, I'll be sorry to do this, Kenny, but now you're in my way."

"You're not sorry, Dolan."

"You always liked to think of yourself as a protector," Flynn said, "but really you're a sell-out."

Kent remained silent. He wanted to give off the air of a man who was preparing to die. Flynn faced him about four feet away and started pulling on his finger joints so that they cracked while the gun swung, hooked on one of his fingers. Kent considered making a move, but a sidelong glance at the gun trained on him by Liam made him hesitate.

"You just want to be serving whoever's in power," said Flynn, pointing the gun right at his face again.

"Flynn, I just tried my best to have a life." Kent tried to swallow and failed. His throat was dry. "There's no life in fighting history."

There was a slight softening of Flynn's face muscles, but he kept the gun steady.

"Kenny, it's not too late! Fight with us. My father died for our people. He didn't have anything to leave us. Is that the best life we can be hoping for? Fight with us. We're so close." Flynn's eyes were swimming with grief-stricken rapture. While he spoke, the boy he once was flashed across his features, the grief he felt, missing his father so much.

If he was going to survive, Kent had to bury the kid Flynn once was. He had to only consider the man. Besides, he'd heard this tone too many times as a prelude to the crushing blows, sobbing boys and shattered bodies that Flynn left in his wake at the schoolyard. Instead, Kent would keep the image of Sarah's white neck, her jugular vein pulsing blue and Flynn's knife draping itself so dangerously across it with its thin trail of blood. He clenched his teeth.

Flynn's joyless grin stretched taut. "Go find out what the hell the boy's doing in there!" he barked at Liam. The taps were no longer running, but Callaghan had not reappeared. Kent prayed that the child prodigy knew what he was doing. He obviously had a plan and was putting it in motion, but Kent couldn't see how he had a hope in hell of achieving it. Liam went marching into the bathroom, gun at the ready, and suddenly there was the crashing sound of a body hitting the wall and then a whoosh of water. Callaghan did not have the physical strength to have thrown Liam O'Rourke down – the body falling into the tub had to be Callaghan's. Kent's heart felt like someone had wrapped it in wires and was tightening them with pliers.

Flynn startled at the sound, and for a fraction of a second looked over to the bathroom door. Kent lunged at him. He crooked his arm and raised it up, sharply dislodging the gun from Flynn's hand. He bent in one fluid motion and pulled the revolver from his leg and trained it on Dolan. Without taking his eyes off Dolan, he kicked his gun under the couch.

Again the twisted smile. "Ah, well we're going to be having a real showdown you and I, Kenny, because when Liam comes out, he'll kill you."

The door opened a crack. Callaghan peered out and seeing Kent holding the gun on Dolan, pushed it open all the way. "Thank goodness you finally took charge, Sir."

The boy was soaking wet. Kent looked beyond him into the bathroom where he could just make out the dark form of Liam, motionless in the tub.

"Callaghan, did you knock him out then?"

"Sorry about your new razor. I'll get you another one from my dad's shop."

Callaghan took his glasses off and went to polish them on his shirt, but it was all wet. With a sigh, he put them back on.

Kent struggled to understand. "My razor? I thought I told you—"

"I pushed Liam O'Rourke into the tub and then threw in your electric razor." Callaghan said. "It was quite a sight."

"Are you telling me you electrocuted him?"

"I am. And I'm not one bit sorry, Sir."

Flynn, although covering it up well, looked a little frantic. He glanced at Callaghan and then back at Kent. His hands were clenched and he turned on the boy. "You're dead and your parents are dead. I won't stop until—"

"Shut up, Dolan." Kent's hands were tight on the revolver, but there was a roaring in his mind. He could feel the tendons in his neck becoming so taut they were going to snap. There wasn't any fear in Dolan's eyes, only pride. He would love to die for Ireland and it enraged Kent even more. He cocked the revolver's hammer, taking his aim, but he was distracted. There was an irritating voice edging into his consciousness.

"Please don't do it, Sir!"

"What?"

"Don't do it, put the gun down."

He lined up the barrel right between Dolan's eyes.

"I'm begging you, Sir, to stop."

Kent widened his scope just slightly more than the look in Dolan's eyes. At the edge, he could see the glinting round spectacles of the child prodigy who spoke a little louder now. "Sir, *don't* do it."

"Shut-up, Callaghan."

As soon as he spoke, his fury collapsed.

"Just hand him over." Callaghan moved toward the phone, his shoes squelching in a most aggravating manner. Kent considered killing both Callaghan and Dolan.

"You've always been unable to commit, Kent," Dolan sneered at him. "That's ultimately what I most hate about you. You're an opportunist. A mercenary. You have no ties to anything but your own self. That's why anyone can hire you. All you are is a gun for hire, Kent. It makes me sick."

The fury started welling up in Kent again. Just to be able to silence that sneering voice, once and for all. He wanted to take the slight smile that played on Dolan's twisted mouth and blast it and all his memories right out of this world.

Callaghan's boyish voice came wafting across the void. "Don't do it. Think about your father, Sir. Think about Sarah."

Suddenly Kent felt weak. He started laughing a shaky, strange laugh.

"Christ Almighty, Callaghan, if you call me 'Riley', I'll let you make your telephone call."

"Riley, don't pull that trigger," Callaghan commanded loudly. "Riley, Sir, I'm dialling right now." Kent turned to him and a dark shadow flickered between them. Dolan lurched forward with the speed and force of desperation. He got his hand clamped around Kent's hand clenched on the revolver. They hit the floor with Dolan's elbow in Kent's side while Dolan's knee smashed onto his fingers gripping the revolver. Kent cried out in agony. A table flipped, missing Kent's head by a fraction. Callaghan's calm voice speaking rapidly into the phone rose above the pain jabbing into Riley's hand and kept him fighting. Only Callaghan would make a telephone call while Kent was fighting for his life.

Kent kicked out and hit Dolan square in the mouth. He screamed as blood spurted from his split lip. Then Dolan got his hands on the revolver as they continued to fight for control on the floor. For some godforsaken reason, Callaghan had dropped to his knees and was rooting around under the couch. Kent's fingers were wet with sweat and he could barely grip the gun. His muscles ached with resisting Flynn's twisting. Abruptly, Flynn wheeled back his head to smash Kent in the face, but his head stopped with a jerk. Callaghan had Dolan by the hair. He trained a gun on Flynn's temple. That's what he had been looking for under the couch.

The boy pulled Flynn's head back another inch. "Make so much as the smallest move," he said in his bossy way, "and I will shoot you dead." Then he addressed Kent. "Get out of the way, Sir. Go to the door. Help should be on the way."

Kent rolled away from Dolan to the right. He got up slowly. He extracted his fingers from the revolver and breathed in sharply. Two fingers, at least, were broken. He looked over at Callaghan, who still had Dolan by the hair with his gun pressing into the back of his skull. The boy looked different. His face wasn't so round maybe. He never took his eyes off of Dolan.

"Callaghan, nice work."

A faint smile surfaced on the boy's face. "Thanks, Sir. Thanks for that."

Kent looked down at his watch. It was getting on to eleven. "Callaghan, did you call the Staff Sergeant?"

"Yes, Sir. I explained the situation and conveyed the need for absolute silence with the Queen and Prince trapped next door. I mean if they've got Fenwick Chisholm—"

"Yes, there's something—" said Flynn.

"Shut-up, Dolan!" Kent ordered. "I don't think we can trust anyone, Callaghan."

"I've got men everywhere, men who—" Dolan threatened.

"Shut-up!" Kent said.

What was the best plan? The bomb needed to be dismantled. Too risky to leave Callaghan alone with Dolan and bursting into the Queen's room alone might just result in her death.

"When I spoke to the Staff Sergeant, I asked that he send additional officers and ambulances, Sir."

"Smart, that's very smart," Kent said his mind racing. "As soon as we take care of Dolan, we'll move next door. Tell me about this bomb you made."

"Dolan made the bomb. It's in the stairwell, Sir, but it'll never go off. I rewired the remote and receiver. It's nothing more than a hodgepodge of wires and putty."

"You don't have a chance, Kent," Flynn said with a sneer. "You can't be stopping what will happen here tonight."

Callaghan leaned down and shoved a starched white linen napkin from the remains of the room service into Flynn's mouth and pulled out his handcuffs which he promptly lost hold of and they clattered to the floor.

"Just leave them for now." Kent peered out the door and checked up and down the hall. No one. He turned back to Callaghan. "How the hell did you get involved with them? When did you get involved with them and why didn't you tell me?"

"Well, Sir, it's like you told me, the less people know, the less they get hurt."

"Don't quote me to myself and don't say 'hodgepodge,'" Kent said.

"They were waiting in a car outside my house," Callaghan explained. "Liam O'Rourke pulled a knife on me and demanded I go with them."

"Why would you do that?"

"They said they'd burn down *Electrolife* and kill my parents if I didn't."

"You should have told me."

"I thought we'd have a better chance of finding out what they were planning if I pretended to be on their side."

Flynn was trying to say something through the fabric napkin, his eyes flashing.

Kent cautiously opened up the door for the second time and glanced down the corridor. Everything was quiet. No police back-up in sight and not a sound in the room next door. It was as if time had stood still. Chisholm had been outsmarted and was in serious trouble or possibly dead. Kent's thoughts were spinning. He was trying to see all angles at once. Suddenly three plain-clothes officers materialized at the far end of the hallway and made their way stealthily down the corridor and into the room. Constable Dan Smythe was one the first through the door. Kent's heart sank. Kent didn't know the second officer, but recognized the third one as Constable Macdonald, no longer in his 'hotel desk clerk' disguise.

"Where's Staff Sergeant Jones?"

"He's at Government House. They're transferring the Queen and Prince to a more secure site," Macdonald said.

Smythe must know the Queen was next door while the other two officers didn't – unless they were working with Flynn too. Kent had to pray they weren't and keep a close eye on Smythe at all times.

"I need a doctor, I've got a couple of broken fingers."

"Here I'll take you downstairs. We've got help waiting."

Kent knew Smythe would take the first chance he could find to immobilize Kent. Kent had to tell Callaghan that he'd be going to the Queen's room after dealing with Smythe. He hoped the boy was smart enough not to let slip anything, but he would need him for backup.

"Come on, Investigator Riley, let's go," Constable Smythe said soothingly. "Let's get you to a doctor, you did good here. Come on now."

Smythe gave the child prodigy a wink. "Nice work, Callaghan! I'm impressed."

The boy smiled like he had just won a blue ribbon for his science experiment.

"Callaghan, it's a shame that Dolan will mar a cell in Canada," Kent said.

"Yes, it is Sir," the boy agreed.

Did he understand the code for *Marvel*?

"You go on now, everything's under control and coming up lilacs," Callaghan said brightly. "I'll do the paperwork."

Lilacs, just like the soap in the turret room, the boy was smart.

Kent leaned on Constable Smythe as he went into the lift. "My hand's broken in several places," he said, "I can barely stand the pain."

"We'll get you taken care of in just a moment, Investigator Riley."

The lift door shut and before the Smythe could so much as press a button, Kent smashed his good fist hard into his gut. Then he slammed him in the nose, hearing it crack and knocked him down to the floor. Kent struck him one more time in the head to ensure he was out cold. He handcuffed him and dragged him to the fifth floor stairwell.

He took the stairs silently, quickly slipped past 702 and put his ear to 704's door, but couldn't hear anything. No sign of Callaghan. Kent would have to go it alone. He tried to hold the revolver in his right hand, and an agonized gasp wrenched out of him. Taking a deep breath, he moved back and then kicked at the door. The heavy door shuddered, but didn't give way. With all his might behind it, Kent slammed his foot against the lock and the door-jam gave way in a burst of splinters.

Marcel Chasseur had a firm hold on Queen Elizabeth's arm. His upper arm was bleeding and his jacket was torn. The Queen was dressed in her nightclothes, but her face was as hardened as any man's he'd seen during the war. A heavy-set man Kent had never seen before was holding a gun to Prince Philip's head.

"Put your gun down or I kill him." The heavy man spoke in a strained, heavy accent

Dressed in gold and burgundy striped pyjamas, Prince Philip was sweating through the cloth. "Pay no attention to me, Investigator," he implored. "Save Elizabeth." His chest was heaving. Kent slowly put the weapon down tossing it on the floor to Chasseur's left.

"Where's Flynn? If you've messed this up for us Riley, I'm going to drop you where you stand."

Kent measured the bleeding gash in Chasseur's arm. Where was the knife now?

"You can't shoot me, Chasseur," he said buying time. "The cops on the floor below would be up here in a flash. Besides, how are you going to get out without Dolan or his bomb? My men have got him in custody. The bomb has been deactivated and Liam O'Rourke is dead. It's all over Chasseur."

"You either get us out of here, Riley, or I kill the Queen. I don't mind dying for the cause. It's your choice." Chasseur grabbed the Queen's arm more tightly. Although a slight wince of pain registered on her face, Kent saw that she was actually assessing the situation. She did not look afraid. The bathroom door was open a crack and from his position Kent could see a seriously smashed-up Chisholm standing immobile, listening and biding his time. Kent looked away and turned his attention back on the two Royals. The Prince had seen Chisholm too. Where the hell was Callaghan?

"You're trapped, Chasseur, and you too," he directed his comment to the heavy man towering behind the Prince.

"Not if we're walking out with Her Highness, we're not. Now come on. Move back to the far wall. Get away from the door Kent or I will put a bullet in the Queen's head."

Chasseur took a step toward Kent, pulling the Queen with him. She resisted and Marcel paused. Her dark brown hair was curled around a very pale face. She looked tired, but straightened up and said evenly. "I have two small children. Could I please write them a good-bye note?"

"No," Chasseur snapped.

The Queen began to cry. Prince Phillip said under his breath, "My God, Elizabeth."

Chasseur wavered. Putting her hand on his, the Queen turned in his grasp and looked up into his face. Chasseur looked away. Kent's mind was working fast. She'd given him a moment. Chisholm eased the door open, just a fraction more. Prince Phillip caught Kent's eye. The heavy man remained oblivious to what was happening right under his nose.

"Okay, okay, fine." Chasseur said, "you have exactly one minute."

"May I sit down?" She asked.

He led the Queen to the writing table near the large window overlooking the pitch black harbour. The heavy man kept his weapon trained on the Prince's head and everyone in the room watched the Queen prepare to write. She moved the near empty cheese platter off to one side then reached over for a silver fountain pen lying next to monogramed stationary and a stack of envelopes. She uncapped the pen and began to write. She took in a shuddering breath. A tear fell onto the page and she brushed it off smudging the ink slightly as she wrote what could be her final words to her young children.

Kent felt ill. His hand was aching. His gun was unreachable. He was listening with every ounce of his being for a sign of Callaghan or for Chisholm to make his move. Suddenly there were two gunshots from 702. Jesus and Mary. He could hear footsteps careening down the hall and the sudden rush of fear instantly became relief as Callaghan came roaring into the room with his gun out. Rooke fired a shot. Crying out in pain, the Prince dropped to his knees. Kent turned to see Flynn at the door. Handcuffs hung loosely from one hand and he had a gun in the other, but couldn't seem to decide on his first target – Callaghan or Kent.

"I can't be going back to prison, Kenny," Flynn cried, setting his gun sights on Kent. "It's the one place I can't ever go again," Kent braced himself, but Flynn hesitated.

"Shoot him!" yelled Chasseur.

Chisholm sent the bathroom door crashing against the wall and barged into the room. The Queen leapt up and threw the silver pen to Chisholm who caught it and lunged at Chasseur, jamming the silver pen into his face. Chasseur let loose an inhuman wail as he keeled over onto his side crimson blood gushing from his face onto the carpet.

Kent flew forward, scooped his revolver up off the floor and, instinctively ducked as two more gunshots reverberated and a bullet whistled past his shoulder. Kent swung his gun up and around at Flynn, but he knew in that moment he could never shoot him. A shot rang out and

Flynn collapsed against the door, blood pulsing from a dark red circle in his throat. Eyes wide with shock, he slumped into a seated position in the doorway and began to drown in his own blood. Callaghan slammed the gun down on a marble topped table as if taking the shot had cost him his balance.

Kent spun to his right in time to see Chisholm fighting for his life with the heavy-set man. Another shot blasted high as Chisholm's boot cracked the man's knee sideways, finally he was able to wrench the weapon free and stagger clear.

Two quick shots from Chisholm and the big man collapsed, smashing through a dainty table and sending a vase crashing to the carpet as he landed face down by the window.

"Callaghan," Kent shouted, pointing at the still-screaming Chasseur, "for God's sake get his gun!"

The boy stood there, his back to Kent, wavering. He must be in shock. It's not easy to kill a man. The Prince jumped up off the floor, moved in quickly and grabbed the gun grasped loosely in Chasseur's hand. Chasseur clutched desperately at the pen jutting out from his left eye where Chisholm had jammed it.

Chisholm, badly battered and bleeding, manoeuvred the Queen into the bathroom. Callaghan was at the phone, calling for backup. His voice was hoarse. He had to be terrified. The Prince tossed Kent the heavy man's gun and followed Chisholm and the Queen. The Prince appeared uninjured. How was that possible? The Prince had cried out after the heavy man's shot. Kent trained the revolver on Chasseur while he forced himself to look over his shoulder at Flynn. Kent swallowed the bile rising in his throat.

Flynn looked startled by death.

The Queen emerged from the bathroom, straightening her dressing gown. "Thank you very much, Investigator Riley, we can't thank you enough for everything you've done. My husband and I are most grateful to you and Constable Callaghan."

"Of course, Your Majesty."

Kent stared at Chasseur who had finally collapsed into unconsciousness. Kent shuddered at the silver pen protruding from his bloody eye-socket. Callaghan stumbled to the couch and slumped onto it. The poor kid had to be exhausted.

"You did a good job, Callaghan. Damn fine code work back there too by the way."

Callaghan was resting in an awkward way. Something seemed wrong.

"I knew we weren't done and Marcel was going to make his move," Kent said knowing that if he talked long enough, Callaghan would chip in or ask one of his aggravating questions.

"Jesus, Chisholm, you look terrible," Kent exclaimed. Chisholm's face was almost unrecognizable. The Queen led him over to one of the wing backed chairs, sat him down and started to very carefully dab his swollen face with a warm washcloth the Prince had fetched from the washroom.

"It's okay, Investigator Riley," the Queen said gently as if he was talking too loudly.

Kent's hand was starting to throb once again as the fear and adrenaline eased. "I knew we were in trouble when Dan Smythe showed up." He kept talking so that he didn't have to see Flynn with blood now soaking in a pool around him. His voice sounded strangely in the room where everyone was still.

"I knocked out Smthye in the lift and handcuffed him." Kent started to laugh shakily.

The Queen straightened up and regarded him. "It's all right now, Investigator Riley," she said again.

"He's probably still riding up and down from floor to floor. We should send an officer to track him down."

The Queen waved her husband over and began what seemed like an urgent conversation with both the Prince and Chisholm. Kent dropped into the second wing backed chair and took stock of the situation. Flynn was dead on the floor by the doorway, the big man was face down near the window and looking very dead, and Chasseur was unconscious in a huddled mess not far from the bathroom door. Why was Callaghan being so quiet? Kent finally forced himself to move toward the boy who was now slumped between two pale pick throw pillows. He stopped and caught his breath. Callaghan had blood seeping through his jacket from the abdomen. Rushing over, his heart pounding, Kent dropped to his knees by the boy's side and tried to unbutton his suit jacket. "No, no-no-no! Callaghan. Speak to me. Come on. Talk to me."

Pounding feet, rushing into the room behind Kent caused him to whip around, gun at the ready. Kent's heart was thumping so loudly he could barely concentrate.

"Hold on there, mister! Don't shoot!" The first of two medics dropped his medical kit and raised his hands in the air. "We're here to help."

Kent let his gun hand fall to his side. And the medics stepped over Flynn and hurried over to Callaghan. Kent backed up to let them work. Staff Sergeant Jones and Constable Macdonald ran into the room. And then a revolving door of people in and out of the room began.

Kent watched closely as the medics tended to Callaghan. "Is he going to be okay?" Kent asked, but no one answered. Two more RCMP officers arrived and took sentry outside the door. Another was speaking into a portable radio. An older medic put two fingers on Callaghan's neck and cut away Callaghan's blood soaked clothes. One medic moved Flynn to the side and Macdonald helped him put the lifeless body into a bag. A third medic entered pulling along a starched white stretcher. They were going to save Callaghan. Another stretcher was brought in for Chasseur. Staff Sergeant Jones was taking notes and speaking with Chisholm and the Prince.

"He is going to be okay, right? I mean—"

The Queen came over to Kent. He felt numb as her slender hand squeezed his good hand. "Investigator Riley," she said quietly, "let the medics to do their job."

The older medic, with the help of another, carefully lifted Callaghan up into a sitting position, but his body slumped sideways. Blood came trickling out of his mouth and Kent tightened his grip on the Queen's hand. The one medic was talking so rapidly to the other that Kent couldn't quite follow, but the urgency was clear. They lifted Callaghan onto the stretcher. "Come on, come on," the older paramedic commanded, but Callaghan remained lifeless, almost as white as the sheets he now lay upon. The medic rested his hands on the edge of the stretcher in defeat. There was a moment of stillness in the room that Kent recognized as death. Kent's head bowed of its own accord as tears welled uncontrollably in his eyes.

"I'm so sorry," Queen Elizabeth whispered.

Staff Sergeant Jones cleared his throat and Constable Macdonald took his hat off. Both Prince Philip and Chisholm looked on in stricken silence. The older paramedic went to pull a sheet over the boy. "No," Kent commanded. "Leave him for a moment." He went to Callaghan's side.

Kent polished and straightened Callaghan's glasses. Putting his hand on the boy's cheek, Kent closed his eyes and prayed to God for his soul's release. He took a step back and spoke formally as if Callaghan could still hear him. "I'm so proud of you Callaghan, so incredibly proud of you."

More medics arrived and one attempted to tend to Fenwick Chisholm who shooed him off. "I'm fine," he insisted. "Leave me alone."

The Queen stepped forward. "Fenwick, stop it," she said. "You look awful. Let the man do his job."

In her pale yellow dressing gown, standing in a room filled with blood stains and dead bodies, for a moment the Queen appeared small and slight. But neither Kent nor likely any of the other men in the room doubted for even a second who was in command. She went over to the stretcher and leaned close over the lifeless form of Michael Callaghan. She put her hand on his forehead and smoothed back his hair. Her shoulders curled forward and began shaking. Prince Phillip was at her side in an instant. He spoke quietly to her as he steered her away.

EPILOUGE

Paris, France
Sunday July 24, 1957

Kent walked along the carefully tended Luxembourg Gardens. He rolled his shoulders, tense from the long flight. His broken fingers still ached in their splints. The morning was humid and the air hung heavy. Gravel walkways flowed like little grey streams bordered by carefully pruned box hedges on either side that occasionally rounded into half-moon shapes to accommodate the marble statues sprinkled throughout the gardens. The delighted shrieks of children came from up ahead where there was a fountain. Wooden slatted chairs were scattered aimlessly around. Kent looked down at the card again in his hand; this was the place.

He sat in one of the garden chairs. It took him a few minutes to spot her. Her hair was short and dyed blond, pulled off her face by a white headband. She wore a short blue coat with a pale, rose-coloured dress peeking out from underneath. Her face looked older, but still beautiful despite the scar across her neck. He could feel her sadness. Kent noted the flickers of fear that caused her to constantly look over her shoulder. She chatted with the other girls watching the children run about carefree. A little boy ran up to her and showed her something. She got down low to see it clearly. She jumped back and the little boy laughed. She put on a serious face that was in no way convincing and the boy returned what must have been a bug or worm of some kind back to the bushes.

Kent got up and started to walk over. She fixed her eyes on him and then just soaked him in. Her eyes never left his as he approached and when he got about six feet from her, he stopped. It was like he couldn't move any closer. She began to walk to him and it turned into a skip and then a run and she flung herself so hard at him that he could barely hold her with his one good hand. She pulled back in his arms and he laughed.

"Sarah, my God, it's so good to see you, holding you—"

"You took so long Kent. What happened to your hand? I didn't know if you were alive or dead."

"You're with me now. I'm safe and—"

"What about Flynn Dolan?"

"Flynn's dead."

"Dead! How?"

"He was shot."

She lifted her head up and put her hands on either side of his face and began kissing him with all of the lost moments of their separation.

The little boy Kent had seen with Sarah earlier came up to them and he pushed at Kent, his little chest puffed out like one of the pigeons in the garden.

"*Monsieur, vous ne pouvez pas embrasser Sarah. Elle est ma nounou.*"

"What did he say?"

Sarah started laughing. "He says you can't kiss me because I'm his nanny."

Kent smiled at the boy. "Tell him that I *can* because you're my wife."

They spent the afternoon in the Hotel du Champ de Mars. The room was exquisite, but tiny. Soaking in the Eiffel Tower off to the left, Kent leaned out the shuttered window looking over flower boxes into the busy thoroughfare of strolling and dining Parisians. As night began to fall, he and Sarah set off in search of a restaurant. Kent held Sarah's hand tightly as they walked the streets of the seventh arrondissement answering her every question. He still didn't let go as they sat at a table with a flickering candle and crisp white tablecloth. He still couldn't believe she was actually there before him. He rested his broken hand on her knee and she gave him sips of a dark wine that tasted like the sloes he and Flynn had eaten by the handful as boys.

"I know the painter Charlie Crawford's work," Sarah said. "It's spectacular. I can't believe you got to meet him. He's done a series on boats that are not the nautical paintings of old. They're very bold; the ships dominate practically the whole canvas and they are in jeopardy."

"The horse painting Charlie Crawford was working on reminded me of you."

"Really? A horse painting?" Sarah lifted her chin. "I think of myself as much more lady-like than a Crawford horse which is always on the verge of breaking down the bar and careening out of the stable."

Kent leaned in more closely. "When I went back to tell Charlie Crawford that I had recovered his Brancusi *Muse*, he gave me his latest painting as a thank-you. I told him how much you loved art and he wanted me to give it to you."

"No, you're teasing me! Where is it?"

"I had to leave it at Dad's place. I was worried it would get damaged if I brought it here."

"Of course, of course. I can't believe it. What does it look like?"

"It's a night scene of a deer standing on a road, illuminated only by car headlights and the trees are swirling around as if there's a high wind. In the background, he's painted his own house and the sea beyond. It's really quite something."

"I can't wait to see it. It'll be the first thing we put in the new house."

A waiter brought a dish of butter, lettuce, tuna, and olives. "*Merci,*" said Sarah. "*Et nous voudrions avoir plus du pain et pourriez-vous porter des haricots-verts quand la viande est prête? Merci.*"

Kent loved hearing her speak French. The little boy cried that she wasn't staying home that night and Kent felt only slightly guilty about taking her away from the Parisian family she had been staying with the past two years.

He told Sarah about Michael Callaghan from beginning to end. She shook her head in disbelief that Kent had ever thought he might kill him, even in fun. She laughed out loud at the child prodigy's obsession with the electric razor and her eyes blazed when she heard he used it to electrocute Liam O'Rourke and save Kent.

Liam and his despicable cousin, Paul O'Rourke, Constable Smythe and Marcel Chasseur, all sounded like characters in a story, now that they were either jailed or dead.

Sarah sipped her wine. "Callaghan was *not* portly! He couldn't have been."

"He was! He loved to eat."

"He didn't *really* polish his glasses on his shirt-front."

"He did! Just like a jeweller."

"He did *not* call you 'Sir'."

"Oh, but he did. It was absolutely maddening."

Every word Sarah said, every gesture, every facial expression reminded Kent why he loved her and now he didn't have to be afraid. It was like walking out of an iron lung that once made every breath burn. Now he took in great gulps of summer air.

"When do we go back to Canada?" She asked.

"The Deputy Commissioner says I can take some time off. There's going to be a ceremony in Ottawa, but it's not until September."

Even after two years apart, he saw right away that she could sense his sudden upwelling of grief.

"Kent, what's wrong? "What is it you're not telling me?"

"Sarah," he clasped her hand, "they killed Michael Callaghan."

"Oh, no!"

He nodded unable to speak. She clasped his hand as he fought back tears.

"No, Kent, no, please tell me it's not true." Sarah started to cry.

"That's who the ceremony is for — it's for Constable Michael Callaghan. Queen Elizabeth will posthumously award him the Queen's Police Medal in September."

"Oh, I am so sorry. His poor, poor parents."

Sarah handed him the wine and it eased his throat.

"And what about you, Kent? You deserve a medal for what you did."

"Me?" He considered. "I'm not interested in medals. I couldn't breathe for fear, Sarah, and now I have you safe."

She reached over and kissed him, then whispered by his cheek, "I want to go back home."

ACKNOWLEDGMENTS

Thanks to Tom Brown for endless responses to research questions. Thanks to Susan and Don Prins for connecting me with RCMP Chief Superintendent, Dave Critchley, who corrected policing gaffs. Thanks to Lucy Bashford, Murray Browne, Ben Coles, Jay Connolly, Dede Crane, David Fraser, Jessica Fraser, Eve Joseph, Katy Karadag, Carol Matthews, Janice McCachen, Mark Thorburn, Patricia Young and Terence Young for critiquing and commenting on the manuscript as it evolved. I am very grateful to Integrated Publishers, especially Michael Marson for his inspired, detail-oriented editing and Simon Troop from CS Creative for a beautiful cover design.

Royal Dispatch is dedicated to my mother. From an early age, she would ask me: "What would you do if you were having tea with the Queen?" This was not a rhetorical question. It was meant as a way to assess one's own personal conduct and to smarten up, if found wanting. As Executive Assistant to the Mayor of Vancouver, during both Gordon Campbell and Philip Owen's tenure, my mother *did* end up having tea with Queen Elizabeth II. Because of her high standards for self and others, she knew exactly how to conduct herself on such an occasion.

Made in the USA
Columbia, SC
07 October 2017